VIPERS RUN

A Skulls Creek Novel

Withdrawn

Stephanie Tyler

A SIGNET ECLIPSE BOOK

SIGNET ECLIPSE
Published by the Penguin Group
Penguin Group (USA) LLC, 375 Hudson Street,
New York, New York 10014

USA | Canada | UK | Ireland | Australia | New Zealand | India | South Africa | China
penguin.com
A Penguin Random House Company

First published by Signet Eclipse, an imprint of New American Library,
a division of Penguin Group (USA) LLC

First Printing, July 2014

Copyright © Stephanie Tyler, LLC, 2014
Excerpt from *Surrender* © Stephanie Tyler, LLC, 2013

SIGNET ECLIPSE and logo are trademarks of Penguin Group (USA) LLC.

ISBN 978-0-451-47046-1

Printed in the United States of America
10 9 8 7 6 5 4 3 2 1

For LEO & CMO

Chapter 1

The office phone rang at 4:55 p.m.

On a Friday.

When I had my keys in hand, bag over my shoulder, ready to lock up behind me.

I debated ignoring the insistent ringing, but since I didn't have any actual evening plans, I walked backward a few steps and glanced at the caller ID. And froze.

Bradley Industries.

I snatched up the phone before I could stop myself, forgoing the usual niceties of "Bernie's Investigations" in favor of a clipped "Calla speaking."

"Calla, it's your father."

Jameson Bradley.

As hard as he'd tried to be a part of my life, we didn't speak very often, so "Hi, Dad" wasn't exactly a major part of my vocabulary. "What's going on?" I asked instead.

It was the way my mother had always greeted him, so I guessed, Like mother, like daughter. But just like all the times I'd spoken with him before, his voice soothed me. And, as I always did, I tried to ignore the brief moment of comfort. I was desperate for family but I'd grown up unable to trust any of them.

His tone didn't change—it wasn't chiding or cold, but still warm and comforting when he said, "Actually, your boss called me."

"Bernie?"

"He was worried about you."

"I'm fine."

"You don't have to pretend with me. I know your brother stole your money. I know you had to sell the bar," my father said.

"When did Bernie tell you that?"

"The first day you went to see him."

Bernie had betrayed me from the start. I didn't understand how someone I'd told a bit of my family history to, in order to find my thieving shit of a brother, could so easily take that information and hurt me with it. "That's true. But I'm not homeless. I'm working and I'm fine. Bernie never should've involved you. I didn't ask him to."

The first time I ever spoke to my father, I was fifteen and in the hospital.

Because of that, I associated him with the very worst thing that had happened in my life. The entire conversation was like a knife stabbed through me. And maybe I was being dramatic, but my father and I never had the typical father-daughter relationship. Or any relationship at all.

My father sighed, like he was reading my mind. "Bernie contacted me in case I heard anything from your brother. That was all he asked. And I hadn't heard from Ned, not until last night."

Ned was my half brother, and Jameson Bradley wasn't his father. "Ned contacted you?"

I heard a hard swallow on the other end of the line, which meant this couldn't be good. "Does your brother know about what happened to you?"

My mouth opened and closed. My world spun. "Yes," I managed. Ned was a year older than me, but we'd never been close.

"He's got the pictures," my father admitted reluctantly.

"What? How?"

"I'm still trying to figure that out."

"He wants money," I said hollowly.

"Yes."

Which meant he'd blown through everything Mom and Grams left, including the money from the sale of the bar that he'd sold from under my nose. He'd always had far too much influence on both of them, and he'd twisted it to his advantage, even though we were supposed to make joint decisions regarding the bar and any money to be split. "I'll find a way—"

"I took care of it. I am taking care of it. With Bernie's help. I didn't want to keep you in the dark, Calla. You have a right to know everything."

Something about the way he said "everything" concerned me, but Bernie's cell phone began to ring. And Bernie wasn't in the office. He never went anywhere without that phone, and I knew that ring—an urgent one reserved for only a select few clients. Clients I never spoke to.

"Can I call you back?"

"Please do, Calla. I'd really like to talk to you . . . about more than just this." He sounded so sincere and I convinced myself it was just years of practice. The rich were different.

So was I. "I will."

I hung up and went into Bernie's office, rooted around and found the phone on the ground. "Shit."

I debated answering, when whoever it was hung up. And called again two seconds later.

There were also texts from the same number with 911, and I knew what that meant.

My voice was tentative when I picked up with, "I'm not Bernie."

A man's rough voice countered with, "I'm dying."

Okay, then, the dying man wins.

I never knew words could haunt, but those would. Fear raced through me even though I wasn't the one in direct danger. I took a breath and started, "If you'll just . . ." *If you'll just hang on a minute, dying man, I'll try to track my boss down* . . . "Can you tell me your location?"

"Where . . . the fuck . . . is Bernie?" His breathing was labored, his speech peppered with pauses, like he was trying to gain the strength to get the words out.

"Please, sir, if you tell me where you are I can send help—" I started and he broke in, saying, "No. Time." And then, "Sir? *Jesus Christ*," but his voice was so weak and slurred, I had to strain to hear it.

"Bernie's not here. He dropped this phone in his office. Please, let me try to help you—I'll send an ambulance and the police."

"No."

I had no idea what else to do, but I wouldn't hang up on this man. I took a deep breath, forced the words past my tightening throat. "Okay. Tell me what you need me to do."

"Talk."

Talk? "I want to help you."

"Might be . . . the only . . . one."

"I've never had this happen."

"Me . . . neither."

He was drawing in harsh breaths between each of the words. He sounded so labored and I figured the more I talked, the less he'd have to. "My name's Calla."

"Sounds . . . soft. Pretty. Fits you."

Soft. God. "Please don't—" I took a deep breath and stopped before I could say *die.* "What happened to you?"

"Shot. Knifed. Beaten. Hit . . . by a moving car."

"Just that, huh?" The sarcasm slipped out because I was nervous.

He huffed a laugh and then drew in a sharp breath and muttered, "*Fuck.*"

"Sorry."

"Don't be."

"What's your name?"

There was a pause and I thought I'd lost him. But then he said, "Cage."

"Cage. I like that nickname."

"S'my middle name. First . . . is Christian."

Christian Cage. I liked it.

"Talk," he commanded, and God, I couldn't let him down. So I asked the first thing that popped into my mind. "What do you look like?"

"Gonna . . . set up a dating profile . . . for me? Better do it . . . quick."

It was my turn to laugh. "I can certainly do that for you."

"Just don't . . . call me 'sir.'" There was a long pause and heavy breathing that sounded like he was in tremendous pain. I glanced out the window, hoping to catch sight of Bernie's truck. He never went very far if he went out at all during his time on in the office. "Six foot four. Dark . . . hair. Green eyes. Your . . . turn."

I was cute, certainly, but not a head-turning supermodel type. "I'm five foot five. And a quarter."

"Quarter's important."

He was teasing. Dying, and still teasing. Dammit, where was Bernie? "My hair's blond. Shoulder length. And I have blue eyes."

"Pretty."

He wasn't asking, but telling. "If you ask what I'm wearing, I won't answer."

Another laugh, another gasp of pain. "Won't . . . ask. But I can picture it."

"Should I even ask?"

"I'm not picturing clothes."

My cheeks burned at the roughness of his voice. "You're dying and you're picturing me naked?"

"I'm a guy," he said. And he did sound better, so who was I to argue? I laughed, then put my hand over my mouth simultaneously to keep from crying. "What . . . were you doing . . . before I called?"

"I was on the phone." I didn't mean for the words to come out so clipped.

"You sound sad. Can't be . . . for me."

"Why not?"

"Calla . . ."

The way he said my name was like a warning and a command. The oddest thing, but I blurted out, "It's just my family."

Because a dying man needed my drama.

"Do you get along . . . with them?" he asked.

God, I didn't want to talk about this. I felt the blurred edges of a panic attack closing in, sure that if I looked up I'd see the room glazed over. Instead of looking up, I forced myself into tunnel vision. "My mom died a couple of years ago. My Grams died early last year." *And I'm all alone.*

"I know what being all alone's like."

I hadn't realized I'd said that out loud. Cage and I shared a silent moment together, and I wondered if he realized the irony that, finally, neither of us was alone. "Grams used to tell me that being able to keep someone's company is the most important thing in the world, and that the hard part was finding the person who you could tell your deepest, darkest secrets to."

"What are yours?"

I almost didn't answer, but knew I had to. "I'm scared I'll always be alone."

"By choice? Or . . . by design?"

"Both," I admitted.

"Don't . . . let that happen."

I swear, it sounded like an order despite the hitch. "You sound better."

"Yeah. Feel . . . beyond the pain."

That couldn't be good. I gripped the phone hard as I forced myself still.

"God, Calla, I really fucked this up." He laughed, but it came out more like a groan. "Should've known . . . I tried to fight them. My whole life, I tried . . ."

"Don't let them win, Cage. Please . . ."

"You sound like you know what it's like."

"I do. And I let someone win and I hate him for it."

There was such a long pause that I thought I'd lost him—I closed my eyes and just waited for what seemed like forever.

And then he said, "Fuck, Calla. Would strangle the son of a bitch who hurt you" in a voice so strong and fierce that I actually took a step back and hit the wall.

"I'd let you," I said softly.

"What did he do to you?"

"I can't tell you." I couldn't tell anyone. It had been all locked up, put away. Except it never really was. "There was this guy. I was fifteen. He—" I couldn't say much more except, "He took so much from me."

I waited for him to say he was sorry, that he wished he could do something, because there were so many *wishes* associated with what had happened to me.

Instead, he growled, "Did anyone make him pay?"

Even though that's not what Cage was asking, I thought of the money in my account. The pictures. "No," I whispered.

"He will pay. I promise."

How many broken promises had I waded through? "Don't."

"Don't defend you?"

"Don't promise."

"Too late."

"I don't goddamned believe you, Cage, so take it back."

"Who gets into a fight with a dying man?" he asked out loud.

"I don't believe in promises."

"And I . . . *don't* . . . break them. You need to be . . . prepared."

Prepared? What did that mean? "Don't do this to me."

"What are you afraid of?" he challenged, sounding more resolved by the second.

"That you're going to want to know what happened to me. That you're not going to want me."

"I think you're really . . . scared that I might . . . want you, and you'll have to let . . . those walls . . . all the way down."

I wanted to tell him this was a hypothetical conversation, that I was happy he was going to live, but that I'd make sure he didn't find me.

And what are you going to do, Calla? Quit Bernie's and run away?

"I don't want to believe you," I told him.

"But you do."

"Maybe," I admitted.

"Fucking meet my angel in the middle of hell," he managed, more to himself than me. "Gotta go, Calla. Remember . . . what I said."

"Cage, please let me do something for you."

"Babe, you have no idea what . . . you've already . . . done. I . . . . Shit."

"Please."

"I'm . . . coming back."

"I believe you," I said, because how could I not? Because I wanted him to. "Let me help you."

There was a silence and then he coughed and then, "Gonna give you a number. Remember . . . it."

"Of course."

"Bernie . . . tell him . . . immediately. Important."

"I will." I memorized the last thing I'd know about Cage. Ten numbers that meant nothing. "I've got it."

"Say. Back."

I repeated them and he sighed. "Good. Sorry . . . so sorry."

Sorry? For dying? For giving me a relatively simple job? For not letting me help him? "I'm sorry I couldn't do more, Cage."

"Jesus. You did . . . everything."

"Cage . . ."

But the line clicked off. I blinked back tears, unable to stop the small sob that made my shoulders lift involuntarily. I was yelling then, slamming the desk with my fists before I pulled my shit together.

Feeling like I'd failed.

Another loss. My whole life was loss and pain,

and why I thought it could be any different, I had no idea.

I looked up at a picture behind Bernie's desk, hanging low on the wall. I'd never really noticed it before, because if I was in here, Bernie was in his big chair, which partially covered it. Why it was hung so low was another story, but I finally realized that Bernie was one of the men wearing an Army uniform. I grabbed a magnifying glass to look at the names on the uniforms. There was one man, his head turned to the side . . .

"Calla?"

"Bernie!" I dropped the magnifying glass and turned, wanting to hug him. I handed him his phone and started babbling about Cage and the numbers.

His face paled. He looked behind him, out the window and then tossed me a set of keys. I caught them instinctively. "Black truck in the corner of the lot. Walk to it like it's yours. Get in. Hit the GPS and follow where it takes you. Money's in the glove compartment. Do you understand?"

"Bernie—"

"There's trouble, honey. Please, do what I say. Now."

He walked out then. I don't know why, but I

grabbed the picture from his wall before I went out the back, grabbing my bag along the way.

Two weeks earlier, he'd gotten a call that made him close his office door. He never closed the door. And when he'd finally emerged, he'd been pale and distracted. Twitchy, even.

For the rest of that week, he answered all his own calls. But then things seemed to go back to normal. We dealt with the usual cases . . . some heartbreaking, some frivolous.

I supposed I could call in my father, ask for help. Or I could throw off everything, once and for all, and thank Cage by actually going free.

When I got into the black car and turned the key in the ignition, I'd made the choice. As I pulled the car out of the lot, I heard gunshots, four in a row, and I forced myself not to go back and check on Bernie. Instead, I followed his orders and got the hell out of there. Running from my past and present . . . and realizing I had no clue where my future lay.

Chapter 2

My mind swam as I forced my attention on the slippery, rain-slicked roads ahead. Thankfully, the truck gripped the road, as if it knew I didn't have the strength to focus. Normally I'd never drive like this, but the roads were clear and I figured the only one I'd be hurting was myself.

Mom was killed by a drunk driver and then two years later, Grams died. I'd come home from college for the funeral and found out that my brother had taken everything out of Grams's accounts, using her debit card. Except for my settlement money, which he couldn't touch. My mother had never been able to either, which was why my father had put it into a trust for me in the first place. I had money at my disposal, but I wouldn't give in and use it. It was blood money, as far as I was concerned.

I was supposed to start a job in London this past fall. Instead, I'd found myself sitting in the office of a private eye named Bernie, explaining that I needed to find my brother and get the money and the deed to the bar back.

Bernie had looked at me a long time before he'd said, "Sweetheart, even if you had money, I wouldn't take your case. You've had everything taken from you already."

I'd refused to break down in front of him.

He'd continued. "I knew your Grams. She was a good woman. Your brother's an ass. Put it behind you, live your life."

"How?" I'd asked, trying not to sound pathetic.

"Work for me."

And from there, I'd started to rebuild. And I realized that a lot of people had it worse than me. Taking pictures of husbands for suspicious wives— and vice versa—was the bulk of his business, but there was so much more he did for people.

Bernie had given me my life back. A job, a place to stay, and he was kind. His wife and daughter had been killed by a drunk driver ten years earlier, and he'd spent the rest of his days helping people get justice. We were drawn together by the pain of circumstance and I worked hard to help him.

And now I was going someplace Bernie had sent me. He'd done everything to protect me from the seedy side of his business. I had to trust this was no different.

I followed the GPS, driving for about six hours nearly nonstop to pass the North Carolina border. I took one quick break once I was across that state line, for gas and the bathroom at a busy enough rest stop peppered with minivans and tired children asleep in their seats.

Happy families. At least they appeared that way on the outside. I got back into the truck and drove away from the appearance of happy as fast as I could. I was more focused, but I hadn't been able to stop shaking. The heat was turned up so high that the windows fogged.

Finally, I was directed up a long private drive that was close enough to the beach for me to smell the salt water. I had a choice there—I had a truck and some money and I could just cut and run.

But Bernie had never steered me wrong. He'd never given me a reason not to trust him. And whoever was at the end of this driveway was now my only real connection to Cage.

I pulled all the way up to the big house, parked and stumbled out of the car. The whole day—my entire past—swirled around me like an impending storm. The worst hadn't come yet, the pit of doom in my stomach unsettling me to the point of shaking.

I barely pulled myself together to make it up the path. The gun from the truck was barely concealed in my bag, and the man who stood in the now-opened front door of the house caught sight of it immediately, his eyes casually flickering from it to my eyes.

"That's more dangerous for you if you don't know how to use it," he noted. He wore dog tags, a black wifebeater and jeans with bare feet. He was good looking in an almost movie star kind of way, but there was nothing plastic about him.

I wanted to say that I knew how to use it—and I did know how—but those words wouldn't come out.

But I did hear some moaning in the background, and I wasn't imagining it, because he called over his shoulder, "Guys, can you stop rehearsing for a minute?" before turning back to me and saying, "Are you here for a job? Because I don't take walk-ins or women."

I'd dropped my voice to a whisper. "I'm not here for a job. I'm here for—"

Bernie.

Shots.

I couldn't get his name out. I must've started to shake. I'd been faking strength the whole ride down, and now the thought of this man ready to turn me away had me at near collapse.

"Sweetheart, you took a wrong turn somewhere," he told me, like the command in his voice would be enough to turn me away. But that only served to remind me of Cage, which strengthened my resolve.

I shook my head no. "I have no place else to go."

"There are hotels. Shelters," he started, then stopped. Looked between me and the gun and an expression I couldn't quite place settled there for a moment as he asked, "Honey, whose truck is that? How did you know where to find me?"

I opened my mouth, wanted to tell him, but the debilitating panic took over. I pointed to my throat, tried to go into my bag for the meds I hadn't needed in a very long time. I kept them with me anyway, like a talisman.

But I was shaking and somehow frozen, not an easy combination. I realized he was taking the gun from me and I couldn't tell him what I needed to.

"Shit, Eddie, a little help here." His grip was strong and sure as he led me inside. I heard him say, "Put the truck in the garage and get rid of the GPS and her fucking cell phone. Not a fucking trace of either."

And then he was focusing on me again. His words were low and calm, although they didn't reach me, because I'd already folded into my panic. Or it had already folded into me. Either way, I was overwhelmed with it.

In my mind, I was rifling through my bag, searching for my pills, even though I was cognizant of the fact that I hadn't moved.

I saw him holding up my pill bottle in front of me. I tried to nod. I don't think I managed to. To his credit, he got me to swallow the med. I don't remember doing it, but the next thing I knew, I was sitting on a couch, covered in a blanket, and he was sitting next to me.

"Sorry," I managed, my voice thick and drowsy.

"Drink this," he instructed, pressing a glass into my hand. I did, mainly because he sounded scary, but I spilled some of it. "Pull yourself together and drink it."

I glanced at him. "Frankly, I think you're a little judgmental of my panic."

He took the glass from me, stood and trapped me against the back of the couch, his arms on its back on either side of my head, his body blocking me from going anywhere. Like I could even get up. "Where'd you get the gun and the car?" he demanded.

"Bernie," I whispered, my throat raw.

The man blinked. "He just gave them to you?"

"Yes. He's . . . we're in trouble. He sent me out. There were shots."

He held up the picture I'd taken from Bernie's office, his expression tight. "Did you shoot him?"

"No."

"If there's something you need to tell me . . ."

"Bernie said that the GPS was in his car—take it to where it was programmed."

"That's not his car."

"No, not the one he drove every day," I agreed. "He started using it two weeks ago. Today he told me to take it. That there was trouble."

"You said you heard shots. How did you manage to get away?"

"I just told you—Bernie sent me out." I stared at him. "Do you think he's . . . ?"

"I don't know."

"You should call."

"Not until I know more."

"Do you know Cage?" I was going to wait for him to say yes, but he didn't hide his expression. "I think he's hurt."

"Think?"

"He told me he was dying." A few tears ran down my cheeks but I refused to break down.

Because Cage had promised, although I couldn't tell the man in front of me that.

"How do you know him?"

"I . . . didn't." I stared at him, waiting for him to tell me that I shouldn't cry over someone I didn't know. Instead, he turned around and spit out a string of curses, many of which I'd never heard before. I tried to commit some of them to memory, but he was muttering now, pacing a little, throwing his hands in the air as if having a conversation with an invisible someone in the room.

Then he turned back, poured a glass of whiskey instead of water and said, "Drink this."

This time, I did. "I don't know your name."

"It's Tenn."

"Ten like the number?"

"Two *n*'s. Short for Tennessee."

"Were you born there?"

"Nope. In Tallahassee." He shrugged when I frowned. "My mom was what they call confused. My dad was what you'd call a convict."

The whiskey mixed with the antianxiety pill I'd taken earlier was making it impossible to keep my eyes open. I didn't bother trying, but I wasn't wholly passed out either. At least I don't think I was, because I was aware of Tenn's conversation . . .

"No powder residue on her hands or the gun. What the fuck is happening, Tals? . . .What do you mean, you'll come get her? No way am I exposing her to Vipers. She's already had a panic attack. You try to bring her into the MC, you're not going to like what happens." A pause and then, "No, asshole, she's not another stray. And maybe I can remind you that you were a stray? Yeah, well, fuck you too."

I jerked my head at the harsh growl in Tenn's voice. Then I heard, "Calla said Cage was dying. I haven't heard from the fucker in months and now he's dead?"

"You think I shot Bernie."

At the sound of my voice, he froze, then turned. "I'll call you back. We are not done."

When he hung up, he shoved the phone into his pocket. "That was my brother. He's a dick sometimes."

I knew the feeling, so I simply nodded. But I could never talk about Ned with the affection that Tenn did for his brother, no matter the names he'd called him. "You didn't answer my question."

"Sweetheart, you knocked on my front door holding Bernie's gun, you showed up in his car and you were panicked."

"Have you heard from him?"

He swallowed hard and shook his head. "Why don't you get cleaned up and lay down for a while, 'cause you look like hell."

I stared at him and he broke into a faint grin. I decided I liked him. I even let him help me up and into a room down the hall. He pointed to the bathroom, said, "I'm guessing you don't have any clothes with you."

I shook my head, determined not to cry again. At least not in front of him.

"We'll figure it out, Calla."

When he left, I went into the bathroom and stripped down. I'd been battered. I'd been through an inner war that I'd waged and I didn't know if I was winning or losing, but I was definitely on the edge of one or the other.

I stood under the warm spray of the shower and let it rain down on me. My tears mingled with the water; the sounds hid my sobs. It was because of Bernie, because of what I'd lost in the past already, and it was for sure because of Christian Cage Owens.

I'd asked him the impossible and he'd promised it to me. Promised. Was I a fool to believe him? Because I felt like I'd be a fool *not* to.

Tenn had laid out some clothes for me—shorts and a T-shirt and socks. Brand-new underwear.

Tenn was prepared, and I began to wonder how many people in trouble Bernie sent his way. And how most of them were men.

There was also more tea, with whiskey on the side, plus a plate of cookies. Despite my misery, my stomach rumbled. I nibbled on a cookie, sipped the tea after forgoing the liquor, as I looked around the softly lit room.

I noticed it then, propped in the chair across the room. The picture I'd taken from Bernie's office. I went to it, picked it up and studied it as I padded back to the bed.

"You okay, Calla?"

I glanced up to see Tenn in the doorway. "I'm not sure."

"I left the door open in case you had another panic attack."

I believed him. "You were talking to someone named Eddie earlier."

"Yeah, he works for me. I sent him and the others away, though. It's just us."

"Okay." I stared down at the throw rug, noting how it contrasted with the dark floors, then looked at the picture again.

"That feels like a lifetime ago," Tenn said, and when I looked up he was checking out the picture.

"Was Cage in the Army with you and Bernie?"

He tilted his head. Didn't answer.

I still believed that "C. Owens" was Cage. "I told Cage something and he said . . . he said he was coming back for me. He promised. And I hate him for that, because everyone always breaks their promises."

I said it so fast that I thought maybe Tenn didn't even understand. Even though I knew what I said, I was confused, and unwilling to tell Tenn what exactly I'd told Cage.

He didn't ask anything else and his expression softened. "You can stay here."

I was already planted against the pillows, planning on doing just that. "I sound ridiculous, I realize."

Tenn shook his head. "You don't. What Cage told you isn't ridiculous—not if you know him. Sounds like you do."

I couldn't deny that, but I wasn't sure if I'd dreamed the whole thing up.

And for the next couple of weeks (and I only knew the length of time when I'd come out the other end of the tunnel) I stayed in bed. Cried. Slept. Dreamed of a dark-haired man with rough hands and a rougher voice telling me he'd protect me.

Even as I mourned him, mourned my other life, mourned everything I'd lost, I held on to

Cage's promise. I didn't care if that was stupid, because not only was it all I had, but it was all I wanted.

I'd slept around to get rid of the ghosts of my past, but I'd never felt anything remotely like I did with Cage just talking to me. His voice did more to me than any man's hands ever had.

It was impossible to fall in love with someone from a ten-minute phone call. Impossible to fall in love with a man who'd been dying as we spoke.

Impossible.

Somehow, *I'd* managed the impossible.

Chapter 3

Those full two weeks later, I got out of bed only when Tenn threatened to forcibly shower me. After a turn under the warm water, I did feel better. And then Tenn lured me out into the open with the smell of food, the bastard. Normally, he'd bring it right into my room, but today he was Mister Tough Love.

I went out into the living room with my hair still wet and found a couple of guys there. They didn't pay me much attention, but they weren't rude or anything. I continued along until I found Tenn in the kitchen.

There was a tall, slim boy there too. Maybe seventeen or so, I guessed, and he was sitting alone at the table, writing in a notebook. Whether he noticed me or not, or if he was so absorbed in the writing, he didn't let on.

"Sit." Tenn pointed to the enormous helpings of eggs and bacon and pancakes he'd put on two plates, all for me. And then he pushed a big cup of coffee in front of me.

"I feel like you're going to give me bad news."

"I am. No more sleeping for weeks."

"Yeah, I got that message."

Tenn leaned against the counter and glanced out at the small crowd in the other room. I took those few moments to really study him.

He was tall. Rangy. But somehow I knew he could be deceptively agile if needed. The young man got up and wandered away, muttering to himself.

"That's Kev. He's writing a book," Tenn explained.

"Do the others work for you too?"

"Yes."

"And what kind of work do you do?" I asked. "Same as Bernie?"

"Ah, no. Definitely not." He wrapped a hand around a mug, dwarfing it. "Some of them are escorts."

"Escorts," I echoed, and he nodded. "You run the business from here?"

"Nope. I keep my places separate." He pointed across the street and gave me a half smile and I tried to reconcile the image of him running an escort service. Which he obviously knew, because he added, "We also do some porn, but it's mostly webcam stuff. A couple of my guys are getting a good following, though. It's filmed here, but the guys stay across the street for the most part."

He wasn't saying it to shock me, or maybe he was, but I still managed, "Escorts and porn, huh?"

"Not a bad way to live. Money's good."

"So you get a cut and what do they get?" I asked.

"Something most of them haven't had their entire lives—protection," Tenn said, his voice slightly fierce even though he was still smiling.

"I believe you," I said quietly. "Just wondering why."

"Why not?" he countered. "Money's good. I keep the porn side for the guys only. Easier that way, and they're more than happy to get paid for something they'd be doing anyway."

"All of them?"

"Everything I do here is safe, sane and consensual. If they aren't happy, I can spot them pretty quickly. And they don't belong either here or in the business. Sex is supposed to be happy. Freeing. Good stuff. And the escorting's a different business altogether. I've got bodyguards for both sexes. Everything happens in my place of business, and if it doesn't, there's going to be one of my guards there watching."

I blinked. Tried to imagine Bernie with Tenn, but it fit. Because Tenn was fiercely protective. And none of the guys I'd seen looked upset or any the worse for wear. "Are you in any of the films?" I asked, in an attempt to lighten the mood.

"I'm the brains behind the operation," he said. "Someone's got to watch out for them. But private performances? Now, that's a different story."

"Cage . . . was he working for you? With you?"

"Are you asking if there are any of his performances on tape?" I blushed and he laughed, a rich, throaty sound, and then let me off the hook. "He works with my brother." His gaze fell somewhere over my shoulder for just a second and then landed back on me. "They're part of an MC. A motorcycle club."

"Like a gang?"

"Not a gang. A club," he emphasized.

"I'm guessing there's a big difference."

"I'm guessing you're going to want me to explain it to you."

Escorts. Porn. Motorcycle gangs. What kind of life had Bernie been hiding behind his ramrod straight posture and easy smile? I guessed we really all did have secrets. "Wait a minute—you totally sidestepped the whole question about Cage and private performances."

"I have to respect the privacy of my performers."

Oh my God. "Let's talk about the club versus gang thing."

For the next twenty minutes, he explained what had to be a very simplified version of MCs. How they had ties to the military. How some of them were one-percenters—aka serious criminals—and how the others, although not as hard-core, were still equally as dangerous.

He didn't tell me exactly what the MC Cage was a part of did, but obviously I was somehow involved in bad MC business.

"I think that's enough of a trip into MC Land for the day," Tenn said. "You're safe here, Calla. Me and Bernie and Cage—and my brother—we know what we're doing."

He was still talking about Cage in the present tense. Maybe it was false hope, but I took it as a good sign.

"Thanks, Tenn."

"Welcome. We're going to be doing a little filming. Private room and everything's sound-proofed, okay?"

I nodded. With a squeeze of my shoulder, he

left and I tried to wrap my head around the whole MC thing. Bikes. Leather. Angry men who drank and scared towns and did drugs. It fit with the violence Cage had encountered and it scared me. For him, for me, because what had I been inadvertently caught up in?

I wanted to believe him, to believe in something, but I was dragging a heavy past behind me, one that was strewn with lies and more broken promises than I could handle.

Because of Cage and his promise to return— for me—I was balancing, walking the tightrope above my fears, refusing to look down. Because the drop was steep, and I'd been left with nothing this time. I was rebuilding from zero. I had a roof over my head. I could take Bernie's truck and his money and leave. Start over.

But I couldn't get Christian Cage Owens out of my mind. I dreamed about him, kept hearing his voice cover me like a rough, heavy blanket. I'd heard the fierceness in his voice. He *would* come for me.

Would I be making the biggest mistake of my life by going with him?

Later that afternoon, Tenn left me in the house with the alarm on so he could go check on the escort portion of his business. He left me a throw-away cell phone with his number programmed in and he pointed out where he'd be—literally across the street.

The area was so quiet. He had to have picked this place on purpose so there would be no neighbors complaining about what he did for a living.

"You've come a long way from boarding school and private colleges," I muttered to myself. Mom and Grams would have a fit. My father probably would too, although he knew I was working for Bernie and he hadn't said anything.

Speaking of my father, I'd left him hanging. I didn't know if he'd heard anything about Bernie, and Tenn hadn't offered any information on him. I was treading lightly here, knowing that I was being kept in the dark about certain things. But I wasn't being sold into white slavery—and Tenn wasn't asking me to work for him in any capacity.

I turned the prepaid cell over in my hand. I didn't want Tenn to know who I was calling. It was public record that Jameson Bradley had a daughter named Calla, but it wasn't like I ended up being talked about in the news. Not the way he was. But then I spotted a fax machine with a phone and picked up the line to hear the telltale dial tone. He wouldn't be tracking this the way he would a cell.

And thank you, Bernie, for teaching me things like that.

I found the piece of paper I'd written my father's number on the night I'd run—I'd pulled it out of my jeans and hidden it, since it was the one thing of mine Tenn hadn't discovered and thrown away.

It must've been a number leading directly to him, because he picked up on the first ring and said, "Calla?"

"How did you know it was me?" I said, and quickly realized that the number he'd given me was only for me. I put a hand over my chest and tried to breathe.

"I've had that number in place for a long time, Calla. Your mom told me you had it and didn't want to use it."

God, the mixture of truth and lies stung so badly. "I didn't know."

I didn't *know* he was my father *until* I was fifteen. It was only when my mom called him for help—and told me who he was—that I realized he had no idea I'd even existed.

Before that, she'd told me he hadn't wanted to be a father. I used to dream that one day, he'd reconsider.

From that point on, I wasn't sure who to believe about what . . . so I kept my distance from my father and shrank away from Mom as well. I was cautious, despite the gifts, the attempted phone calls, the pleas to visit. He tried—I'll give him that.

I wanted to forget everything that happened that horrible night I couldn't share with anyone—not fully, anyway. And my father's entrance into my life coincided with that hell. Every time he'd call, my mother got upset and tense. I continued to associate it all together. He tried, but I wasn't having it.

At the time, I was scared. Depressed. Angry. My dad got caught up in that. Fair or not, that was simply the way it was.

And to his credit, my father never made me feel bad about it. For a while, I convinced myself that was because he didn't care. But I'd been wrong about a lot of things.

"Calla, are you okay?"

"Sorry. Yes. I didn't know. Didn't think . . ."

"*I'm* sorry," he said firmly, sounding pissed at himself. "I've been worried—I couldn't get in touch with Bernie or you. Where are you? Your voice mail is full."

I wanted to ask him what he knew, but I didn't want him to worry. "I just needed to get away for a little while, to clear my head."

It wasn't *that* far from the truth.

"Bernie hasn't returned my calls."

"He's on a big case," I lied.

"He was supposed to be finding out some information on your brother."

"And the police?"

"If I go to them, Ned says he's got a friend who'll pull the trigger. I paid, but he'll be back."

My stomach clenched. I stared across the room at the open window. "Don't pay him again."

"What do you mean, Calla?"

"I'm a nobody—who'll care about seeing me that way? I know it'll be an embarrassment for you, so that's why you're doing it but—"

"Calla, you listen to me right now. I will never let those pictures come out. It has nothing to do with embarrassment. You're my daughter and I won't stand to see you hurt."

A lump formed in my throat. "Thank you," I managed. "I'll call you soon."

I hung up before he could hear my sob. It was only one, and I forced it back quickly, putting my fist against my mouth. I shook my head, telling myself I had to cut it out and be strong. The way I'd always been.

I hadn't told my father that I got those same pictures a couple of times a year at random times. Each time, it went long enough that I got comfortable, thinking that was the end. It was a taunt, a tease—a disgusting one, but I had no actual contact with Jeffrey Harris, whose family I'd gotten the settlement from. For all I knew, it was one of his friends who was there that night.

But it had been almost nine months since the last picture was sent to me. And suddenly my brother shows up with it? I wanted to think it was a coincidence, but there wasn't a possibility I could accept that. I figured that somehow, someway Jeffrey and my brother were doing this together to get more money. To humiliate me. Because Ned never liked me much anyway. Especially after I had the police put out a warrant for his arrest because he'd withdrawn the money and signed the lease on the bar over to himself while my Grams was dying.

I assumed that my father hadn't told Bernie everything that had happened to me. Even if Bernie was checking out my past in order to get a lead on Ned, there were some things money would've buried deep. I tried to recall if Bernie had treated me differently over the last month and could only see his kind smile in my mind's eye.

Grams believed in patterns, believed that things followed us until we could resolve them. But this hadn't been anything I'd wanted resolved. I wanted it to go away, disappear, bury itself in quicksand and cement, to dissolve as though it had never happened in the first place.

But that was far too much to ask the universe, apparently.

Apart from my family, I'd never gone as far as to hint at what happened to me. Telling Cage that small bit was a first. I'd never even given a statement to the police. My family had taken care of it, buried it. The problem was, burying it for myself wasn't enough—it wasn't working. I couldn't push it down enough, couldn't bury it deep enough down to where it stopped affecting me.

For six years after, I'd hung out with a group of privileged kids, very much like Jeffrey Harris, and I pretended I fit into their world, all the while wondering which one of them would see through me and do it again.

Therapy had helped. The rich all seemed to be in therapy. Like a badge of honor. Sex became meaningless, a way to make myself feel good and wanted and not dirty, a way to prove to myself that I could still have pleasure, that they didn't steal that from me.

The truth was, it was important for me to prove all that to myself. But afterward, the emptiness, the spiral downward was almost too much trouble. For a while, I closed myself off from all men.

But I left all of that behind. The only man I could think about was Cage. And I couldn't even talk to Tenn about him. All he knew was that I was scared and mourning someone . . . something.

I went to the room I'd been staying in, flopped on the bed and stared at the Army picture for the umpteenth time.

The way his head was turned made it impossible to see his face. Had he done that purposely? I traced the profile. Tenn was laughing—so whatever Cage was saying to him was funny. Cage had been funny, even in his distress.

But Cage hadn't been in touch with Tenn, and I was trying so hard to believe Cage's promise, but for me, cold, hard truths were easier to deal with. Typically, truths and promises were so far apart they weren't even in the same universe.

Jeffrey Harris promised me things. At fifteen, I'd been naive enough to believe them. I believed it when my mom told me that I could fit in with the rich people at the boarding school—that I deserved that. I believed both Mom and Grams when they told me I was different. There was no more believing in promises that ripped my heart out . . . until Christian Cage Owens came along and did so.

Damn him. Because as several more weeks

went by, the seeds of doubt snuck in, no matter how hard I shoved them aside. It brought up the biggest issue I had.

What was I going to do? Were the police looking for me? I didn't think so. Bernie had left no information on me anywhere, had paid me in cash. Simply because of the nature of his business, he would make enemies. He hadn't wanted me to get mixed up in anything.

"Bernie," I whispered. He'd been so good to me and I hadn't been able to help him, or anyone, including myself.

But all that had to change, starting now. Because although Tenn was entertaining—and honestly, so was the porn—I was getting antsy.

I stayed in his loft, which was separate from the house/studio on the same property. We were far enough away from the general population of the small town and I didn't exactly walk in on porn shoots. But I was aware that it was happening around me—and that all these men around me were feeling damned happy most of the time. I wanted that for me.

Most days, I'd join whoever was at the big breakfast table instead of coming down when no one was there. Tenn treated it like it wasn't a big deal at all, and whatever guys were there at the time all followed suit. Tenn poured me juice, Eddie shared a plate of pancakes with me, I ate and listened to everyone talk and laugh about their night and the day's shoots ahead.

It was good to be among the living.

One morning, Tenn hung around after the men split. We had more coffee, made small talk, and finally Tenn told me, "Sometimes, no news is good news."

I wasn't sure he believed that—not fully, because he seemed to be mourning Cage too. He was quiet a lot of the time, and Kev, the young guy I'd seen writing in the notebook, told me that Tenn was too quiet. That this wasn't like him. Which made my heart even heavier.

Instead of retreading old ground, I said, "I need a job," and when he paled, I quickly added, "Not one of yours."

"Good, because that's not happening." He gave a smile. "I can show you how to work a camera."

I opened my mouth but "no" didn't come out. But really, filming gay porn—and really, many of the guys weren't gay at all—wasn't anyone's life's goal, was it? Even Tenn had a side business. "I've got to find myself."

Tenn rolled his eyes. "I didn't realize you were lost."

"You specialize in that."

He sobered and nodded in concession. "You hide it better than most. Or maybe you're not as lost as you think you are."

I swallowed the last of my coffee. "It's just . . . you've been really good to me."

"I sense a 'but.'"

"I can't stay here forever."

I waited for the lecture about the dangers, about how I had no money, no job or car, but it never came.

Instead, he checked his watch. "I don't think we've hit forever yet, Calla. Not even close."

Chapter 4

My eyes opened sometime after four that morning. I woke restless as anything and I wasn't sure why. I tried to read a little, but I couldn't concentrate. I gave up, went to the bathroom, splashed some water on my face, brushed my teeth and figured I was up for good. Maybe I'd go watch some mindless infomercials or Bravo reruns of *Real Housewives*.

But as soon as I walked into the living room, my nerve endings tingled, like they were foretelling something of great importance. I looked around the now quiet first floor, a sense of impending change heightening my awareness, and I simply waited.

He stepped out of the shadows and I knew better than to be afraid. Not for my life at least— though I don't know how I knew. I just did, with the same amount of certainty that I knew that the moon was still there, even if I couldn't see it through the clouds.

His walk was silent, even along a hardwood floor that squeaked under the best conditions, and despite his heavy black motorcycle boots. Because I'd dragged my eyes down there first, certain that once he caught my gaze in his, I'd never escape.

I tracked up his legs, clad in faded jeans that were especially worn in the crotch area—deliciously so—and up his broad chest to his shoulders. He wore a black T-shirt stretched across his chest, along with a black leather vest with a snake patch on the front.

Black leather.

MC patch.

Snake.

I breathed harshly when I saw the scars, bunched like cords along the side of his neck. I didn't know what would happen when I looked up farther, but I wasn't worried. I found myself staring at a pair of angry, beautiful eyes, a calm expression that looked fierce because of scars running down the left side of his face and neck. The fresh scars that riddled his cheek did nothing to diminish his handsomeness. If anything, they made him inexorably more sexy.

"Calla."

The voice was hoarse. Raw. Dangerous.

Calla.

That one word. I'd fallen in love with him when he'd said my name on the phone that very first time. It was him.

Christian Cage Owens.

There were so many emotions flying through me at the moment, they all fought for equal attention. When I opened my mouth, I had no idea what would come out . . .

"I thought you were dead." Not a bad opening.

"I told you I don't break promises, sweetheart."

I'd been led to think he was dead for nearly two months and that's all he could say? "Alive, *and* an asshole."

He gave a clipped nod of his head, but something flickered behind his eyes before they went cold and hard again. "Now that we've got that shit out of the way, let's go."

In every dream, every fantasy, Cage came back for me, and I went with him without hesitation.

But we were firmly entrenched in reality. "Go? I'm not going anywhere with you."

If it had gone smoothly, Cage probably would've flatlined. Again. Instead, he stared at Calla, knowing there was no way to keep the hunger from his eyes. In his mind, he'd already laid claim to her. She'd given him something to hang on to—a reason to fight, to live, something to come back to. He'd come back for her because she'd reminded him that there was always a reason to keep fighting.

He'd rehearsed what he was going to say to her the entire ride here.

Hey, I didn't die. Good to meet you.

Thanks for taking one for the team.

I hope you had unlimited cell phone minutes.

Because really, what did you say to someone after she offered to help you and, in return, you fucked up her entire life? Calla Benson had a bounty on her head, because the Heathen chapter up in New York knew she'd worked for Bernie. And they knew she was missing. And even if she'd run away for reasons entirely unrelated to his shit, the Heathens would be looking for her, just in case.

He had a bounty on his head too, but that was nothing new—he'd been born with it in place.

And since he still hadn't known what to say, he'd almost turned back. As it was, he'd been avoiding Tenn for weeks. Talon too. And Preacher, even though he and Tals had visited him in the hospital, had known he wasn't dead even before

Tenn did. As soon as Cage had pulled through, they'd all walked out and now he was left with finding a way to make amends to all of them.

But Calla was first on the list. Preacher was going to kill him anyway, so what the hell difference did it make?

Calla.

She was gorgeous. He'd had beautiful women before, but Calla Benson was in an entirely different league. He'd researched her as soon as he could sit up. And he hadn't been prepared to play bad boy from the other side of the tracks to her "I'm a rich girl pretending to be something I'm not" act.

Although maybe it wasn't an act.

He stilled as she stared at him. The stare was expected; the softness in her eyes while she did so, not as much. He ignored that part, though, even turned his head so she could get a full look at the scars. They were barely healed, ugly as fuck—and he didn't give a shit. His heart was still beating.

Because of the pretty, cool blond in front of him. She'd turned from soft to goddamned angry in an instant, and if looks could kill, he'd be a goner. "You're still pissed."

"You think?" She wasn't scared of him. She was angry . . . because he'd hung up the phone.

Because he wouldn't let her help. Because he hadn't gotten in touch and because Tenn had kept his secret, knowing she'd be pissed at him for it.

There were a lot of pissed-off people circling him. And here he was, prepared to add another one to the already long list. "Calla—"

"Don't." She took a step back. Watched him, like she was trying to take it all in. He stayed in place for her inspection, watched her watching him. Jesus, he was naked under that gaze, and somehow she didn't goddamned know it. Yet.

Chapter 5

Cage continued to stare at me. His stance was aggressively, blatantly sexual. All anyone would have to do was look at him to know he'd know *exactly* what to do with a woman in bed.

When I didn't say anything, he walked toward me. He moved like a predator, smooth and silent, with more than a hint of danger. Big, strong, graceful. He moved like a motorcycle, sleek, fast, nimble, able to take corners on the fly.

Economy of movement while watching everything without seeming to, and missing nothing. I was vibrating. The need to reach out and touch him was overwhelming, and so I did—ran my fingers along his bare wrist. His skin was warm under my fingertips. Solid. Alive.

Most definitely alive.

Which was good, because now I was going to kill him. Unless Tenn beat me to the punch.

As if reading my mind, he said, "You can't be angry at me for keeping a promise."

The anger and fear that had lodged itself in the back of my mind came out swinging. "You don't get to tell me what to do. You don't even know me."

"I know more about you than most, though, Calla."

"Stop saying my name like that."

He was enjoying this too much and I hated the way my body tugged to his. *Traitorous bitch.* I moved away from him quickly and grabbed the nearest thing I could reach—a glass—and threw it at him. He ducked, it shattered and then I heard a resounding "What the fuck is going on out here?"

Tenn entered, wearing only a pair of low-slung sweats, and he was looking at me, but only for a second. Then he turned his head to Cage. "Four in the fucking morning?"

Cage shrugged, his big shoulders moving fluidly. "Yeah, like you've got a nine-to-five thing happening here."

"Such an asshole," Tenn muttered, and I pretty much vacillated between agreeing and throwing myself at Cage.

I settled for getting mad at Tenn instead, because it was painfully obvious that Tenn wasn't surprised to see Cage alive and kicking. "You knew and you didn't say anything." When he didn't respond, I had my answer. The sense of betrayal overshadowed everything Tenn had done for me. "Bastards. Both of you."

"Calla—" Cage said.

"You two belong together," I told him.

"I don't swing that way," Cage said seriously.

"Impossible. Completely impossible," I muttered.

"And here I thought you'd be happy to find me alive" was Cage's answer.

I whirled to face him. "I'd have been happier not to have mourned you. Do you have any idea what that's been like for me?"

Cage glanced over at Tenn and, yes, I could see he knew all about how goddamned hard it'd been. His expression was guarded. I turned back and focused on Tenn too, because neither of them was getting off the hook. "You knew what I was going through and you let me."

Tenn looked pained. "I won't make excuses for what I did. You came here for help. Help's what I gave you," he said firmly, and then he softened. "There was shit to figure out, Calla."

"There's always shit to figure out. You let me think he was dead."

"That was for your own good. And it's this asshole's goddamned fault." Tenn pointed at Cage, who shrugged apologetically. Tenn went to smack him in the back of the head, but Cage ducked in time.

Ducked, and still defended Tenn, telling me, "It's not his fault."

I refused to let Tenn off the hook, mainly because it meant dealing with Cage. "If he knew you were alive and didn't tell me—"

"You think it was easy, letting you cry yourself to sleep every night?" Tenn announced, and that hung in the air between us. "And you—" He pointed to Cage. "Don't get a big head over that."

I stared at Cage, watching Tenn's words register on his face. Then he relaxed again and said, "As much as I'd love to let you two kiss and make up, I've got to get Calla out of here."

He took what seemed like a single stride over to me, and before I could move he had a hand on my arm, his grip on my biceps gentle but unmoving.

If the electricity that sparked between us was any indication of what could happen if I was alone with him again, I was in trouble. And as much as I didn't want to know that right now, attempting to jerk away from his touch would only prove that

I couldn't. I was tired of proving my inadequacies, tired of always knowing that the other shoe always dropped. "You ruined my life. And you scared me. Anything else you'd like to do while you have the floor?"

"Your life sounded pretty busted before I came into it," he said. And as much as the truth hurt, I hated him for being right.

"So did yours," I shot back.

"You're right. You gave me something to fight for, Calla. Something—someone—to come back to."

"This is crazy. You don't even know me."

"I haven't stopped thinking about you since I hung up. I know what you've been through—I know it's my goddamned fault, so I've got to make it right."

"You made me mourn you."

"So, what—I don't know you, but you knew me enough to mourn me?" he asked.

I blinked, because . . . *yes*.

"You really didn't fucking believe me," he murmured. "I couldn't call—"

"Maybe not at first. But then it became more of a—you *wouldn't* call, right?" When he didn't argue, I asked, "After you recovered, you had time to call. But you didn't. You considered breaking your promise, didn't you?"

"Yes."

I wasn't surprised he didn't deny it. I didn't know much, but I did know that the man in front of me was a straight shooter. And that he smelled so good I wanted to lean in and lick his neck. "Why?"

"Too many reasons to go into."

"Just because you were alive didn't mean that you'd end up coming for me," I whispered.

"I said I would."

"I don't count on promises."

"You need to start with mine," he said firmly.

"You need to start doing a lot of things," Tenn said pointedly to Cage, who I swore growled. "That shit doesn't scare me."

"You know it should," Cage told Tenn pointedly. "Calla, we're out of here."

"I don't know if I'm leaving with you."

"You don't know if you're leaving with me," he repeated, like disagreeing with him was such a rare occurrence that he didn't recognize it. Or acknowledge it.

"I think she's still in the anger part of the grieving process," Tenn offered.

"I'm not dead," Cage said through clenched teeth.

"She thought you were," Tenn shot back.

"So yeah, that's why I'm not sure if I'm going with you," I said.

"While she's deciding, you can make some shit up to me," Tenn said, and by the look on Cage's face, I could tell he knew what the favor was, and he didn't look happy about it, to say the least.

"Don't start, man."

"You started it."

"Could've called to check," Cage said quietly, moving slightly away from me. He still held my arm while going chest to chest with Tenn, who growled, "I did. Would've expected to hear from you at some point. So you want to take her out of here without her consent, you're going up against me."

"I'm not leaving without her."

His words echoed—a threat and a promise. My mouth went dry. He was so damned male. Completely untamed. He looked like he'd been born on a bike, his motion fluid as he swung a jean-clad leg over and revved up.

"Then it looks like you'll have some time to do that favor you owe me while you try to convince both me and Calla that she should leave here with you," Tenn said steadily.

Cage stiffened next to me, the frustration coming off him in waves. "Now is not the time, Tennessee."

But Tenn looked both unimpressed at Cage's

using his full name and also pissed as hell. "I thought you were dead, fuckwad—even after Tals knew you were alive, you made him lie to me. So go play nice for the camera. Lucky that's all you've got to do."

Cage let go of me and walked away cursing. I stared after him for a long moment before turning back to Tenn.

Tenn, who shoved a camera into my hand. "Put it on the tripod. Get everything except his face. From here up." He put a hand on the middle of his nose. "Make sure the sound's on too."

"What are you talking about?"

"You wanted a job? You got it."

Chapter 6

I stared at Tenn, openmouthed, for a long while. It was only the slam of a door behind me that got me talking. "You're not serious about this."

"Dead serious." The awful gallows humor wasn't lost on me, but Tenn wasn't smiling. "You stay in there with him."

"I don't think I can."

"Why not? You said you needed money. You'll get a cut of the profits."

How much could that be, really? And when I asked, he threw out a number, telling me, "That's only the first week."

I headed to the room, ignoring his laughter behind me.

I had no idea what to do once I got in there. Maybe I wanted to let Cage off the hook, especially because he was muttering and pacing.

He stopped dead when he saw me with the camera. "That fucker." He slammed the door open and yelled, "Remember that fucking hellhole in Jakarta, asshole? That's worth a million of these."

I heard Tenn call back, "You let me think you were dead."

Cage slammed the side of a fist against the doorjamb, put his forehead there, and for a long moment I had no idea what was going on. Not until Tenn called, "You're live in five."

"I can't fucking believe this."

"You told me to come here," I pointed out unhelpfully, trying not to laugh.

"No, Bernie told you," he corrected, then mumbled, "Because I told him. Fuck." He turned to stare at me. I ignored the butterflies in my stomach and held up the camera like a challenge.

I don't know what I expected—maybe for him to walk out? And I wouldn't have blamed him.

But I was also an idiot to challenge a man like Cage. The look on his face turned from frustration to kid-in-a-candy-store in a second's span, and I swallowed hard when he shut the door, closing us into the small space.

I turned away from him, put the camera on the tripod and tried to line up a shot for the only chair in the room. Tenn had given me a sixty-second lesson and I tried to concentrate on that, rather than what would be happening. Because I knew what happened in this room . . . I'd just never believed I'd be watching Cage do it. Or filming it for a live audience.

He was standing in front of the chair, staring at me through the lens. I pulled back and stuttered out, "We're going live in a minute. If you're, ah, embarrassed . . ."

Wrong thing to say, apparently, because he shrugged off the leather cut (I assumed because it was too visible) and took down his jeans in an effortless move before he sat, his cock out for the world—and me—to see.

His pierced cock.

Shit.

I couldn't even swallow. How did this man do things to me in a way no man ever had? Maybe it was just this room. And Tenn's living room. And the phone line . . .

"Might want to press the on button," he said with a smirk as he palmed himself and stroked a couple of times, purely for my benefit. "First time behind the camera on this?"

"No," I lied, and his expression tightened.

"Gonna be your best," he said.

Oh God, this was really going to happen. I peered through the camera to make sure the shot was set up correctly. Someone rapped on the door, which meant it was, and that the feed was going live . . .

Now.

I forced myself not to look anywhere but through the lens as Cage palmed his cock again. His legs spread, jeans shoved down, the piercing shining. He twisted it with one hand and I heard him hiss. He ran a hand along his belly and then slid it back down, watching me the entire time.

God, he looked fit and tanned . . . and the way he sat, with his scarred shoulder and neck away from the camera, you couldn't see anything but shadows. All you could see was his cock, big and full, and he was straining for his own touch.

I clenched my fist because I wanted to touch it. I wanted to play with the piercing on top. I wondered if there were more. He bit his bottom lip as he stroked it lightly several times, and what he was doing wasn't an act. That was what made this so damned appealing.

His abs looked like they were cut into his golden skin. His eyes were so green that they jumped out at me through the darkened room.

Had he done this before? Did he want me to get down on my knees for him? Because that's what I wanted, and my face flushed.

He glanced down between my legs and nodded slightly.

He wants you to touch yourself. Here. In front of him.

Instead, I put my hand under my shirt and pinched a nipple. I bit my lip and watched him bark out a soft laugh while he stroked more leisurely now. I'd learn later that the point was to give the people what they paid for.

The fact that others would watch him get off only served to make me hotter. The fact that he could expose himself to a camera—knowing it would be mainly men watching him stroke himself—was so incredibly tantalizing that I made a mental note to ask Tenn for a copy.

As I continued to watch the scene unfold in front of me—less than ten feet away—I noted how the camera really loved him, how it demanded more of the perfection it currently translated. It didn't matter that he was scarred. He had an indefinable quality that would make men follow his lead and women simply follow. He was brooding, promised to be moody as fuck, and if I didn't already somehow believe I'd fallen in love with his voice on the phone, I knew it had happened here. Completely. Inextricably. Unrelentingly.

But knowing and admitting it were two very different things, and I pushed it all to the back of my mind.

He was half naked to my fully clothed, touching himself, being filmed . . . baring everything. And every stroke of his cock throbbed straight to my clit. He'd made himself unbearably vulnerable to me and still he was somehow completely in control.

His hand palmed his rigid length, his flushed face a mirror to mine and his eyes glossy with pleasure. His lip curled hungrily. I fought every rational urge to strip and sit on his lap, lower myself onto his cock until I was full with him.

This man came back from the dead for me. He wasn't playing games, wasn't going to come for me and leave. He was never leaving. This time, having a man tell me this was comforting.

"You like this?"

"More," I whispered, and I saw the hint of a smile on his face.

"You like watching."

I swallowed hard, knowing I couldn't answer, because even though his question wasn't for me but rather the masses watching him, I was dying to. A smile broke his face wide open for a brief, glorious second. He smiled because he knew, and then he said, "Don't stop—focus on me, okay, babe? I'm going to come thinking about you. I need you to know that."

Oh God. I squeezed my thighs together as I

became a giant ball of need, the throb between my legs more intense than anything I'd ever felt. Everything that had bottled up inside of me over the past weeks was threatening to overwhelm me, consume me.

"God, I want you to suck my cock," he ground out. "That's what's going to happen next, just so you know. You're going to get down on your knees and take it in your mouth and I'm going to come for you."

I didn't care that he might be ruining this by talking. I didn't think that was part of it, but maybe he was performing for the camera only.

No way, Calla.

I couldn't stop staring—his gaze had me locked, loaded, mesmerized. I was aware of his hand moving faster along his cock, but that's not where I watched. Not completely. I could see the whole picture, but it was the look on his face, the way his lips parted slightly . . . his lower lip swollen and wet and I wanted to put my finger in his mouth and watch him suck it. I wanted to get on my knees, put my cheek against his thigh and lick his balls.

I wanted to be so dirty with him.

I was going to come from simply watching him. And if I didn't, I wanted to. Needed to. If I could've ground against my own hand or anything else unnoticed, I would've, but everything I had was focused on him. I couldn't tear my eyes away, every muscle and fiber in my body invested in his orgasm.

His climax was brutally beautiful, a rush and a roar and his entire body shuddered, and it seemed like it could go on forever . . . and I would still watch. He ground out a strangled groan as he came, spurting along his belly and chest, a few drops hitting his scarred shoulder. He threw his head back for a moment, closed his eyes, and I wanted a still of that very moment, even though it was burned unduly in my brain.

When it ended—seconds, minutes, hours later?—his gaze through the camera leveled me. I had my hand on the off button, needing to press it, refusing to break the moment.

Could I walk over to him, straddle him, take him? Yes, he'd let me. Was I scared of my own arousal, fierce and needy?

Yes, terrified. Because I'd never thought I could feel even a minuscule portion of what I felt. And he knew, dammit. The self-satisfied, smug twist of his lip made me rethink the getting-down-on-my-knees bit. My body didn't agree, the tight, hot wetness between my legs aching for him.

Jesus Christ.

I yanked my gaze back to the viewfinder, like

I could hide there. But he was still watching me, even though I'd turned the camera off.

Once I'd pressed the off button, I'd expected the heated mood to shut down with it. But it didn't. It got hotter, even as he stood and tucked his half-hard cock into his jeans. His look, his stance—it was all an open invitation.

He picked up his shirt and walked toward me. I got my first up-close-and-personal view of just how far down those scars ran. To me, it looked like he'd been slashed purposely. He'd been tortured, and that would show in his eyes for the rest of his life.

"You shouldn't have been involved, Calla. But you are, even though it might only be peripherally. That's my fault. But I meant what I said about making the son of a bitch who hurt you pay."

"All by yourself? That's impressive."

"I'm sensing sarcasm."

"It's a second language," I muttered.

A corner of his mouth quirked like he was trying not to laugh and failing.

I was twenty-three years old. The guy in front of me was too wild. Too much of everything that was so bad for me, and what I'd just watched had done nothing to get it out of my system.

He brushed past me then, but before he did,

his gaze told me in no uncertain terms that this was far from over.

I'd fallen for him because of the unmistakable command in his voice. It'd been there even as he was dying. But the fact that he'd refused to leave without me was more than I'd ever thought I could handle. My head spun, my eyes locked to his, and I knew there would never be any escape from them.

And maybe I didn't want one.

Chapter 7

Cage went into the shower and jerked off again under the cool spray, because once was not enough. It had been too long for him. Granted, he'd been dying, but still, his libido didn't give a shit. It gave less of one after seeing Calla watching him.

Goddamned Tenn and his ideas. And he'd let one of his best friends completely fuck him over by sending him into a room to jack off in the corner. It didn't matter that all money made from his shoots went to an LGBT charity of Tenn's choice. It was that Tenn knew exactly what he was doing by putting Cage in a room with Calla.

Like fucking TNT in a room full of lit matches.

He stroked his cock with a soapy hand, wondering if Calla was touching herself while thinking of him. He'd bet money on it, and he planned on asking her the second he saw her. Which would be as soon as he dried off and dressed.

Because the whole "I don't know if I want to leave with you" bullshit was something he planned on ignoring. Even if he had to carry her out of there over his shoulder and tied up.

Tied up. Fuck. He put his forehead against the cold tile and stroked faster, his breath hitching as he pictured her lips and how they'd look wrapped around his cock. Pictured her on her knees in front of him, her hands holding fast to his hips, his hands buried in her hair.

He came with a hiss, the orgasm ripping from him, harder than the previous one. It was like being a teenager all over again. He held himself steady with a hand against the wall as he breathed hard. His shoulder and neck ached, like the doc told him it would, especially if he overdid it.

Who knew a hand job would be overdoing it?

Tenn was waiting for him, stretched on the bed, his long legs crossed. Cage slid on a pair of jeans and asked, "Please tell me you don't have cameras in that shower."

Tenn just laughed. And didn't answer him. Fuck. "She put her jeans on."

"And that's a good thing? Because I'd rather her naked."

"First time she's put on her own clothes since

she got here. Maybe give her half a second to adjust to your walking-dead state, Cage."

"Said the man who had me beat off in front of her."

"Had to let her see what she's been missing."

"Aren't you sweet. Definitely Mr. Romance of the Year."

"It was for your own good," Tenn said. "Try to tell me you didn't enjoy it."

Cage didn't lie as he yanked on his T-shirt and dragged his cut on over it. His keys and phone were in his pocket and he checked his phone messages.

Nothing.

"Heard you might not be welcomed back."

"Heard you weren't keeping up with the MC these days," Cage shot back.

"Yeah, like that's possible with Tals keeping tabs on me every five seconds," Tenn told him. "So you've really got no place to go? Because you'd better be seriously kissing Preacher's ass to get yourself back into MC Land."

"I'll be fine."

"It's Calla I'm worried about."

"Why's that?"

"There's something going on with her. Not sure what but . . . don't fuck this up."

Cage had a feeling he knew exactly what was

going on with her—but he couldn't push that with her. Not yet. "I don't intend to. At least not any more than it already is."

"How reassuring," Tenn drawled.

Cage caught his friend's gaze. "Check your phone, asshole. I called you that night. You didn't pick up."

Tenn paled and Cage instantly regretted saying anything. But fuck . . .

"Even if I knew that, I would've filmed you," Tenn told him, and suddenly Cage felt a whole lot less guilty.

"Yeah, I know. Because you're a bigger bastard than me."

"I'm a bastard because I believe in romance?"

"That was romance to you? Jesus H. Christ, Tenn, you're way more fucked up than I thought."

"But she's going to agree to go with you."

"Why? Because of the hand job of love?"

"Something like that. Trust me. I know shit."

Tenn did. He was right about a hell of a lot of things, including relationships. Excluding his own, since he never seemed to have one. Claimed it was by choice, but Cage didn't believe that for a second.

Cage sighed. "She has to come with me. She has to stay with me."

"So what's the issue?"

"You and I both know what kind of life I have. She doesn't belong with someone like me."

"Maybe not. But the way you two look at each other . . ." Tenn shook his head and stared at him. "You're not leaving each other anytime soon."

If Tenn could see it, that meant it was worse than Cage had originally thought. It was bad that Tenn could see through it so easily. The visceral drag between them reached out to grab Cage by the throat when he'd first seen her. And every second thereafter, it had only gotten worse.

One phone call and his goddamned heart was gone. Done. A lifetime of no attachments to women out the window. He'd analyzed it from every angle, thought about it till he drove himself crazy and realized that the only thing for him to do was find Calla. And surrender.

And he'd realized he was in deeper than he'd thought. Because as he lay dying on that fucking freezing cold floor, Calla's voice brought him back to life. And instead of dying he'd been comforting her.

Lying in his hospital bed, he'd practically seethed with rage and vengeance, used those emotions to get himself up and moving, much faster than the doctors wanted. But no matter how much they—and the nurses—threatened, then cajoled, then threatened again, it hadn't stopped him. Because the idea of finishing this once and for all made him move through the pain; it was Calla that got him through.

The entire time he was healing, he heard her voice when he let the shower beat down on his sore muscles, stiff from underuse. Her voice lulled him to sleep. Finding her and getting her out of trouble became the drumbeat of his soul.

He let that thought comfort him while he mourned Bernie.

Laid down his life for me, dammit. And Calla's too, by the sound of it. He'd heard Preacher and Tals talking about it when they thought he was asleep, how Tenn had called about a woman who'd been sent to him by Bernie. And he'd been grateful she'd been with Tenn. He didn't want Tals or Preacher near her, not without him. He didn't want her any more frightened than she no doubt was.

He couldn't have that. Tenn could be scary enough, but he wouldn't say a word about his war with the Heathens, the possible connections. Not until Cage went to him.

And so he'd been relieved Calla was with Tenn. But Tenn wasn't him. And about a thousand times a day, he convinced himself that Calla would be better off without him, that he should just let her go off on her way. She'd disappear and he'd take care of any danger that might follow her. She'd meet a nice guy . . .

And that last part would make Cage rethink his plan every time.

Chapter 8

Tenn had a gym set up for the guys, and during the early-morning hours it was pretty much empty. His guys were late-night partiers, and even if I'd wanted to sleep, it was off my agenda pretty much permanently, replaced by a simple grief so fresh it tended to catch me off guard at odd moments. Like my destiny had passed me by. Call it what you will, even laugh at me, but I wouldn't care. You don't when you connect with someone that deeply.

And now that he's here, you're pushing him away.

Or I'd at least tried. Cage was the first man in my life—the first person—to deliver on a promise. And I was trying desperately to see when the other shoe would drop and the promise would break.

But I'd gotten dressed in the clothes I'd arrived in, clothing I'd let sit on a chair in the bedroom for a month while I'd wallowed in borrowed sweats and T-shirts.

I'd showered too, bringing myself to a tight, quick climax that left me slack-mouthed and tingly. I'd done it like I'd known he was somehow privy to my orgasm.

And so I was sitting there in the gym, dressed and waiting, when Tenn found me, although I don't think he was actually looking for me. His expression was troubled as he glanced at me and asked, "Are you all right?"

"You're not."

He laughed a little. "I didn't pick up the fucking phone," he said, his voice dark. "I was helping a kid and I saw it was Cage. Figured he hadn't been in touch for months, so fuck him, I'd get back to him when I was ready. Kid was really fucked. Beaten and needed a hospital."

The guilt that choked his voice was immense. "Tenn, you didn't know . . ."

"I should've."

"If you'd picked up, I wouldn't be here."

"Exactly," he said.

"Exactly," I told him.

He shook his head.

"Cage doesn't blame you."

"Makes it worse."

"You were helping a kid. That's what you do."

He glanced at me. "It was Kev—the one who's always writing."

I put a hand to my throat. "The night I came here . . ."

"He was in the hospital already. Safe and sound. He came here about two days before I forced you to surface." He stared up at the ceiling for a second. "Most of the guys I deal with are from fucked-up backgrounds. Not all, but—" He shrugged. "It's a type I know well."

"Tenn—" I put a hand on his arm.

He drew in a breath, looked like he was making a decision, and then he began, "I got into porn when I was young. Forced into it." He paused. "I liked it. That's not to say the business side of it wasn't like a second rape. But really, I started the business because of my mom. She was a whore— her word, not mine. 'Escort' was always too fancy for her. No one protected her. I wasn't going to let that happen to anyone else if I could help it. I don't expect you to understand, but the background I came from . . . let's just say, I'd have killed to have someone provide me with a safe way to make this kind of money. They're going to do it anyway. If they do it with me, they've got a shot at getting on with their lives, or to keep going in this industry. Whatever floats their boat."

"So going into the sex business helps unfuck things for them."

"It's not that easy a link. It's probably more about control."

I could understand that, more than he knew, but I didn't say anything. The reasons people made the choices they did were alternately fascinating and heartbreaking. "You take good care of these guys. Of me."

"I try."

"Who takes care of you, Tenn? Was there ever anyone special?"

He smiled. "At one point, yes."

"And?"

"He ran into special forces and never looked back," he admitted. "Probably better that way."

"Or maybe he's thinking about you the same way you are him."

"You're very bad for me, Calla," Tenn warned, then sighed. "You can stay here, hon. But I think you're cheating yourself and I'm not sure why."

"He's dangerous," I blurted out.

"Best things in life usually are," Tenn countered.

"You can keep me safe."

"Of course I can. But the thing is, Cage already set his sights on you. Once that happens . . ." He shook his head, like I had no idea what I was in for.

"He does this with a lot of women?"

"Actually, no. Never. But I've seen him with a single-minded focus before—in the military, with the MC. Whatever he puts his mind to, he accomplishes. He's not an easy man, but he's worth it."

He wasn't easy, but a part of me didn't want—didn't trust—easy. Maybe because I'd never been either easy or able to trust.

"I know you're angry about Cage's promise. Promises can be a freaky thing."

"And the fact that he was alive and didn't tell me," I added. "Let's not forget that."

"Cage and my brother kept me in blackout mode too," he said.

"Why?"

"A couple of reasons. Because Cage is in trouble—there are people still after him. Because it was safer for you, and for me and my business—for the guys involved."

"Because whatever Bernie and Cage were involved in, I'm involved in it too."

He didn't deny it. But he didn't expound on it either, deferring to Cage to tell me. Instead he offered, "Cage saved you in more ways than one. The only thing that stopped that was you taking Bernie's picture."

"Why's that? They'd recognize you?"

"Maybe. They'd definitely recognize Cage. And

if they'd been smart enough to take out the back of the picture, you'd find names and latitude and longitude."

"I should probably leave it with you, then."

"That'd be best. I'll make you a copy, though," he told me. "Wait—you said leave it with me. That means . . . ?"

I nodded. I'd met a protector in Bernie and now I had a friend and protector in Tenn. But with Cage, I might be able to have it all.

I left Tenn and went out to face the music. Cage was waiting, stretched out on the couch, his big black boots on the coffee table. His still-smoldering gaze met mine, as intense as a physical touch.

"I already figured that any woman who fights a dying man's wishes isn't going down easy," he said.

I felt the need to point out the obvious. "You said you weren't going to die."

"So you did believe some of what I told you."

"That situation was one of a kind. Intense."

"So it would've been like that with anyone?"

I crossed my arms across my chest. Shielding myself from him had already proven impossible, but I was stubborn. "Yes."

"Bullshit. When did you start lying to yourself?"

For survival, I wanted to shout. *Because I was*

busy mourning you, when I couldn't finally do with you what I'd never done with anyone else.

So I didn't answer him. He got up in one swift movement, and I backed away a step or two, but no, he wasn't letting that happen. Mr. Tall, Dark and Commanding closed that space rapidly, leaving just enough room for me to not be completely threatened.

"Kiss me."

"You can't order someone to kiss you."

"I'm not ordering *someone*. I'm telling *you* to kiss *me*."

My tongue darted out to lick the corner of my lip as I considered this. Very dangerous—or it could possibly prove that this pretense of attraction was just that. "Okay, fine."

He raised his brows in that "I'm waiting" way.

I put my mouth on him and was rewarded with a bruising, brutal kiss that devastated my nervous system. Hands down destroyed it as he'd proved I'd been lying to myself.

"Damn you," I murmured against his mouth, and then I stopped thinking. His arms came around me, steel bands, but warm. His whole body was so damned warm.

He murmured against my cheek, "Every second I was on that goddamned concrete floor, bleeding and waiting for help, I thought about you. Every single day I was in that hospital, I thought about you."

"You hung up."

"I had to concentrate on not dying, Calla," he said fiercely, then softened. "I want you to realize that I'm not going anywhere. Correction—I'm not going anywhere without you."

I thought about him lying on the concrete floor, then in a hospital bed, clinging to life. Thinking about me. Heady stuff, and I couldn't deny that it made me feel better about the uncertainty I'd faced so far. "You expect women to fall at your feet. I'm sure they do. It's not happening this time."

He leaned into me again, the scruff of his cheek brushing my ear. "It's already happened, Calla. So fucking deal with it."

Was it time to surrender to the inevitable? What could it hurt?

It could break your heart, baby girl.

My mother's voice. Grams's too. Both strong women almost done in by equally strong and dangerous men.

Although no, that wasn't right—those men were dangerous, but not strong. Because they'd never come back to do what was right. Cage was here, despite everything, despite the threats to his own life. According to Tenn, Cage had risked it again to come make sure I was all right. How could I walk away from that?

God, I was in so much trouble. I should run, out the door, down the street, beg the nearest police officer to get me home . . .

Home.

Where's that again, Calla?

But no, I wouldn't do that, because I had nowhere else to go. I'd never let myself be defeated, and I wouldn't start now.

I'd had dark, dangerous men circle me before. I seemed to be a magnet for them. I was independent and they took that as a personal affront or challenge. But that's not why I did it. Not at all.

I saw what dangerous men did to the women in my family, how it left them with nothing, beat up and destroyed. It started with Grams, continued with Mom, who loved a bad man while never giving Jameson Bradley a second chance. And it continued with me trusting the wrong boy.

I'd watched love ravage those women until they'd become nearly unrecognizable. Loving the wrong man wasn't a crime, but I began to believe that it should've been. Because it rendered both my mom and Grams incapable of loving any other man—any good man—and there were several in each of their lives that came calling.

I never went as far as to say my family was cursed, but if you looked at the long line of disappointments, I don't know if you'd agree or not. Or maybe you'd simply say it was a self-fulfilling prophecy. And maybe it was, but I wasn't planning on getting near any dangerous man to find out. I'd already done it with that phone call, fallen in love with a dying, dangerous man who stole my heart in ten minutes and would never let it go.

Or maybe I was just protecting myself. To let Cage walk away seemed like a foolish, selfish thing to do when I'd been given a second chance with him.

I'd already fallen too fast—completely, ridiculously, head-spinningly fast—and there was no escape from it. But I couldn't shake from my mind one notion that my mother ingrained in me.

You take a man's money, you give him power.

And I was never giving the only thing I had away. And that was why I'd never touched the settlement money from Jeffrey Harris's family.

Out of the corner of my eye, I saw Tenn come back into the room. I glanced over at him, then gave Cage a hard stare. "I'll go with you. For protection. Obviously, there's a connection between us. I'll share your bed, but I'm not yours to order around. You don't own me, Cage. No one ever will."

Cage stared. Tenn gave a low whistle, but, smart man that he was, said nothing.

Cage was either very stupid or very brave, because he did speak. "In or out of bed?"

"What?"

"You said you're not mine to order around   is that in or out of bed?"

I swallowed hard, hated the thrill that went through me at the thought of Cage and bed. "Neither."

He shook his head slowly. "You can think that it'll end there, sweetheart. But the MC doesn't work like that. I don't work like that. It's a different world, like nothing you've ever been involved in before. It's going to blow your mind. I'm as goddamned possessive as I know you are. You want to go in thinking we'll play this fast and loose, make it a casual thing—you try it."

"You're saying it's not going to work?"

"I'm saying that my MC doesn't fuck its way through women like you. They'll be hands-off because of me. Every MC woman wants the opposite of what you just said. Every guy too, if he's not too stupid to admit it."

"Do you?"

"I'm here, aren't I?"

"I can't tell if that's guilt."

"I don't fuck who I pity." His harsh language, self-absorbedness all clenched in my belly, fueling the already big ball of want. "So if I don't own you, then you don't own me? You can handle that?"

Behind me, Tenn cursed, a warning, and I had to stand my ground. "I can."

I'd just lied to him, and it wasn't the first time.

Chapter 9

Calla was still packing when Cage heard the un-mistakable roar of tricked-out bikes breaking the quiet of the North Carolina night.

Tenn stilled. "That's not Tals."

Definitely not. "Heathens." They rigged their bikes loud and obnoxious, and their enforcers were rigged the loudest. "I wasn't followed."

"Could've been info in Bernie's office on me. Could just be that they followed her here and they were biding their time, waiting for you," Tenn said as he drew the blinds, then looked through the side.

"Now you say that?"

"Not like I saw Heathens hanging around the beach. I think I would've noticed."

"Some of them aren't as sloppy as the others." He listened again. "They're three blocks away."

"You scare me with that shit."

Hell, this'd been his bread and butter. Still would be, if Preacher would take him back in.

Tenn glanced at him. "You gotta go."

"I'm not leaving you with this."

"You've leaving with Calla."

"This is about me, not her," Cage said.

"I'm sure. But that doesn't change the fact that I've got three assholes to contend with." Tenn paused. "If they find you here . . ."

"Let them."

"You're not up to this. Not with Calla by your side. What's more important this time—the fight or the girl?"

Tenn's eyes challenged him, reminding him why he'd come here in the first place. "Both, Tenn. They're two sides of the same damned coin."

But nevertheless, he'd pulled his keys from his pocket. "Call Tals."

"Already did. I'll let you know what this is all about."

"You're going to give them a chance to talk?"

"I'm feeling charitable." Tenn grinned as he flexed his fingers.

"You know there are more waiting for me to run so they can follow."

"Counting on it," Tenn said. "I'm also counting on you outriding them. You always could."

"I'd rather fight this one than run," Cage said quietly.

"You think I want to see you fight? You think I can't?" Tenn asked. "I want to see you get the girl. So get. The fucking. Girl."

He turned away from Cage, focusing all his energy and concentration on the front door. Calla came out of the bedroom, bag slung over her arm, looking hot in a borrowed black leather jacket of Tenn's.

"What's going on?"

"We've got to go, Calla."

She glanced nervously at Tenn, whose shoulders had squared. The energy in the room had changed palpably. The fight was in Tenn. "What's that sound?"

"Heathens MC."

"Are they after you?"

"And you." Normally, he'd stay and fight, not let Tenn take on the burden. But he couldn't risk Calla, and Tenn knew that better than anyone. And so Cage did what he'd never done before.

He ran.

She paled and he grabbed her, picked her up and walked her out the back door. Took her bag while handing her a helmet, and once she got on the bike behind him, he told her, "Hang on, Calla. That's all you've got to do."

As he pulled out, he noted the Heathens' bikes parked in Tenn's front yard. And where there were three Heathens, more were waiting in the wings. They'd figured that if he'd gotten away, he'd head for the most open road and, fuck it all, they were right.

The bike had the advantage. He slid in and out of truck traffic as Calla held on to him so tightly, her face pressed to his back. He was taking her life in his hands and he'd already nearly taken it away once before.

But there was no choice now. Because saving her, getting her out of this mess was now the only option he had.

He forgot about Calla. Worrying about the girl in the bitch seat was a surefire way to get them both killed. And he could ride the goddamned shit out of a bike better than anyone he knew. And he'd do that now.

He'd ridden for his life before. It took a single-minded focus, and now, with the smell of tar, exhaust and fear swirling around him, the wind rushed madly against his face, battering his body at times, and at others pushing it forward.

His hands tightened around the bars. He had to fight the urge not to clutch the throttle too hard, refused to freeze and make everything stall out.

He couldn't think when he rode like this. He just had to react. Push forward, refuse to look back, ride like the devil was at his heels and his soul was in question.

Wasn't it?

And he wove in and out of the lanes, throwing off the men behind them, keeping the few cars he saw on the road out of his drama. The bike danced for him like a pliant but formidable partner.

I held on to Cage tightly and concentrated on not distracting him. My pulse beat a tattoo and I could barely breathe, but the bike wove through the roads smoothly.

We had to be doing close to eighty miles per hour, and eighty on a bike was so different from what it was in a car. My body vibrated so hard I wasn't sure if I'd break or come, and that had to be the oddest situation I'd ever felt in my life.

The bike swerved as Cage headed off-road, and my body dipped right, the heavy steel horse between my legs powering me along. Saving me.

And at the same time, bringing me right back into the arms of danger.

I heard the roar of the other bikes behind us for a long while, it seemed. And then I only heard the wind and the low purr of Cage's bike. I didn't dare turn around, but even though Cage didn't slow down per se, his body eased. As the bike tore through the dark and dusty roads, I relaxed more into the rhythms of the bike's movements, found myself leaning when he leaned and rubbing my cheek along his leather jacket.

I was never more aware of the throb between my legs as I was now. It was a throb I couldn't ignore for much longer, an ache that got more intense the farther the bike seemed to climb in altitude. My sex rubbed against the metal and leather, looking for some kind of relief. I swore I had a mini orgasm at one point, and I was sleepy and turned on and wired all at once, and I swore if Cage pulled over and wanted to take me in the dirt, I'd be helpless to say no.

When he did pull over, he reached a hand back to hold me steady as I got off the bike. My legs were nearly jelly, and he didn't let go, even as he swung his own leg over. His arm caught around my lower back, keeping me upright and propelling me toward the cabin. He'd parked alongside it, in a lean-to with a canvas cover he pulled down before we walked onto the porch.

"These are seriously creepy woods," I murmured. "Serial-killer woods."

He snorted but didn't argue. The door was open but the low hum of a set alarm comforted me. He hit some buttons, keeping me in front of him, then closed the door and reset the alarm.

Then he flipped on the lights.

Okay, so we were cut off, but there was a bed and running water—I saw a sink—and, hopefully, heat?

When I glanced up at him, I realized I had all the heat I could need. There was a connection, an intense, inexplicable one strung taut between us, that yanked us closer until the electricity crackled.

I didn't know what to do or say. All I could think of was, "Thank you."

"You don't have to thank me. You're going to be with me. You're mine, whether you're ready to admit it or not."

I wasn't. Instead, I focused on his hands going under my jacket and my shirt, caressing my bare skin. His hands were large, rough and extremely capable, like the rest of him. That thought went straight to my sex. I was already wet for him, and his tongue touched the corner of his mouth for a brief second, lingered there long enough so I could picture it licking me. Spreading my legs and taking me with his tongue, tugging my clit in his teeth . . . making me scream.

God damn, get a grip, girl. "We talked about this, *Cage.*"

"You're flushed, *Calla.*"

"Warm in here," I lied as coolly as I could.

He hadn't let me go, though, and what had started back at Tenn's was about to culminate, a freight train without breaks. There was no stopping it.

His mouth came down on mine, a brutal, heart-stopping kiss. I moaned into his mouth and I swore he smiled against mine before capturing my body against his. His grip was insistent and there was no missing how hard he was. My arms wound around his shoulders, a hand cupped the back of his neck, and I surrendered, just like that.

I sucked on his tongue the way I'd wanted to suck him earlier, and when I pulled back, I caught his bottom lip in my teeth for a second. And he ground out a groan.

"You're in so much goddamned trouble, Calla."

"Good," I told him. "Show me."

He laughed, a dark, rich sound that bit me with a hard shiver. I could lie and say it was the adrenaline of the ride, the promise of almost being caught . . . the fact that we'd made it safe and sound was what made me want to rip his clothes off. But I'd wanted to do it from the first moment I'd heard his voice.

"You. Naked. You've already seen me."

"I've seen your dick," I corrected.

He pulled down his fly and put my hand on his cock. "I've been hard for you since I walked in. The bike ride made it worse."

I don't think he expected me to stroke him, but I did. He stilled for a second, especially when I brought my thumb up to play with the piercing. And then he smiled and it told me that I was in trouble. The good kind. "Maybe you should get naked first."

He obviously had no problem with that. He pushed his jeans down and pulled his shirt off. "Gotta untie my boots," he said.

Reluctantly, I released him. He had the boots and jeans off and he was carrying me over to the couch, practically over his shoulder. He pulled open the couch bed with one hand and put me down.

He hovered over me, completely naked. "Your turn."

He wasn't right on me, wasn't holding me down, and he wasn't trying to strip me. He was watching me with a mixture of lust and concern, and while my heart tugged for what he was doing, I planned on wiping the concern right off.

I sat up slightly and pulled my tank top off. Unhooked my bra as he watched, and made short work of my own jeans. For a long moment, he just stared at me, then murmured "Beautiful" and "Mine" before kissing my belly. His hands covered my breasts, my nipples tender to his rough touch. I arched beneath them, pushing them against him. I was so wet, my legs spread, hooked around one of his thighs as his cock drove into my belly.

While at Tenn's, I couldn't fantasize about him. I was ruthless about cutting off my needs because I was certain that would curse us. Now, coming off my fast, I was starving, my core aching for him.

The truth was, I hadn't enjoyed sex before this. I pretended to, made myself have and take all the power because I thought it would soothe me. It just allowed me to stay in control.

There was no control when I was with Cage—and no pretending either. He'd never allow it.

But with him, I didn't have to pretend anything. Not with his hands on me, leaving trails that were a combination of fire and ice—intoxicating, exhilarating . . . liberating.

I'd come for him if he touched the right spot. Or anywhere close to it. And when his mouth closed on my nipple, my entire body writhed and I climaxed with a surprised, low moan.

He simply sucked harder, rubbing my sex with his thigh. And then he prepared to take me over the edge again.

"Have to taste you," he told me, moving down between my legs, lifting my legs over his shoulders. I was completely open to him, and he licked along the seam of my sex, his tongue driving inside me. He held my thighs open as I threaded my fingers through his hair to keep him close.

"Cage . . . please," I whispered urgently, the need for release clawing through me like a fever. The second orgasm tore through me faster than I'd ever thought possible. But Cage didn't stop, and even when I thought I couldn't come again, I did.

He watched my face the whole time. There was nothing sexier than that, knowing I was under his gaze, unable to escape his pleasure assault in so many ways.

I'd dreamed about this, but my dreams were always a mix of heavy sadness at knowing what I couldn't have. This was pure, unmitigated pleasure, and I reveled in it. I swore I still smelled the scent of adrenaline from his body—the outside air that enveloped us on the ride up to the cabin.

And when I couldn't take it any longer, he kissed his way up my belly and positioned himself over me.

His hold was strong, but it wasn't making me panic. No, exactly the opposite, because for the first time ever—in bed—I was safe. I sagged with relief against him and his grip grew more insistent. I didn't think it would be possible to get closer to him, but that's what I wanted.

He could hurt me, really and truly, but his control was so finely tuned that he didn't. It made me breathe out in wonder, enjoying the heavy weight of every part of his body on mine. His erection was pressing my belly . . . and then, when he moved down, it pressed against the tight, hot bundle of nerves between my legs.

I shifted my hips to press back just as wantonly, murmured, "Please."

"I'll please you, Calla."

I grabbed his shoulders, still dazed. "This is make-believe."

He pushed up into me, filling me. I gasped. "That feel real enough for you?"

The man inside me became my world. And I was okay with that. More than okay with it.

"Stop thinking," he growled. "I want to make you forget."

As we rocked against each other, I knew for certain that I'd never forget him.

Chapter 10

"So much for not sharing my bed," Cage murmured several hours later.

"Technically, this is a couch."

"A pullout, making it a bed."

"There were extenuating circumstances," I told him. "And I never said I wouldn't share your bed—just that you couldn't order me around."

"Right." He didn't look convinced at all. I wasn't either, but I frowned and tugged the covers over me. "Pull those down, babe."

"No." I paused. "I will if you check on Tenn."

"I can work with that." He reached behind him and held up his phone. There was a photo of Tenn crouching next to two men in leather vests on the ground.

"He showed them," I murmured. Cage gave a small smile, put the phone down as he pulled the covers away from me. He covered me with his body instead, and I wrapped a leg around the back of his thigh. He had the heaters going—I'm guessing he didn't use the fireplace because we were technically hiding. "What's this place?"

"Vipers owns it. We call it the Cabin of Secrets," he said with zero irony. "When the club's got an issue, guys come here. Admit stuff. Like a confessional, without the priest."

"And here I thought that was Tenn's specialty."

"Tenn's dealing with his own shit in his own way," Cage explained.

"You were in the Army together?"

"We went through basic together. Ended up on different platoons for a while—that's how I met his brother, Tals. Then Tals went to a different unit and Tenn and I served under Bernie."

"I'm so sorry."

"It's not your fault, Calla. It's mine. Can't stop my past from hurting people. The harder I run, it seems like the easier they catch me."

"So stop running," I told him. "What if we both stopped running and turned and fought instead?"

"I'm afraid we'd just be fighting for the rest of our lives."

"I'd rather fight than run," I admitted.

*   *   *

Later, I woke with a start, alone in bed under a warm blanket. I wound it around me as I looked around the darkened cabin.

I caught sight of Cage. He was sitting in a chair by the window. The soft light made him look young. It didn't hurt that I was looking at the unscarred side of his face, although I decided then and there I liked both sides together, because both sides made the man.

"Hey," he said without turning his head.

"I didn't think you noticed me."

"I notice everything about you, Calla."

It was odd to be shy around him after sex, and I still was, but I fought for boldness. "I would've shown your face on the tape. That was everything, the whole show."

"That part of the show was just for you." He gave a fleeting grin, and if it wasn't so dark, maybe I would've seen a slight flush to his cheeks. "Half face is standard for shots like that. No pun intended. My scars wouldn't have worked for everyone."

I moved close to him. He shifted on the chair, making room for me on his lap. Even if I'd wanted to refuse, he was tugging me down and I curled in his lap. "Are the Heathens the ones who did this to you?"

Finally, he ground out, "Yes. Five of them."

Five. And Cage had been shot, stabbed and beaten severely. He'd be feeling those injuries for a long time to come. He rubbed his hand along his scarred neck, like he was revisiting the scene. He wasn't self-conscious about the scars.

His jaw clenched and his eyes snapped fire. I should've been scared enough of him to move away, because I knew what he was capable of surviving. I could only imagine what a fair fight would be like for him.

"Why do you want to know this, Calla?"

"Because you almost died. Because I think you're taking me into the same world where this happened."

He clenched his jaw and then ground out, "Fair enough."

I had a feeling nothing that happened to Cage was fair.

With Calla in his lap, Cage told her how he'd gone to the underground garage with the promise of information. "I've been trying to get information I could use against the Heathens. They've been giving my club trouble for years, and I finally had a way to stop them. There was this guy who'd been working for the Heathens on and off, but he wasn't a member. And he was easily flipped for the right price. So I met him and got what I needed."

"The numbers," she said quietly.

He nodded. "It wasn't in my source's best interest to tell the Heathens what was going on, and as far as I know, he's still working for them and he's been calling me too. I'm still trying to figure out how the Heathens found me, but I've never run from a fight before tonight." From anyone or anything.

"I consider tonight about saving me."

He brushed hair from her shoulder and nipped at the unmarred skin, reddening it a little. She ran a hand over his scarred cheek—it tingled every time she touched it, like she was bringing the nerves back to life.

He leaned his head back and recalled that night. He'd been surrounded, and the fact that it was familiar faces only added to the warning bells that indicated he should've been up and out of there an hour before.

He could still hear Troy's voice.

Dad says hi.

Jesus, how he'd ended up with such a dick for a brother, he'd never know.

He'd heard the sirens in the distance before he'd called Bernie's phone. They'd scared Troy away—even though they'd known the ambulance was ten minutes out, Troy figured Cage would be dead by the time the EMTs found him. At that moment, lying on the cement floor, he'd been beyond pain, didn't feel the coldness of the cement under his body as much as his entire body was cold. He'd blinked, but it hadn't cleared the blurriness from his eyes. He saw the blood from his wound spreading under him rapidly.

Shot and stabbed. His idiot brother was always one for overkill.

You always knew you wouldn't die in your bed peacefully. He'd known he wouldn't live to any kind of ripe old age, but he'd lived longer than he'd expected to.

But he didn't let Calla in on any of that—his history with the Heathens wasn't something he let out easily. Instead, he told her, "I just knew I had to hang on until the ambulance got there. I hung up on you because I had to crawl through the garage—I was all the way in the corner, behind a Dumpster. They might've missed me."

She stared at him. "I would've stayed on."

"I know that."

And he'd known he'd been potentially fucking up her life by giving her the intel, but choices were so limited. He couldn't let the Heathens win. And he wouldn't let the guy who'd put that pain in her voice win either.

He'd crawled on his hands and knees out of the parking garage, and when he couldn't crawl anymore, he'd commanded himself to keep going, ignoring the pain in his chest and the fact that he'd begun to wheeze. He'd been freezing by the time he'd heard screams and attracted attention from two older women coming to collect their car.

One of them had pushed the hair out of his face and told him that he was going to be okay. She'd smelled like flowered perfume and her touch was such a mom's touch, so much like his own mom before she'd gotten hooked on that shit. He'd closed his eyes and thought about her . . . and Calla . . . and Calla was his first thought when he'd opened them.

He'd even said her name, and the nurse told him, "You haven't shut up about her. She must be pretty special."

"She is," he'd agreed, and then he'd done everything in his power to stay the hell away from her. And he told Calla all of that, then said, "I was in the hospital. I didn't know Bernie died. Preach—Preacher Jones—he kept it from me because I wasn't in any shape to deal with it. The second I woke up—"

"You were in a coma?"

"Yes."

"When did the Heathens find out you were still alive?"

He glanced over at her. "When I called them and told them they'd have to try a hell of a lot harder than that."

She bit her lip, then ran a hand over his scars. "This isn't going to be an easy ride."

"No one ever promised it would be."

"The Heathens know I'm with you."

"Yeah."

"And Tenn said they know I worked with Bernie. That they'll come after me in case I know something."

"They're ruthless, Calla. I wish I could tell you otherwise. I didn't think that they were already watching Bernie. I thought I was smarter . . . that I could do it on my own, without backup." He stared at her eyes, and there was understanding there.

"You didn't want anyone else to get hurt," she said quietly.

He nodded. "And in the process, look what happened. I made you a target. For me, that's normal. I was born with a bull's-eye on my back."

"Can you use the information you got against the Heathens still? It's not too late, is it?"

"Never too late, babe. But I've got to be careful who I give the information to. Law enforcement and motorcycle clubs aren't exactly on the best of terms." He sighed. "In the meantime, I need to find a way to stop a few of the higher-ups in that club. And I don't want to talk about the Heathens anymore."

It wasn't fair to her at all—she had a right to ask all the goddamned questions she wanted to, even if he couldn't give her the answers. But she looked at him, nodded and said, "I don't either," and he knew he was a goddamned goner.

Chapter 11

Cage took a long drink of his beer and I did the same when he shared it with me. I was warm and tingly inside already, so I didn't need much else to help. I was untouchable here with Cage. I'd take it for however long it would last.

"Storm's coming," he said. Until then, I hadn't noticed the wind, but I quickly realized that the wind slammed the cabin doors. At any other time, the storm might've echoed the rising storm inside of me, but Cage eased the mind-numbing fear.

"How far away from Skulls are we?"

"Hours. Whole different world in these hills."

"Whose world?"

"This is near Havoc territory," he said.

"Is that a metaphor?"

"Another MC. Bad motherfuckers." He handed me a beer.

"So, not friendly, then?"

"Better than the Heathens."

I took another long drink from the bottle. "That's not very comforting."

"Not meant to be. This is dangerous shit."

"And here I thought you weren't scared of anything."

His smile was easy. "Fear keeps you from being stupid, if you're smart enough to see it." His smile had been easy for a moment and then he turned serious. "The MC world . . . it's nothing like you've seen."

"We had MC members come into my family's bar."

"Seeing a couple of bikers in a random bar's a lot different than living with an MC man," he said, not unkindly, and I recalled the information Tenn had already provided me with. "But for the moment, I've ensured you've got no choice. You're not safe without me, Calla, but that's not the only reason I want you with me."

How he could admit that so openly amazed me. Cage stated it like an immutable law and I didn't want any other choice but to believe him. And rather than delving further into that, I asked instead, "Did the Heathens follow you to Tenn's?"

His jaw tightened. "I think they were waiting there to see if I showed. They were still actively looking for you. They know Bernie, Tenn and I were in the Army together. Makes sense they'd stake us all out. Tenn said you didn't leave the house, but I'm sure you went out on the back deck. Who knows if they saw you there and waited for me." He paused. "You made a phone call from Tenn's fax line."

"Do you think . . . Was that traced somehow?"

"I don't know, babe. I wouldn't think they'd go that far but . . ."

I steeled myself for the anger, but none came. "Then you know who I called."

"Yes."

I pulled the blanket tighter around me. "He's my father."

"Did you tell him where you were? Or what happened?"

"No. I didn't want him to worry about me. I'm sorry." I kept the rest to myself. "Do you think the Heathens were tracking me through my father's calls?"

"I wouldn't think they'd be that smart to re-search who your dad was."

The thought of my father being in trouble be-cause of me made my stomach turn. "Bernie was helping my dad. Maybe someone made the con-nection."

Cage watched me silently, waiting for me to

spill everything. God, I didn't want to. "Is this about the guy I'm going to find?"

My throat tightened. "No. Bernie was looking for my brother. He—Ned—stole money from me."

"And your dad was helping?"

"Yes. He's not Ned's father so . . ." I shrugged, hoping that would end it. "I'm sorry—if I'd thought for a moment . . ."

"That you'd have a rabid MC on your ass, you would've behaved differently? I'm thinking not," he said. "But from now on, you need to."

"The way you talk about your club . . . do you like it there?"

"Most of the time, yes." He paused. "I'm not sure how any woman survives it, though."

His honesty floored me. "But some do, right?"

"Yeah, some do, Calla."

I swallowed. "If you want to be with someone enough, you'll deal with almost anything. As long as you're doing it together, right?"

When I was younger, I looked for a love that would tear me up and have its way with me. I wanted to feel battered. Satiated. Terrified. The ups and downs of my mother's love life made me think that was the only way it should be. It wasn't until I got a little older—and wiser—that I realized that all I really wanted was a love that would set me free from all the pain of my past.

I knew it was out there, if for nothing else, because of all the time musicians and authors spend on the subject. It's the Holy Grail and compromise is out of the question. Still, I figured that, after what happened with Harris, I'd never really be able to trust any guy again. That didn't mean I didn't try. I pretended I didn't care. And while I never had another situation like that one, it didn't mean I was happy. I'd had some good sex—I'd needed to in order to make up for the worst first time ever—but the attraction postsex was never there.

Not like this. "I'm going with you by choice, Cage. Not because I don't have one."

"Good."

"Whatever happens . . . I don't have any expectations. I don't even want any. It's all too complicated anyway. Sex is simple."

He raised his brows. "You might be the first woman in history to say that. Even if I know you don't mean it."

I didn't bother arguing.

I woke to the sound of bodies thumping against the wall, hard. I heard grunts and cursing and tried to make myself invisible against the back of the couch while I watched the shadows, really hoping that one of them was Cage.

"Son of a—"

Yes, Cage. I sagged in relief, especially when another man's voice said, "She would've been proud to be called 'bitch.'"

"Asshole."

I blinked and watched the men stand, saw Cage shove the other man away hard. When the man I didn't know turned to me, I immediately saw the resemblance to Tenn.

"You shouldn't have done this shit alone, Cage."

"Heard it from your brother. Don't need to hear the same shit from you."

"You're going to hear it, and a lot more where that came from."

"Calla, this is Talon," Cage said, and Tenn's brother smiled and corrected, "Friends calls me Tals."

"She's not your friend," Cage replied.

Tals shrugged, unconcerned. "Now I can see why you didn't want any of us near her."

Cage groaned. "Ah Jesus, Tals. Shut it!"

Tals's laugh was deep and booming. "You've got it bad."

I, for one, was glad to hear it, but I wasn't happy about the world intruding. Cage had warned it would happen, sooner than I'd want it to.

Cage ran a hand through his hair and sighed. "Why *are* you here, Tals? Coincidence?"

"You're the one who always says there's no such thing. No, sir, I'm your escort back to Skulls in the morning."

Cage tensed immediately—and I wasn't the only one who noticed it. Tals clapped a hand on his shoulder and said, "Preach is not happy."

"How much does Preach know?"

"He knows everything," Talon said simply. "Calla, honey, we're just gonna step outside for a few minutes."

"Knock yourself out," I told him, then wrapped the sheet around my body and headed to the shower. I could've sworn they both whistled at me.

And I liked it.

Cage watched Calla's retreating back until she shut the bathroom door behind her. Tals had whistled with him, but then his friend had turned away and was already on the front porch when Cage joined him.

"Tenn wouldn't let me come get her."

"He's the smart one in your family," Cage told him, and sidestepped a swipe at the back of his head.

"I wouldn't have let anything happen to her. Christ, hers was the only name you kept saying, over and over and—"

Cage held up a hand. "I've heard it before."

"You're keeping her with you, then?"

"Yeah."

"Why?"

"Lot of reasons. But I pulled her into this, and I'm the only one who can get her out."

"Keep telling yourself that," Tals muttered.

His friend was more pissed than Tenn after being shut out. Even though he'd known that Cage wasn't dead pretty much the whole time. But before that, Cage had dropped out of sight for months, and he'd refused to return any calls. "I'm sorry, Tals."

"Yeah, that you got caught."

"Gonna make a great father with lines like that."

Tals pointed at him, fear of the devil in his eyes. "Don't you dare fucking curse me like that."

Cage snorted. "Did Tenn get anything out of the Heathens?"

"They weren't in a chatty mood and Tenn doesn't have the patience for that shit." Tals crossed his arms and stared at him. "Going to finally tell me what the hell really happened? Because I don't believe the Heathens just happened to sneak up on you."

"Got some intel."

"Gonna share?"

"Tapes. Wiretaps."

"Enough for a RICO case against them?" Tals asked.

Cage nodded. "It's locked up tight, though. I won't risk giving it to the feds until I know who I'm giving it to."

"Your dad know you have it?" Tals asked, then paled. "Shit. That's why?"

Cage kept his mouth shut. He wasn't sure he could get the words out.

Tals whistled softly. "I knew it was Heathens, Cage . . . but . . . your dad?"

"He sent Troy." And Cage didn't know if that made it better or worse. "A lot of this is about me, Tals. But some of it's about her."

"We've had to tread lightly where Bernie's concerned."

Cage agreed. It was the only thing that kept him from breaking into the police database to see what they knew. The only thing that stopped him from calling Bernie's sister. He thought about the burial, how he and Tenn and Tals had to avoid it . . .

"He always knew what he was in for with us," Tals told him. "He went into things with both eyes open."

"Calla didn't." Tals looked like he wanted to say something, but he didn't, and so Cage continued. "Need a favor."

"You're serious? Beyond this saving-your-ass thing?"

"Where were you when I was trying to lose a Heathen tail tonight?"

Tals snorted. "Go for it. Just remember, you're really racking them up."

"Bernie was trying to help Calla."

"And while you avoided all of us, you were figuring out a way to help her too."

He nodded. "Her father's Jameson Bradley."

Tals whistled and shook his head. "And you got his baby girl in trouble."

"I don't think they're exactly close. But she's got a brother. Need to find him."

"Take it we're not paying a Welcome Wagon call."

"As far from it as we can get," he agreed. And there was also another guy out there who hurt her. Cage had that tucked into the back of his mind. Because as much pain as he'd been in that first night they'd talked, the pain in her voice when she'd admitted that a guy had hurt her in her past was unmistakable.

Every time he thought about it, his fists clenched, the way they were now.

Tals noticed, of course. "I'll help."

"Thanks."

"S'what we do." Tals touched the scarred side of his face, shook his head. "Helps that you were always an ugly motherfucker."

"Better than you on your best day."

Tals hooted, and for a second Cage was back in better days. Then again, the woman inside the cabin might just be the start of more.

Tals told him, "I'll be back tonight to escort you back to Skulls. Preacher's orders, so don't try to say no."

"Where are you going?"

"Figured I'd visit Havoc and give you two some privacy."

Cage shook his head. "You getting involved in shit I should know about?"

"You're one to talk. Don't worry about me, brother. I'm just fine. See you in the morning." Tals jumped off the porch, got on his bike and gunned it up the road.

For a long moment, Cage stood in the mountain air, letting what Tals said settle in.

Preacher swore the hills of South Carolina were the perfect place to soothe—and save—men's souls. And that might be true of North Carolina too, because Havoc thrived there, while boasting the rep of being both calm and deadly.

What that MC did was far enough removed from civilians and the law to give them some kind of mythological, legendary status.

Cage knew some of them, had visited their compound. Their rep was well fucking deserved. They had no desire to play nice with anyone. They just stayed to themselves and out of most wars, unless an MC fucked with them. And then their army came down from the hills and let their fury loose.

Whatever Tals was doing up there, Cage hoped it was for pleasure and not business.

Cage had been putting bikes together for as long as he could hold a wrench. The irony of being born in the back of a van—and being named after the incident—was something of an inside joke among the Heathens, because "cage" was a derogatory name for a car, which civilians drove, as opposed to the freedom of the bike.

For Cage, it referred to his Heathen lineage and his royalty, so to speak, because his cage was a beat-up Ford Bronco in which his mom had been in active labor, and it had a line of hogs leading it to the hospital. He'd been too damned impatient to wait, a trait that followed him his entire life. He was the firstborn, the golden child, and at that time his mom had been a hot-as-hell old lady his dad had been lucky enough to bag.

She'd run away from a very wealthy family to be with his father and, by extension, the MC, and Cage knew she'd regretted it. Not at first, but for sure it was a part of the reason she'd turned to drugs.

She'd been trapped. She'd seen no escape and, in reality, there was none. So whether or not she'd planned to kill herself, she'd already been doing it slowly, years before her actual death.

Which was why everything about Calla concerned him. More often than not, the old ladies of the clubs had grown up around the MC, and if they didn't, they were well enough versed in the ways of club life. The real version, not the romanticized one.

And then there were the MC groupies. The mamas. Similar to the women who looked for soldiers to marry. They knew what soldiers were capable of, and they knew that the job involved more than wearing a uniform.

Calla knew more than most civilians, unfortunately because of what he'd put her through already. But once that situation was over . . . no matter how hard it was for him, he was going to have to give her the choice to walk or push her out the door.

He knew he was trouble, more than any one woman should have to deal with. He also had an expiration date—if his family had anything to say about it. By running off on his own to get Calla, he knew he might be cutting himself off from the only family who'd ever given a shit about him.

But for now it seemed they were standing by him. He'd go back to Skulls and take whatever he had coming to him.

Chapter 12

It was almost time to head to the Vipers MC, and I felt like mourning that. At the cabin, for a little while, at least, we were just Calla and Cage, no pasts, only present. Even though we were both wanted, we were also hidden from the world. We had each other all to ourselves.

Until Tals showed up to rip the curtain away and drag us back to reality.

"Did you ever just want to escape everything? Escape who you are, who you're supposed to be? Run from the expectations until you know what you expect from yourself?" I asked Cage now.

He gave a small smile, almost rueful. "I know a little something about all that."

As foolish as it may sound, this cabin was our literal escape. Maybe a little too literal for my tastes, but now that the imminent threat of danger had passed, it was just us. And I didn't want to argue or worry anymore.

I just *wanted*. "So we're going to Skulls Creek."

"I don't know if I'm welcome there anymore. But for you, I'm willing to try."

"Suppose they don't welcome you?" I didn't know much about MCs, but what little I did convinced me that the Vipers wouldn't just wave and let Cage walk off into the night.

"We'll be okay, Calla. They're good people."

I ran my hands over the tattoo on his biceps, the viper curled around the knife, the grim reaper skull with the not so grim smile, like he held the secrets of the world. I sighed. "I don't want to leave this place."

"No one does."

"Then maybe the MC should move here."

"Wouldn't be special anymore. Besides, who's got that many secrets?"

"You'd be surprised," I murmured, and he smiled a little.

"You're going to let me in on all of them, you know. You've already started. No going back now, no matter how hard you try."

And did I really want to go back? My future was scary as anything, but that future promised me a life.

"So what does the MC do for you?"

"We watch out for each other. Help through hard times. Keep the town safe. Drink, fight, tattoo, screw. And ride." He smiled at "ride."

"You're dangerous."

"If you're the wrong person, yes." He shrugged. "No different than any family."

"Any gang or mafia family."

"We're a club, Calla," he said seriously, before pulling me closer. I escaped his grasp, though, and sank to my knees in front of him.

He ran a hand through my hair as I knelt between his legs. I'd never wanted to do that for anyone else in my twenty-three years.

Ran a hand along his thigh, his muscles tensing under my palms.

I wanted to make him lose it. Completely, one hundred percent lose it. He'd nearly done so at Tenn's, but now that we were alone, would he let the facade drop more? Or was this him?

No, it couldn't be. I had walls high enough for armed guards, so I could recognize similar boundaries.

I unzipped his jeans and tugged them down. He shifted to help me, and ran my finger over the head of his cock, avoiding the piercing for the moment.

"Yeah." He smiled as I looked up at him. I tongued the piercing and he hissed with pleasure, and then I took him into my mouth.

His entire body tensed and he groaned my name as he bucked his hips up into me. I took him in again and again, sucking harder as he got more frantic. Until finally he tugged at me, saying, "Fuck, Calla . . . need to be inside of you when I come."

Reluctantly, I rose and stripped as he watched. And then he picked me up and flipped me to the couch bed and covered me.

I was simply greedy for him—there was no other way to put it. I needed him to be mine, all mine—and the feeling seemed to be mutual, judging by the way he held me down and nipped along my tender flesh. Marking me.

"Harder," I told him. "I want to see marks there."

He stared down at me, his eyes blazing with lust. "You're trying to kill me, Calla."

"Why would I do that? You couldn't fuck me then."

He groaned and slid halfway down my body. He licked my cleft as I watched, unable to do more than grasp the sheets and pant. Between my legs was a pulse of pleasure. And then he licked his way back up my body, driving into me, hard and fast, like he couldn't wait any longer. I knew I couldn't.

I buried my nose in his hair, the crook of his neck, and hung on while he took me. He was so completely, intensely male, and right at this moment he *was* one hundred percent mine.

How he could so quickly demolish all the heavy walls I'd built around me—around my heart—I didn't know. The tears that ran down my face did nothing to diminish the ferocity of my orgasm. And even as my core convulsed, I wanted more.

It was a beautiful, brutal race to orgasm for both of us. My climax was a quivering, heated roll of delight as it uncoiled, rushing through me.

Affection was the most painful thing of all—the most dangerous too—because it dug into Cage's heart and lied to him, told him everything would be all right.

She was afraid of it too, maybe as much as she was of him. She didn't trust it, or him, or her feelings.

But goddamn, they made each other feel. He was all revved up and so was she. Her cheeks were flushed, her eyes shone, and even with the death-defying race, this experience had proven something. They were both alive.

Did anything else really matter now?

Chapter 13

The long ride chilled Cage out for a while, mainly because it was uneventful. No Heathens to be found. Their MC was several hours away from Skulls Creek, in the opposite direction of Havoc. There were other MCs and gangs along the way that were friendlies with Vipers and just as many that weren't. But the friendlies would let them know the second they spotted a stray Heathen, because if there was one thing Heathens didn't do, it was stealth. They were proud to let you know they were coming for you. They valued brute force, and their numbers had grown.

Once he passed the familiar sign for Skulls Creek, his unease grew. Tals had trailed him for the ride, and dawn broke as they pulled through the main strip of town. Store owners were just

starting their day. Some waved, others ignored—
business as usual in the town.

And the prodigal son returns.

He could practically feel Preacher's reprimand
from here.

Behind him, Calla held fast, although her grip
got easier the longer they rode, and the trip was
nothing like the chase the night before. Still, she
was as tense as he was, and nothing he could say
would make it better.

He'd gone rogue from the Vipers six months
earlier. He'd lied, said it was because his sister
needed him, but Marielle was safe and sound, in
sunny Florida (which she hated), and he was
tearing up the strip between the Vipers and the
Heathens, looking for any intel that would fry
those motherfuckers.

And, oh, he'd found it all right. Way more
than he'd bargained for, and he'd laid his life on
the line. If he didn't see it through, then people
died for nothing. And no one who'd ever helped
him would die for nothing.

He pulled into the long driveway and parked
behind Vipers clubhouse. As he helped Calla off
the back, Tals was already headed inside, clap-
ping a hand to Cage's shoulder as he went.

Calla stood next to him as he surveyed the

place. Had he been expecting a change? Did he think he'd feel differently, coming back?

"Are you all right?" she asked now. He slung an arm across her shoulder protectively and nodded. They walked toward the back door together.

He didn't know how she'd feel about Vipers. He'd lived this life for so long that he barely noticed it, but he was trying to see it from Calla's point of view.

It was big and loud and clean . . . it looked masculine and lived-in. It was a safe place. A party place. His home, his family. There was more sex happening here than he'd ever imagined. Sex and violence and guns and love. And that was what he'd grown up with, until the drugs had taken over the Heathens, and his mother.

Preacher was watching him carefully from the moment they entered. Preach was forty—but had acted more like a father even though he was only ten years older than Cage. Mainly because Cage had been only ten when he'd stumbled into Vipers at midnight, a refuge from the Heathens. And Vipers had circled him, because you didn't just get a present like that from a rival gang and do nothing, no matter how old the kid. Especially a boy.

Preacher made sure they'd done nothing. And then he'd abolished any kind of revenge exacted on children for any MC. And he'd kicked guys out of the club for doing so over the years.

That was all because of Cage. So for him to see the betrayal on Preach's face now . . . Well, fuck . . .

"There's nothing you can say to make it better."

With a starter like that, where the hell was Cage supposed to go?

"I'm guessing you're not welcome?" Calla asked him, the uncertainty in her voice making him hold her hand tighter.

"I'll let Preacher be the judge of that," Cage said.

"You're damned straight, Cage. I'm the goddamned judge, jury and executioner," Preacher growled. "And who the hell is she?"

Preacher knew exactly who Calla was and why she was there, care of Tals, but that didn't mean Preacher wasn't going to enjoy the hell out of Cage's discomfort.

"Calla's staying here. With me. Until I can figure out a way to get the Heathens off her back."

Calla stiffened beside him, especially when Preacher said, "You didn't even ask if you were invited back inside, Cage."

"Didn't think I had to."

"Well, you fucking do."

He wasn't scared of Preach, not like he'd been

that first night, ten years old and fucking terrified. But anything had been better than staying
with the Heathens. Anything had been better
than watching his mother burn down their house
because she was high.

Anything was better than another goddamned
beating because he'd flushed her drugs down the
toilet, and any others he'd found in the clubhouse.

"Hey, Tals? Come show Calla where she can
catch a breather for a few minutes," Preacher
called, and Tals came out of the back.

"It's okay—he'll grab you something to eat.
You can hang out in my space and I'll be there
soon," Cage assured her. Bent down to kiss her
cheek.

"I'm not going anywhere," she told him.

He should've known better than to think that
the same woman who'd argued with him when
he'd been almost dying would go down easy now.

I knew I should be afraid, but I was really tired
of men ordering me around. With Cage, it was
different, though. I knew he was trying to keep
me safe and away from the impending argument
with Preacher, but I wasn't having it.

Preacher studied me for a long moment, not
saying a word. Maybe I was supposed to look

away or kowtow or something, but I thought about how, somewhere over the last forty-eight hours, I'd begun to admit that I could believe in his promises.

I didn't walk away from a guy like that, especially not when he might be in trouble. "He saved me," I told Preacher firmly.

"He got you in trouble in the first place," Preacher pointed out.

"Men get women in trouble all the time. Most of them don't bother to make good on it."

Preacher frowned and I swore I heard Tals chuckle. Cage just watched me, like I was a ticking time bomb, especially when Preacher came closer.

He ran a finger across my jawline. I had to admit, he was sexy as anything, even with the shaved head, except I wasn't used to being treated like I was best in show. Before I could react, Cage growled and Tals said, "Down, boy," except I wasn't sure which one of them he was referring to.

I don't think they knew either, but Cage ground out, "Keep your fucking hands off her. She's with me."

Preacher looked over my shoulder at him. "You claim her?"

"Damned straight."

Preacher took a couple of steps back, and I breathed, just a little. "Calla, this is my house. Go with Tals, get some food and let me talk to this asshole alone."

I sensed that arguing would just make things worse between the men, but at least some understanding had been reached—he acknowledged me, used my name. And so, with a squeeze of Cage's hand, I followed Tals.

At first glance, the clubhouse reminded me a little of the dorms in my first boarding school. The community room was packed with furniture and a bar, and I could look down a hallway to see all the rooms spreading off from it. There was a staircase at the end of the hall too.

And it was pretty quiet in here, save for a couple of bikers who played pool, beers balanced on the edge of the table. They looked up to acknowledge Cage, and one of them whistled as he stared.

"Calla, that's Cage's place—bathroom's in there too. I'll make some breakfast—come meet me out here when you're done." Tals directed me into an unlocked room, and I closed the door behind me, sagged against it and simply breathed.

The dynamics would continue to shift now that we were at Vipers. I'd known that. But it was a huge change. I went from being his focus to being left alone, told to stay put. And I didn't know what else to do but listen to him. To all of them.

It was day one here. I was already freaking out. I'd been brought into another world where I didn't belong, where I needed to figure out how to pretend to get along. No matter what, my past was always in my way.

Speaking of pasts, I tried to get a sense of what Cage's life was like here before he'd left Vipers . . . maybe even before the Army. His room was scattered with pictures—of him with Tals and the others, leaning on his bike . . . partying. A couple of him in uniform. There were some clothes in the drawers. A bed. The sheets looked clean, but I'm sure if it could talk . . . I'd want it to shut up.

As well as I felt I knew him, there were whole sections of his life that were missing. I'd have to cobble together puzzle pieces.

My mind was spinning from exhaustion but I was too wired to even try to sleep. It was light out now, had barely been so when Cage's bike drove past the sign for Skulls Creek. Tals had been slightly behind us and to our right, and they'd ridden in this synchronized formation for the past four hours. I'd been hypnotized by most of it, once we'd gotten on the smooth highway roads. In the dark, Cage went fast and I'd tried to settle my nerves by concentrating on the feel of the bike under me, and how this was something Cage loved. He had to in order to be a part of an

MC. And even though I had been only on the second ride of my life, I could easily understand the headiness of the freedom of the open road.

"Just because Tals came around doesn't mean the other guys will," Preacher started out.

Cage stared at him steadily. "Guessing that includes you?"

"I am so not in the mood for your shit today." Preacher ran a hand over his shaved scalp. "You didn't ask permission to go rogue."

"I knew you'd say no," Cage countered.

"I should beat your ass," Preacher muttered. But he knew—Preacher always knew why Cage did the things he did. "None of what happened the night you came home from the Army was your fault."

"Keep trying to tell me that," Cage said quietly.

Preacher tried a different tactic. "How's Marielle?"

"She's okay. But she wants to come here."

"Not raisin' your whole fuckin' family, Cage."

"Didn't ask you to, Preach. So fuck off." He slammed the nearest wall with a fist, several times—mainly because it felt goddamned good to hit something—until Preacher said, "Stop."

His voice was sharp and calming, like he knew

where Cage was headed. "You're having the nightmares again."

Cage shrugged as he shook out his hand. "They always come back. Not a surprise."

"They're back because of what you're doing, trying to win a one-man war against the Heathens."

"Like I have a choice."

" 'Course you do," Preach growled.

"Not getting Vipers involved in a war. They stay out of Skulls, it's not your problem."

"But they're not," Preacher said with an uncharacteristic quiet that made the hairs on the back of his neck stand up.

"Come again?"

"You heard me, Cage. They're pushing back. They've been selling about an hour away from here, thinking we won't get word. Using skinheads to push their agenda when the local law won't fold."

Shit. Cage ran a hand through his hair, missing the length it was before he'd asked the nurses in the hospital to cut it all. They'd had to shave a part of it to stitch him, and he'd been only too happy to start over. He felt for the familiar leather thong he'd always tied it back with, still in his pocket. He always tied it back when Vipers went to war. And he'd nearly missed the first battle. "Now what?"

"You and me, we're taking a little joyride in the

next couple of days. I've got something to show you." Preacher stared at me. "Calla stays here while we're gone. That shit can't be a problem."

"She gets it."

"Does she really?"

If she didn't, she would soon. And by then, it might be too late for both of them. "I don't think we'll stay here tonight, though."

"I think your apartment's best," Preacher agreed. "But the pleasure of your goddamned company is requested at the bar this evening."

It wasn't a mere invitation, and Cage nodded his assent at the directive. Preacher dismissed him with a wave of a hand, and normally any authority doing so would rankle him. But it had always been different with Preach.

Cage wandered toward the back to where Tals was cooking breakfast. His friend glanced over his shoulder. "Might want to check on your girl— she locked herself in your room."

"Windows are barred."

Tals grinned. "Things are that bad you think she'd try to escape from you? Brother, what're you doing wrong?"

"Fuck off, Tals."

Tals leaned against the counter as he flipped pancakes with his usual array of chocolate chips in them.

"Gonna tell me to fuck off when I've got the information you asked for?"

"That fast?"

"I'm that good. Thought we'd take a road trip later on."

"How far?"

"Closer than you'd think. I talked to Bear and Rocco. They'll stay outside your apartment for you to keep watch over Calla."

At least two more club members were willing to not give him shit about leaving the MC high and dry. He sighed in relief. "You don't have to go with me."

"Of course I do—I'm the only one who can keep you from getting into deeper trouble."

"You really believe your own shit." He pointed directly at Tals. "And you're not stealing any cars along the way."

Tals shrugged. "They jump out at me. Make it so easy."

Cage rolled his eyes but smiled internally. It was good to be back where he was understood, no matter how angry Preach and the others might be at him. And they were, for sure, but Calla was safe here until he figured out the meaning of the intel he'd gained.

Chapter 14

After we ate, Cage and I took another ride through town. I'd never been down this far south, and even though we didn't stop, I knew this place was different. For one thing, I was used to states with a faster feel, where you didn't slow down until forced to. Which was typically never. Even in Connecticut, where my schools were, there was a feeling of elegant intensity. Like it was preparing us to head back into New York and her frantic pace.

Here, things sprawled with a quiet dignity that made it seem almost offensive to rush. There was more land, more room to just slow down and breathe.

Skulls Creek was along a river, the main drag making it appear more small town than the moderate-sized city it actually was. The busier section, with the big office buildings and the more commercial restaurants and shops, was on the north side. The Vipers' influence was most strongly felt on the original strip near town hall, where residents seemed to be used to the roar of Harleys. I suspected it worked that way because the clubhouse was actually pretty far removed from either section of town, tucked away from prying eyes and curious teens.

"Vipers own this block?"

"Preach bought real estate back when a lot of this place crashed. Got in cheap and made a killing. We fixed the buildings up, rented the shops and now this place looks like it did way back when."

It had a small-town feel, where everyone looked out for everyone, but was big enough that you could get lost if you needed to. The town was a municipality that appeared to be thriving. Lots of cars and foot traffic. Stores were open, pretty. Clean.

If this was what having an MC in your town meant, I guessed that very few complained.

"So the MC is good for the town," I said, once we'd parked behind a building along the outskirts.

"We are. Most of the time. It's a balancing act. Vipers keep drugs out. They'd ruin this place. We've seen it happen to other nearby cities."

It seemed as though he'd seen it firsthand, up close and personal. Again, I was frustrated at his refusal to share, but I was hoping that the further he let me into his world, the more he'd reveal.

Granted, I hadn't revealed a lot either, but he knew the basics. And for me, that was enough to make my gut tighten just thinking about what might happen if I had to reveal everything. "How did Vipers start, anyway?"

"There were four original members," he explained as he used his keys to let us into the locked building. There was an alarm too, and he locked up, realarmed and got us into the large service elevator. He hit the button for the sixth floor, which was the top floor. "They came back here after Vietnam, kind of all fucked up, and they built the club from the ground up. Bought the block of run-down stores and apartments and the big lot on the corner, and built their clubhouse and the place for them to fix their bikes. It wasn't ever open to the public, just a place for club members to fix their bikes and cars. The clubhouse was where the guys lived for a while."

"Are any of their sons still with the club?"

"Rally's a great-grandkid of an original."

"So why isn't he in charge?"

"That's a long, boring story."

"Somehow I doubt that."

He let me off the elevator first, then pointed to the lone door in the hallway.

"This whole floor is yours?"

"Yeah. Preacher's big on investments in real estate. It's way too big for one person." He unlocked the door and motioned me in first. There was an alarm buzzing too, and I guessed better safe than sorry. And I was feeling safer the deeper I went, like those Russian dolls where each doll was protectively encased in another and another. All the layers helped.

I looked around his apartment. It was sprawling and mostly empty, with floor-to-ceiling windows. I could see the view of the river all the way down. On the other end, there was a locked door that seemed to be in the middle of nowhere. He didn't explain what it was, and I didn't ask. I went to the window, where I could see the river instead. I could see the clubhouse if I strained a little.

Finally, I turned back to him. He stood in the middle of the place, looking around like he didn't own it.

"You don't spend a lot of time here."

"I don't spend a lot of time in any one place, no," he agreed.

The walls were bare, a soft beige. The floor was a gorgeous dark stained wood and there were two leather couches and various kitchen appliances. A big mattress and box spring on the floor in the bedroom. And wooden blinds. "It's a great place."

"You'll be hanging out at the clubhouse most of the time, so don't get used to it."

Great. Because even though it had been fine that morning, there was something about it that made me uneasy. I couldn't put my finger on it, though, and I didn't want to make a big deal of it right off the bat. Going up against Preacher had been enough for one day.

I crossed my arms and sat on one of the couches, watched him rifling through some bags on the floor. He pulled out clothes and stuffed them in a bag. "A couple of the women will go shopping for you, okay? I think it's better if you stay with club company for the moment, until I make sure this shit with the Heathens isn't entangling you in it."

"Sounds good. So where do you spend time, besides at the clubhouse?" Because that room hadn't looked very lived-in either. Cage was slipping away already and we'd barely been in Skulls for two hours. The whole broken-promises thing was starting to tug hard at me, and I didn't want to go to that dark place again. "I mean, I know you were in the Army with Bernie. And Tenn. And Tals."

"Yeah, I was. Tenn and Tals got out before me."

He had a faraway look in his eyes. I wanted to know how long he'd been out, how long he'd been a part of the MC. Instead, I asked, "What have you been doing since you got out of the Army?"

What have you been doing since you got out of the Army?

It shouldn't have been a hard question to answer. He'd been in for a tour, and then his inactive reserve status hadn't lasted long. He and Tals had gone back in—Tenn joined them for six months. But then Cage had volunteered to stay active until his eight years were up. Tals and Tenn went back on reserve, and as of eight months before, they were all out.

The fact that he couldn't answer Calla's question alerted him to the fact that, for the last six months, his sole focus had been revenge. He'd never outgrown it, and while there was nothing inherently wrong with that stance, it was dangerously close to the blood-for-blood mentality of the Heathens. And he was tired of blood for blood.

That was the reason he'd gone into the Army in the first place. He'd skated the edge of insanity that went along with vengeance for so long that he'd started hating himself. The Army gave him what he needed, worked his mind as well as his body.

But when Preacher told him things had gotten worse with the Heathens, the choice was made. Drugs were pushing in closer, and as much as law enforcement didn't want to need the Vipers MC, the officers and the mayor realized that, without them, they'd lose their stronghold completely in the war against a meth invasion. Meth brought more dangerous MCs to town—not that the Vipers weren't dangerous themselves, but they simply couched it better—and meth also brought the skinheads. And nobody wanted those guys in their backyards.

The Vipers were an insular crew. Occasionally, they'd take in a rogue, but more often than not it was a member's brother or cousin or son. It added to the family mentality.

Tenn hadn't wanted anything to do with the MC, but because of Tals, he'd be protected anyway. The guys who worked for Tenn would be too intimidated if they'd known just how close their boss was to a one-percenter MC, but, for the most part, the MC respected the fact that Tenn could kick the majority of their asses enough to not give a shit that he was running a gay porn Web site . . . or that he was gay himself.

"I've been doing MC business," he told her finally, ignoring what looked like betrayal in her gaze. Betrayal or hurt at being shut out. "You all right to stay here while I go do a few things? I won't be more than a couple of hours. I've got a few guys who live in the building keeping an eye out. The whole thing's locked up tight and their numbers are right by the phone. They won't leave the building without checking with me first."

"You've got guards on me now?"

"Yes."

He'd been conscious of the fact that she was the daughter of one of the wealthiest men in the country, and could probably compete for that title worldwide. Calla hadn't grown up with her dad, but Cage had been right about the look of a rich girl. He could spot them a mile away, and more often than not they meant trouble.

"Okay, then." She glanced toward the bed. "I haven't slept in days. Not much, anyway."

"We're making an appearance at the bar tonight, so catch some shut-eye while you can."

"Are you going anyplace I should be worried about?" she asked, and when Cage didn't answer, she sighed. "Forget it. Just be careful."

He would.

Chapter 15

Ned's place was a dump of a motel that sat in front of a flophouse, about thirty miles from Skulls, right beyond the mountains, where people were sparse and land was abundant. Why he'd come here, and why he was hovering so close to Calla, had been Tals's main concern for getting Cage out here so quickly. They'd discussed it briefly when they'd made a pit stop to grab food and take a piss, but Cage needed to keep going, to see the motherfucker instead of talking about him.

Cage had also checked in on Calla, through Rocco.

"I just texted her to check on things. She's okay," Rocco assured him. And then he hung up, pocketed the phone and realized Tals was staring at him. "What?"

"You got it bad, brother."

"Problem with that?"

"Depends on how far it takes you from the club. You made a commitment to Vipers first."

He had. And the MC had saved his ass in more ways than one. But he'd be damned if he'd let it get in the way of a life with Calla. "What the fuck do you think I've been doing the past six months, jackoff?"

Tals held up his hands. "Just trying to get the love dust out of your eyes and your mind focused on the fight."

"Never left," he growled. "Let's just find this asshole."

"What's the plan when we do find him? Threaten? Because I think we need to bring him back with us and let Calla deal with him," Tals said. "Women need that kind of closure."

Cage eyed him. "Who are you and what have you done with Talon, the bastard?"

"Someone left an old chick magazine in the john. There was nothing else to do." Tals shrugged unapologetically. "Well, after I beat off."

And then Tals was back, just like that. "I don't think Calla wants him anywhere near her. Which is why I don't want him to see our cuts."

Tals reluctantly peeled his cut off and stored it in the back of the van, as did Cage. Ned would probably know they were MC members, because from what little Cage had found out about the guy, he wasn't stupid.

He and Tals had been breaking into places unnoticed since they were small. The Army had continued to hone their covert skills, and with the amount of drugged-out people wandering the area, they probably could've walked naked through the outside hallways of the motel and no one would've noticed.

"Jesus Christ," Tals muttered as they stepped over a woman who was passed out by a doorway. She was skeletal—looked to be in her fifties, but Cage would bet anything she was in her twenties.

"Fucking meth," Cage replied, sliding into Ned's locked room using a magnetized-strip card he'd grabbed off someone he'd passed in the hallway. The people staying here were all too stoned to realize there was one card that opened every room.

Once inside, with Tals standing guard, Cage systematically went through Ned's things. He found nothing of interest, beyond some stubbed-out joints. If he was taking anything harder, there wasn't evidence of it.

"Anything?" Tals asked as he came out.

"No, but he's here. Found a take-out box with his name on it."

"So we come back." As they headed to their bikes, Tals told him, "You know Calla's freaked, right?"

He knew, because he was the one responsible. Balancing her and the MC wasn't easy. He was just about to address it when he noticed a few of the local skinheads staring at them.

"Did they see me in the room?" Cage asked.

"No, but they saw me." Tals looked damned pleased with himself. "You need a good fight later."

"And let me guess—you know where to find one?"

"Stick with me and I'll hook you up. One's going to follow us home."

Chapter 16

I was really nervous by the time Cage came back. He'd brought me some clothes—cute jeans and boots and shirts—and I'd already showered. He was still distracted, and Tals was with him, which meant that we couldn't talk much.

I dressed quickly. Thought about telling him I wanted to stay here instead, but I really didn't want to be alone. But when I'd hinted at that, he'd said that he'd been ordered to a command performance by Preacher.

The bar was walking distance from the apartment—two short blocks—but we rode instead, parked in a line of bikes along the back and walked into the darkened bar.

It wasn't too different from any of the bars I'd been in. But it was crowded already since it was after eleven at night, and the drinking was going full swing.

I'd known it wasn't going to be easy, coming here and meeting a good portion of the Vipers crew, plus their women, plus hangers-on. And it was more crowded tonight than usual, Cage told me, because they all knew he was back in town.

Many of the guys watched him with guarded expressions. Some of the women did too. I got outright contempt from more than a few, but smiles and waves from others. Still, I was nervous as anything. I was sure it showed, and I didn't want it to. But I was out of my element, and while I might've felt that way in boarding school and college, I knew how to fake it. Here, I really didn't.

I mean, I felt stupid because what could I do? Look up, "My boyfriend's a biker, what next?" Because Cage wasn't exactly my boyfriend. Although I wasn't sure what calling me "his" meant exactly.

I'd watched *Sons of Anarchy*, along with the rest of the world, and that aided with the pictures Tenn had drawn for me in my mind of what a real MC was. These men lost tongues and noses and balls. They were hard-core. And maybe Vipers wasn't as hard-core as some of the MCs, but there'd been guns in Cage's apartment.

He was in the Army, I reminded myself. But that

hadn't settled the questions in my head. So I just stayed by his side and studied the women. I quickly realized there was a certain way of dressing, a certain bearing to each group—there always was, and the MC women were no different.

It was easy to spot the old ladies from the mamas. There was a natural confidence to the old ladies, like they knew they were untouchable. I was dressed somewhere in between, and I wondered which one of them had picked out my clothes.

At some point, Cage parked me by the bar next to a few women he'd introduced me to and told me he had some club business to attend to. As soon as he left, they stopped talking to me, and I sipped a Diet Coke and looked around.

Cage was hanging out with a group of women who were basically all over him. I wasn't sure what the hell was going on at this point, but club business, my ass.

The depth of my jealous feelings was too intense and it surprised me. A woman was talking to Cage with far too much intimacy for my comfort. The jealousy I'd known twisted with misery, and instead of going over to him, showing the woman that he was mine, I turned away and walked toward the back room.

"You can't let him get away with it." I turned

toward the source of the voice. A pretty, dark-haired woman, curvy in jeans and a tank top, bracelets of silver and beads of different colors traveling up her arms. "I'm Amelia. You're Calla, yes?"

I nodded, not trusting my voice.

"Calla, look—these guys, they're going to get away with whatever they can. Some women deal with it. Others can't. But Cage will never respect you if you don't fight for him."

"I would like to punch that bitch out," I muttered, and Amelia laughed and clapped her hands together once lightly.

"That's the spirit. But, honey, fists aren't the way to win this game." She looked me over. "I see what I bought you fits well. If that's not to your style, tell me what you need."

She didn't question why I couldn't do my own shopping, didn't seem to think it was odd at all. So of course, I blurted out, "I told him I wasn't sure I wanted commitment. I told him we were both free to do what we wanted," and wondered how the small, dark hallway had suddenly become a confessional.

"So? We're not allowed to change our minds?" she asked. Then she rummaged in her bag and pulled out a couple of wrapped bracelets. "Here, put these on. It's onyx and these are worry beads. They'll help."

I'd take whatever I could get. I unwrapped it and slid the pretty black and wood beads on my wrist, rubbed it a couple of times with my opposite hand for good luck.

"Who are you dating?" I asked.

"Me? No one," she said with a smile. "I just work here. Manage the bar. They stopped hiring their own guys because they were drinking too much of the profits."

"Thanks for being nice to me."

"The others will, once you're with one of the guys. Until then . . ." She shrugged, then gave me a crash course in life, MC-style. "MC men fuck whoever they want. Old ladies are expected to be faithful, but most of the time any guy who's got an old lady's off the market."

"Since I'm not attached, I'm a threat," I said.

"Right. Means all the women hate you on sight, especially because you're gorgeous." She glanced at Cage. "My suggestion? If you want him, if you think you made a mistake, it's time to claim him."

Yes, I could do that.

I'd grown up between two worlds, not feeling entirely comfortable in either. It was like I didn't know the entire story behind my life—was I supposed to be a bar chick or a rich girl? And in the end did it really matter? I'd been faking everything for so long it had all become a matter of course.

I understood now, watching Cage, just how much I missed. So much lost time to make up for. Because everything I'd thought I'd wanted at the cabin went straight out the window the first time I saw another woman chatting Cage up. My heart raced in my chest and I wanted to rip him away from her, rip her hair out. And I could've flirted with any number of MC members in the bar—and I should've.

Instead, I stared behind the bar and said, "Do you need help tonight?"

"Honey, I need help every night. Bar business isn't my thing. I'm good with numbers, but this other stuff? Preacher promised me he'd find someone to take this over. So go take a spin."

"We don't need more help." A woman who looked to be in her mid-thirties brushed by and went behind the bar. She was all boobs and butt, curvy, undeniably hot. She eyed me like I'd crawled off the bottom of her shoe, then called, "Rich girls don't know what work is."

I raised my brows to Amelia and pointed behind the bar. "Mind?"

Amelia held the swinging half door open. The other bartender watched me as I walked through the bar, taking stock of where things were kept and what kinds of liquor, including top shelf, they kept there.

It had been a couple of years since I'd been behind a bar. But in a matter of five minutes, I was pouring drinks and shots. Flirting. Ignoring Cage in favor of having fun.

For a little while, I didn't feel like a pretender. This is what the Benson women did. I might not belong in this world, but at least I got to be me, didn't have to fake anything.

When there was a lull, I couldn't help but scan the crowd for him. If he'd noticed me behind the bar, I didn't know.

I didn't want to flirt with anyone but him. And so I didn't. Not in the traditional sense anyway, but when Amelia cranked the music up, I got up onto the bar and started dancing.

For Cage.

When Cage heard the catcalls, he looked up and saw Calla. Dancing. On top of the goddamned bar. She was laughing too, having found a group of women to dance with, and he sat back in his chair and watched her letting loose and having fun, because she was twenty-goddamned-three and obviously hadn't had enough of it. Her hair had come out of the knot she'd tied it in earlier when she'd become the in-demand bartender, and now she was reaching under her shirt, pulling out a lacy bra and twirling it.

He could see her peaked nipples through her white cotton shirt. Someone would soak the girls with water soon enough, and he'd watch that show. Because other men could look, but they couldn't fucking touch, and it didn't matter what he'd told her about that.

The thing was, she knew it. He could tell. But if she wanted to play this game, to prove whatever it was to both of them, who was he to argue? Either way, she'd be in his bed tonight, and sooner than later.

She was in control. Protected. Worshipped by Cage's eyes. She was safe here, for the moment, and she wasn't being judged for taking her bra off, dancing wildly. No, the crowd wanted more from her and the two other women she was up there with . . . and she had all the power.

And he'd tried his best to give her space, to give himself distance. It wasn't working, and it never would. She was his. He'd known it from day one, so why he'd bothered to fight it was beyond him.

She got down off the bar and danced her way

over to him, threw a leg over his. The woman he'd been talking to glared at her, but Calla smiled at her, then brought her mouth down on Cage's.

"Done fucking teasing me, babe?"

"Not even close," she murmured.

"You could suck me off right here."

"Wouldn't we get arrested?"

"Never happened before."

"How many women have sucked you off in this bar, Cage?"

"I'm a wise enough man to not answer that question." He dug into her pocket and pulled out several phone numbers—he'd seen some guys handing them to her—and crumpled them before dunking them in his beer mug. "If you're out looking to get laid, that's not going to fly."

"You agreed that we didn't own each other," Calla reminded him.

"You agreed—I never did, so take a walk back through your memory bank, sweetheart. You want to fuck, I'm right here. I'm not letting someone else fuck what's mine."

"I'm not—"

"Mine," he repeated firmly, backing her against the wall, his knee sliding between her jean-clad legs. Her thighs clamped around his in an effort to stop it from pushing against her sex, but it was useless. "I'll get it through your head however I have to, even if it means fucking you right here in the middle of the bar."

"You wouldn't."

"You think no one's seen that before?"

"You're a goddamned caveman."

"And you're a cocktease." He looked over her shoulder and saw Rocco motioning to him. Urgently. "I've gotta take care of a few things. Tals'll take you back to the apartment."

She looked pissed. He was pissed too, but he wasn't exactly sure why. But now wasn't the time to pick it apart, not when he saw Tals throw himself into the crowd of skinheads outside the bar.

"Jesus Christ, what happened to waiting at the town border?" Bear asked. "They've got a lot of nerve coming in here."

"Then we gotta make sure they never want to come back," Cage growled. Although reluctant to leave Calla, he'd been furious enough to do so, and he recognized this opportunity for what it was . . .

Tals had found their fight.

I stared out the window at the melee in the middle of the street. Last call had people pouring out half an hour earlier. At this point, there was a skeleton crew of men, including Cage, and the fight looked brutal—on the skinheads' end. The MC guys seemed to be doing just fine.

I refused to turn away, as if doing so would cause any of the MC guys to get hurt. I'd seen fights before—teenagers in bars, an occasional punch thrown—but melees like this were reserved for the movies.

This was no movie. This was my real life now—and the skinheads who'd come into Vipers territory were bringing it back up.

"Amelia, what the hell?" I asked. But it wasn't Amelia. It was Hot Blond Butt. And she looked worried.

"They're the guys who were caught here a couple of weeks ago. They're pushing meth for the Heathens in Skulls Creek," she said. "My kid goes to the middle school. He told me he saw these guys trying to sell there too."

She glanced at me, like she was waiting for a judgment.

Instead, I told her, "Cage came back to try to help."

"Maybe he shouldn't have left in the first place."

"Maybe. But that's not going to change any of this." I looked back outside. The Vipers were outnumbered, but it didn't seem to matter. I saw the glint of something metal—Blond Butt did too, because she grabbed my forearm and we both could only helplessly watch the Vipers defend their town.

With all the tension, I hadn't noticed the sirens in the distance. Now they were close enough for me to see the flashing lights coming down the street parallel to the bar.

"You've got to go," Blond Butt told me.

"I'm Calla," I said.

She smirked. "I know." Then, "I'm Allie. My old man's Jimbo. I'll keep an eye on them."

"Are they going to jail?"

"For a little while at least," she said. "Go. They'll try to question you."

I'm assuming she'd been questioned a lot. For me, right now, it could be the worst thing. And when I turned around, I saw Rocco was waiting for me by the back door. I was waiting for Amelia to grab my jacket.

She handed it to me, staring around me and out the window toward the fight. "That's a beautiful thing."

"The fighting?"

"Yes. So primal. God, I love it when they kick some ass." She turned to me. "By the way, this whole tension between you and Cage? It's him."

"I guess that's supposed to make me feel better?"

"It's supposed to make you stop feeling sorry for yourself." Amelia leaned into me. "They don't like to break down their walls or let us in, darlin', but I hate to break it to you. You're already over the goddamned wall, so stop fucking it up."

I was quiet on the ride back to Cage's. Rocco didn't press for conversation, just put the music on loud enough to drown out my thoughts for the short trip. He walked me up, made sure I got into the apartment all right. I took a shower and was just pulling on a flannel shirt of Cage's I'd found when I heard him come into the apartment.

I practically ran out there, in my bra and underwear and my shirt unbuttoned, only thinking that he could've brought someone back here with him, when it was too late. He stared at me and I pulled the shirt around me, because my nudity was distracting him and the way he watched me was distracting me. We had our own fight to finish, dammit.

"Are you all right?"

"Do I not look all right?" he asked. He had a day's worth of stubble on his cheeks. A cut above his eyebrow that had been stitched. His hands looked like they'd gone a few rounds, but other than that . . . No, he looked *good*.

"Did they arrest you?"

"They tried."

"What does that even mean?"

"Means you shouldn't ask questions that will get you in trouble later, if it ever comes down to that."

The protection thing again.

"You don't have to keep holding your shirt closed like that," he said. I moved to button it and he snorted. "You want to tell me what's going on?"

"Nothing. Except you go out and fight and come home and the first thing you worry about is the fact that my shirt is open."

He shrugged. Smiled. "You look cute."

"Cute, huh?"

"Still pissed?"

"Yes. Actually, more than I was before."

"Why? Because I want to take care of you?"

"Well, you can't keep taking care of me any way you see fit."

"Why not?" Cage demanded. "Fucking hell, woman, why the fuck not? It's all I want to do. It's exactly what I will do, and you're not stopping me, so you might as well stop fighting this battle and pick another."

"Why? So I can lose that one too?" I crossed my arms and stared at him.

"There are some battles you can most definitely win, Calla. Battles you like. Battles that leave you screaming my name and coming so hard you'll swear you won't see straight."

"Try me."

"Try you?" he echoed. "You've already tried me tonight, with your dancing."

I swallowed hard, because that's exactly what I'd been doing. And he'd known it. The game I'd played had worked, and I'd both lost and won.

He advanced, picking me up so I was slung over his shoulder, and that's when I realized I might've pushed this battle thing a little too far. Because even though I might win a battle, he was about to win the whole goddamned war.

I was on the couch, the shirt sliding back to my shoulders, his hand down my underwear and on my sex. I was helpless, impaled on his fingers as he explored me leisurely. I couldn't sit still, but I didn't want to hump his hand. But that's exactly what I ended up doing, especially after his mouth sucked one of my nipples through the thin cotton. He jerked the fabric up with his teeth, ripped my bra off and caught the nipple lightly between his teeth, flicking the end with his tongue as his fingers made me wetter than I'd ever been.

I arched against him and tried to squirm away at the same time, but he wasn't letting me escape. The biggest part of me didn't want that either.

My belly tightened, my voice thready as I moaned his name, and he knew he had me. He knew it, caught me in his gaze as surely as his hands made me his. My body responded to him in a way it would for no one else. I'd been sure it would happen that way, but now that it was actually happening, it made me want to beg him to just hurry up and fuck me.

But his hand set a leisurely pace, like he was teaching me a lesson about control. "I know you wanted to pay me back for the video. But having you sit there and stroke yourself for me, that would let you distance yourself from me. And I don't want distance between us, baby, you got that?"

"Yes," I managed, threw my head back as my sex contracted around his fingers, wet, slick and needy.

"I've got you, Calla. I told you that from the beginning. I've got you." He looked down at his hand and back up at me and—fuck, it was so dirty . . . and I was going to come.

"Cage, I—"

"Go ahead and come," he said casually and my body betrayed me by following the command immediately. The air sucked out of my lungs with the intensity of the pleasure that followed, a long string of contractions that tortured me in the best way possible.

"I'm going to fuck you tonight, more times than you can count. I'll fuck every last bit of worry out of you, because when you're with me, I don't want any worry running through your mind."

"Cage, Jesus . . ."

"I know you like dirty talk, Calla. Don't try to deny it to me."

I wouldn't. Couldn't.

"I'm going to taste you now," he warned as he threw one of my legs over his shoulders and bent in to grab my clit between his lips. He sucked hard, then licked my slit slowly, probing inside. He flattened the bundle of nerves with his tongue, then speared me with it, hard, sending me into a shattering, all-consuming orgasm.

"Stop," I told him, but he was still licking me, sucking me, tasting me. He watched me too, and I realized I really couldn't do anything but enjoy him. This was all about me. I was safe. Pleasured. Cared for.

It was the most primal pairing I'd ever had, one I never thought I'd be able to enjoy. I was used to being the aggressor, picking out men who were a little afraid of me, picked exactly for that reason, so I didn't have to be afraid of them.

I was so afraid of Cage, but for reasons that captured my heart and not my fear. And as I lay on the couch, he moved up over my body, nuzzling my neck.

"Talk to me," he said.

I didn't want to tell him that everything balled up inside of me, that I didn't know where I belonged—but I told him exactly that.

He took me fiercely, rolled me underneath the weight of his body and said, "You belong with me. You belong to me."

And strangely, the thought of being owned comforted me instead of scaring me. "Do you belong to me too?" I asked.

"Is that what you want?"

I nodded and he smiled. The pull to him was indescribable. There wasn't a chance of denying it, or a reason to do so. No, the attraction was as palpable and obvious as the sun. If we touched, we imploded, for better or worse.

I don't know why connections happen, but this one took me by surprise—and by the throat—and wouldn't let go. I didn't want it to, no matter how bad or hard it got, no matter how scared or unsure I became at times.

Like now.

It would become all of those things, but I'd been through both bad and hard and I'd come out the other side. And I was prepared for whatever happened between me and Cage to destroy me. Destroy Cage. Destroy both of us.

But we'd been joined.

"You hear me, Calla? Mine," he emphasized as he drove his cock inside of me, reminding me whose I was, of who I was. Cage's girl. And that's what I'd wanted.

Taking the consequences was simply a part of that.

Maybe I'd fallen too fast and too hard for my dangerous man. He was in my blood—and that need had always been there too. I couldn't deny it. But it would cost me. It would cost us both.

Chapter 17

The next evening, Cage went out on his own. He'd spent the whole day with me, and I didn't press when he told me he had more club business to attend to. He didn't look happy about it, so I assumed it wasn't another night at the bar.

I waited up for him—because I was worried. Because I missed him. And when he came home around three in the morning, I had to force myself not to run out to greet him. I waited in bed until he came in. And he didn't look surprised to see me awake.

There was a bruise on his cheek and his hand was scraped along his knuckles, and that did get me up and out of bed. "Cage . . ."

"You told me you'd rather fight than run," was all he said.

"Who did you fight?"

He sat heavily on the edge of the bed, still not talking. I went to the bathroom, got a washcloth and washed his cuts. Stripped him out of his shirts. Bent to take off his boots. He shifted to get out of his jeans and I paused to admire his long, lean body.

Whatever had happened tonight was bothering his soul more than his body.

I grabbed him a cold soda. He guzzled it. Told me, "You're acting like an old lady."

"I'm acting the way you should when you care about someone," I corrected. But I still smiled at the "old lady" thing. "Am I allowed to ask questions?"

He motioned to the bed and I climbed in. He followed, tucked in next to me, then said, "They're bringing drugs right into Skulls. To the fucking high school—and tonight we stopped them."

"The Heathens?"

"Gotta be. They're using some low-level dealers to do their dirty work."

"Do the Heathens know you're back here?"

"Yeah. And word will spread more after tonight." He paused. "I'm sorry, Calla, but I can't hide forever."

"I don't want you to."

He shook his head. "If they succeed in getting the drugs in here, Skulls won't survive. I won't let that happen."

He sounded so fierce. So protective. Because he'd grown up here. Preacher had too, and although the town didn't love the Vipers MC, tonight Cage had stopped the Heathens from selling meth to a group of high school kids. He'd saved lives tonight, and I wished the town could know that.

"Go off to war. Come home . . . still a war. Same goddamned war I've been fighting for what feels like forever."

I knew all about those kinds of wars. "I wish I could fix it for you."

"You are, babe. Just coming home to you like this . . . you have no idea what it helps to fix."

The MC men weren't angels. I was pretty sure that the Vipers garage was a front for a chop shop—one of my mom's boyfriends stole cars, so I was pretty familiar. No, none of these guys would ever be accused of being an angel.

But tonight, it appeared they'd won a battle.

Several days later, we'd fallen into a predictable, if not comfortable, pattern. Often I'd stay in while Cage conducted club business, and then we'd go out—sometimes to dinner and sometimes to the bar—and I gradually began to meet all the men and women of Vipers.

But even though Cage had claimed me, I didn't have true "old lady" status. Because even though we'd given up the whole pretense of me not owning him and him not owning me, the fact was, I was in hiding here.

I'd planned on calling Tenn that afternoon, because I needed to hear a familiar voice from someone who semiknew me. But Cage and I ended up heading to the clubhouse for an afternoon barbecue, which stretched out to early evening. The men were fixing their bikes and running around after small kids, and the women were handing out plates of food, and it all looked so normal, like we could be anywhere in America. Anywhere where there were lots of leather jackets. And patches. And tattoos of snakes and reapers and skulls with knives through them.

Still, this gave me a chance to see a different side of the club, to see the guys being gentle with their kids and their women—everything was softer, albeit still rowdy.

I was sitting on the back steps with Cage standing next to me when an olive-skinned woman dressed in black pants and a crisp white shirt under her blazer jacket came around the corner. It was warm out for such an outfit, but I noticed the holster that ran along her side when she moved.

"Cop," Cage said under his breath at the same moment she chose to focus directly on me.

"How can I help you, Detective Flores?" Cage asked.

"You're just the man I was looking for. You, and Calla Bradley."

How did she know me? And by that last name? It's not like I'd registered at the post office, and I was pretty sure the MC hadn't announced my name in the local police blotter.

Cage stared steadily at Detective Flores, and I told her, "It's Benson, not Bradley."

"But your father is Jameson Bradley, correct?"

"What's this about?" I asked, and Cage's hand went to my shoulder.

She made a note on her open pad as a tall black man came around behind her. "My partner and I need to speak with you. We could do it here or down at the precinct, if that would be more comfortable for you."

"I thought you needed to speak with me," Cage said.

"I'll get to you," she said with a curt smile.

"She being charged with something?" Preacher asked. I hadn't seen him come up to her.

She looked up at him, unsurprised, and said, "No."

"Then you can ask her the questions here and she can decide if she wants to answer them or not. All within her rights, correct? Or did you forget about that whole innocent-until-proven-guilty rule?" Cage said.

Flores's mouth jerked to the left in a vicious smirk. "Right. I'm supposed to believe that anyone associated with this MC can have the word 'innocent' attached to their name."

"Calla's not attached to the MC," Cage said, and although I knew why he was saying so, it still made me wither. He stood next to me, not touching me, and God, I wanted this over with.

"How do you even know who I am?" I asked.

"I have my sources," she said, and I swore Cage growled next to me.

Was that source the Heathens? What the hell? "Can you tell me what you came here to say?"

Flores motioned to Cage. "We'd like to speak to her alone."

"I'd like a lot of goddamned things, but that's not happening," he replied.

Preacher hadn't made a move to leave either.

I put my hands under my thighs, because I wasn't sure if they'd stop shaking or not.

Flores continued paging through her pad, no doubt trying to see how nervous I'd get while I was waiting. Bernie used to say that the most nervous people were often the most innocent. If that was the case, I was the most innocent person ever.

"Miss Benson, where were you on Wednesday night?"

"I was out with Cage."

Flores's gaze never left mine. "Where was that?"

"The bar—Wally's."

"Ah, the MC bar. Let me guess—you've got an alibi all night."

She was being so sarcastic and Cage's tone matched hers when he said, "That's right."

"What time did you arrive?"

"Why don't you check with the owner?" Cage suggested. "She was at the door."

"Why can't Miss Benson answer the question?" Flores shot back.

Instinctively, I knew I was supposed to lie. Because we'd gotten there late. Because of the fight. Because I didn't go home with Cage and there were hours unaccounted for. "We got there around eight. We left after ten. Maybe eleven."

"And then?"

The MC must've been rubbing off on me, because I relaxed, glanced up at Cage and smiled. "We took a ride. And there were no witnesses to that."

Flores's expression grew tight, even more so

when Cage said, "I'm sure we could find some-one, babe. You were pretty loud."

I bit back a laugh, because I really didn't want to piss off the police. "What happened Wednes-day night?"

Flores flipped her pad closed. "We'll be check-ing your alibi with the bartenders, of course."

My alibi? I went to say something but Cage's stony look stopped me.

Flores smiled and then said to Preacher, "Why don't you show me around your chop shop?"

"Shop's not open to the public. Just where we fix our bikes, Detective," Preacher said easily.

"I've never bought that bullshit, Preacher."

Preacher shrugged. "Don't know what to tell you. But all these bikes? They're my club mem-bers'."

"Your gang members' bikes."

"We're not a gang. We're a club. And I don't see you producing a search warrant." Preacher was unruffled, and I guessed this happened pretty regularly. Because even I didn't believe what Preacher was selling, but I had to admit, there was zero hard, cold evidence to prove the existence of a chop shop. "If we're done here, you're interrupting a family barbecue."

She snorted, and her partner, who'd been si-lent until then, simply said, "We'll be back."

"You always fucking are," Cage muttered.

I let them walk away, waited for Cage to sit next to me. Waited for him to say something about my alibi, the fact that I'd lied to the police for him. But he didn't.

Instead, he said, "They always hassle us."

I glanced at him and his expression was guarded still. "I take it you don't like the police."

"I like them well enough when they're not bothering us because of our club association," he said. "The old detectives . . . they were good to us. My record's clean, Calla. I even had to prove myself when I enlisted, because of my MC status, and the cop who vouched for me was a former gang member from LA turned police officer."

"What did you do in the Army?"

He grinned a little. "I learned how to build bombs, but I can also disable them."

"There's a metaphor there."

He relaxed against me. "I thought Flores might be asking questions about your brother," he admitted.

I tensed up. "What about him?"

"I went to pay him a visit the night she's talking about. He wasn't there. I went back last night. Place looked like it'd been cleaned up— although his stuff's still there. I figured maybe someone took care of him already, which is no loss to you."

It wasn't, but the fact that Detective Flores was sniffing around wasn't good. "How did you know where to find him?"

Cage didn't answer me. Wouldn't or couldn't—I guessed it didn't matter. But my head started to throb a little bit. The party moved inside the club-house and I noticed that moms were taking their kids home. The majority of the women who stayed were old ladies, but there were a few mamas there with the single guys, as Amelia had pointed them out to me. They were nice enough, once they knew I was with Cage, but I knew not to trust them.

"Can we get out of here?" I asked him now.

"Sure. My jacket's inside. Come on."

I had to use the bathroom anyway, so I followed him in. He stopped to talk to Preacher for a second and I continued walking toward the bar area so I could go through to his room. My mind was swirling. I was thinking about Ned, wondering if I could have a normal life here. I couldn't say yes completely, no matter how well the past week had gone. But I was trusting Cage more and more each day, so I'd been willing to make it work.

I was so focused on getting to Cage's that I

almost missed it. I'm not sure how, since there were wolf whistles and cheering, and when I stopped dead in my tracks, Cage nearly ran me over.

"Babe, what?" He put his hands on my shoulders but I was immovable, staring at the scene in front of me. I'd seen men and women looking like they were going at it in the bar, but this was different.

There was a woman—one of the young mamas that Amelia had warned me about—sitting on the pool table, her legs spread, and a man kneeling with his head between them. People watched and cheered as she cried out.

"S'all right, babe. Slim just got out of the Navy. Six months on a sub," Cage explained. And that was fine—I could understand, even deal with it. But not the way the other men eyed her, men I'd sat and talked with. They were getting closer, a few with their hands on their crotches.

"What's going to happen to her?" I asked.

"Whatever Slim wants," he answered back.

"He'd share her?"

"She's not his old lady. She knew what she was in for."

"Jesus, Cage." I turned and tried to push past him. His grip was like iron. I tried one of the moves on him that I'd learned living with Tenn, and he practically howled but wouldn't let go of me. "Goddammit, he said that would work on anyone."

"Anyone but me, Calla. Why don't you believe me when I tell you I'm not letting you go?"

He didn't seem to care that we were in public, and no one cared that I was actively fighting him. We were in the clubhouse and this was expected even and, for the most part, ignored by the other men unless there was a gang bang involved . . .

I stopped. Pulled away. Twisted in his arms and he was backing away, his hands out.

Trigger much, Calla?

"Please . . . I have to get out of here." I heard the woman's cries now—of pleasure, it seemed, but the crowd was chanting and I couldn't watch, couldn't be here.

"Calla—"

"What if that was me!" I yelled finally, and he froze against me. Then he picked me up and carried me out of there, out into the parking lot. He didn't say a word, just strapped the helmet on me, climbed onto the bike and waited for me to do the same. And then he drove away from the madness happening inside Vipers and he took me to his apartment.

Chapter 18

He carried me from the bike into the building. Wouldn't let me go in the elevator. He talked to me like I was a wounded animal, telling me I was safe, and I let him, because I was still shaking from being in that crowd. I clung to him, feeling stupid. Vulnerable. There was no way I could survive in this world.

It wasn't until we were upstairs and I was huddled on the couch, a blanket wrapped around me, that I focused on his worried green eyes.

"I didn't realize, Calla."

"How would you have?"

"You told me that a guy hurt you. I should've known . . ."

Honestly, I should've known too. But the way Cage treated me, the fact that he'd stripped down first and bared himself to me, had stopped all the familiar feelings of dread. Because he turned me on more than any man I'd ever met. The connection that solidified during our first phone call had never weakened.

But I'd avoided talking about this subject—and he hadn't mentioned it except to tell me he hadn't forgotten his promise.

But this morning, while I was answering Tenn's e-mail, another, all too familiar one popped up. I didn't want to open it, but I had to. I always had to, just to check. Somehow, I felt as if Jeffrey knew, that he was tracking whether or not I opened them, and if I didn't, something worse would happen than just being sent a picture.

After I'd glanced through the pictures, I'd immediately gone into the bathroom and gotten sick. I'd shut the computer down and didn't even think about it again. Until now. "I don't know if I can do this."

"You don't have to go to the clubhouse anymore."

"That's not going to work. That's your home, Cage."

"You're my home," he said fiercely; then his tone quieted. "Babe, come on. Deep breaths, then talk to me."

"I'm not strong enough."

"Maybe not right now. But I'll be strong enough

for both of us." God, that soothed me almost immediately. But I still remained on mute, and he continued trying. "Calla, come on, just talk to me. Lay it all out, because—fuck, I can't help you with anything if you keep me in the dark."

"I don't want you to know things. I don't like what you know already."

His voice lowered to a dangerous octave. "What the fuck happened to you, Calla?"

"It doesn't matter. I'm fine."

"You're lying. And I'm the guy. I'm supposed to say everything's fine. You're not."

I crossed my arms over my chest. "I'm not like other women."

"No, you're not. And that's why I'm here with you. You're not getting rid of me, so it's either tell me now or I'll start digging."

"Don't you dare. You bastard . . . you wouldn't."

"Yeah, I would, if it meant getting to the bottom of all this shit."

The glint in his eye meant business. I knew he had the will and the means to try, but what was buried by Jameson Bradley was intended to stay that way. I couldn't let Cage dig. Which meant . . . I'd have to tell him the truth.

I curled up into myself—I didn't want him touching me when I told him what happened, and even though he didn't look happy about it, he seemed to instinctively understand. He sat next to me, giving me plenty of space.

I took a breath and looked at him, saying, "I was fifteen and he was seventeen. He'd been my boyfriend for a couple of months. And it started out consensual."

"Didn't stay that way."

"No. I mean, we had sex. I was drunk but I didn't say no. I thought . . . I thought he loved me. Fifteen and stupid, but I wouldn't have been the first girl to sleep with the wrong guy. But while I was passed out . . . I don't remember what happened but when I woke up, I was in his dorm suite. They'd drawn on me," I said, my voice hollow, my body numb. "I woke up covered in black and green permanent Magic Marker, on my body and my face. I was naked. I was bleeding between my legs. And I was all alone in his room."

I didn't want to go on, not after seeing the anger in Cage's eyes. But he put a hand over mine and didn't say a word.

I took a deep breath. "My phone rang. I picked it up and it was Jeffrey. He told me to check my pictures and I did. Me, naked, with guys' naked bodies around me. No faces, though. It didn't make sense until I realized that he'd let the guys watch us having sex, and then he'd let them jerk off on me, draw on me and take pictures of it for keepsakes. And he told me, 'Last night was great, honey. Anytime you want to do it again . . .' "

Cage let go of my hand and I didn't look at him. Not until I heard something smash and I turned to see he'd thrown the coffee table against the wall, letting it shatter into a thousand pieces. There was a dent in the wall.

He was taking all the anger for me so I could remain calm.

I don't know if I was the first—or the only—girl he'd done that to. I suspected not. I could still see the goddamned pictures when I closed my eyes, so right then I kept my eyes wide open. "I want to get over it. I need to. But I haven't found the right guy to make me forget. I hadn't . . . until you."

Cage reached his hand out and waited for me to grab it. I did. "I don't remember much after that. I got sick in the garbage can before making it to the bathroom. I just wanted to get clean—I couldn't leave his room like that, so I showered. Scrubbed myself raw trying to get the marker off me."

It would take weeks before my skin was unblemished again.

"I didn't think about the police. I was sick and confused, and obviously Jeffrey had counted on that. I was goddamned fifteen and had had sex with the guy I'd thought loved and protected me. At first, I didn't even understand his part in the betrayal. Not until I saw the pictures. My father contacted his friends in the police department. They went after Jeffrey hard. Jeffrey's family had a lot of money too, and my mother didn't want any of this public. I don't blame her—I didn't want it getting out either. So there was a settlement and everything was buried."

I took a deep breath and then said, "There's more."

"Okay," he ground out.

"Remember . . . I told you my father was working with Bernie? Because my brother stole money from me?" I didn't wait for him to respond. "That was true, but it was only partially why my father got in touch with me. Ned has the pictures and he was blackmailing my father—if he got money, he wouldn't publish the pictures online."

Cage's eyes were stormy when he asked, "How did Ned get them?"

"I don't know. He knew about them when it happened." I swallowed past the lump in my throat and ripped the Band-Aid off. "But Jeffrey has sent them to me at least once a year since it happened. He's not supposed to have any contact, but he sends them and I don't say anything to anyone, and the rest of the time it's fine."

"When was the last time he sent you those pictures?"

"This morning," I whispered.

"Why didn't you tell anyone?"

"Because I thought I could handle it," I told him, my voice low and angrier than I'd intended as I took a step toward him. "Because he only sent me the e-mails a couple of times a year."

Cage held his ground even as the earth seemed to tilt under my feet, but I managed another step. "Because I thought he couldn't get close," I told him, even as I closed the distance between Cage and me. I grabbed his shirtfront, fisted it in my hand and yanked as I practically whispered, "Because I didn't want it to be goddamned real."

Cage's eyes flickered over my face, his expression something I couldn't place. Melancholy, maybe? "I get it, baby."

"Do you, really? Do you know what it's like to have someone following your every move, watching you . . . waiting for you to break?"

I still held his shirt tightly. He didn't try to pull away, but his tone matched mine when he said, "You'd goddamned better believe I do. I've known what it's like for my goddamned entire life. And you shared that with me. And I promised to come back and take care of this guy for you."

"I don't understand why. For me, a total stranger."

"You're not a stranger, Calla. Don't bullshit me. You knew that maybe the second you picked up the phone and you definitely knew it by the end of the call." He went and got the laptop and brought it to me. "Log into your e-mail."

I wanted to refuse. But my fingers hit the keys. I was so beyond numb by this point. I hit the e-mail. No text. Just attachments. But I hesitated, with my finger hovering over the delete button.

I couldn't press it, though—doing so wouldn't actually erase what happened. It wouldn't be that easy. I was going to have to let Cage see the pictures and I knew that could ruin us. It was one thing to explain it and entirely another to see it.

How was he ever supposed to be with me again after seeing that?

I turned the computer back to him. "I don't want you to open them. I want to tell you that I'll hate you if you do . . ."

Even though we both knew that last part wasn't true, he looked so torn. I wanted to take it back, but I couldn't.

"When you see them, you'll never look at me

the way you do now. It will never be the same. He will ruin my life again. It's like he gets to violate me over and over . . ."

"I have to, Calla." His voice was as raw as my emotions. He clicked the link and I closed my eyes. Turned away and tried not to be sick. Because I didn't have to look to know what he was seeing.

It was enough that I could feel his rage, palpable and violently so, slam through me.

This was it. Knowing about what happened to me was bad enough, but the fact that he was actually seeing the aftermath made my stomach turn. He'd never touch me after this, or he might try but he'd never be able to rid himself of those images.

He closed the laptop and turned to me.

"Do you ever think about those pictures when I'm fucking you?" he demanded.

"No!"

"Is that the truth?"

I stilled, because it was. "Yes. Never."

"Then why would I?"

"It's different."

"It's not, Calla. Do you have any faith in me at all?"

"Yes."

"If you did, you wouldn't say things like that

to me." He pulled away. The pictures had driven a wedge between us—maybe not in quite the way I'd thought, but they were a wedge between us all the same—just as I'd feared. So I sat in Cage's apartment in a high-security building guarded by MC members, and I'd never been more afraid in my entire life.

I hugged my arms around my legs, pulling them tight to my chest. "I need to be alone."

"Babe . . ."

"Go. Just goddamn go."

"I'm not leaving."

"Get the fuck away from me, Cage. I don't want you here. I don't want to see you or talk to you. What don't you understand? Get out."

He stared at me hard, but he complied. He didn't fight, just told me, "The guys are at the door. No one's getting through them."

And then he left me alone in his apartment.

Chapter 19

"Cage, you look like shit."

Rocco came up the stairs—he never took the elevator. "What's up?"

"I need you to make sure the building's secure as fuck."

"Threats?"

"Against Calla, yes."

Rocco nodded. "Want me to stand guard here?"

"I'm not leaving the front of this door."

He turned away, but not before Rocco said, "We do what we have to, brother."

Brother. How easily Vipers had accepted him into the fold, once, twice, and back again. Each time, he'd expected anger, and each time, he got understanding.

But his anger—that could swallow him. Engulf him. It already choked him so hard he was like a mad dog straining on a leash.

He'd survived more than his fair share of accidents and not so accidental things. He'd been born into violence—it surrounded him, followed him when he tried to leave and sucked him back in.

The Heathens lived by the concept of an eye for an eye. Blood for blood. But the problem with vengeance was that it was a never-ending lineup of death and more death. Cage didn't want to find himself simply surviving in between taking revenge on anyone who hurt the club or Calla.

Surviving in between trying to stop his family from ruining his life and the lives of everyone he cared about.

Christian Cage Owens had come to Skulls by way of the goddamned motherfucking Army, which had promised to make him a man but actually ended up making him a better criminal. He'd been a Viper for ten-plus years, bred to that MC life as surely as he'd been born to it.

Except he'd been born a Heathen, not a Viper. And while it had taken the Vipers a long time to believe him or trust him completely, once they had, they'd had his back completely.

Now the woman who'd kept him from dying, the one he swore pulled him back from the dead with her *Don't go into the light* voice and her fucking sweetness—a sweetness he swore he didn't deserve—was in front of him. And she was scared to death of him.

Which was, of course, the way it would go down for him. Why he'd expected it to be any different was beyond him.

He'd been born a Heathen, uncivilized in every sense of the word. But knowing what happened to Calla was something he could never, ever stand for. He figured that sometimes being uncivilized might be the best thing going for him in a time like this.

He didn't know how he was going to get through to Calla, but he had to try. He had to get through to himself too. They were both in traps of their own making and he had to figure out a way they could free themselves.

I woke with a start. I'd fallen asleep, half slumped on the couch, and the sun was blaring through the open shades. I didn't have to look in the mirror to know my face was swollen from crying, and my head throbbed from the stress and worry.

Cage wasn't here. Because I'd kicked him out.

And what, you secretly wanted him to break back into his own apartment for you? I'd even put the chains and dead bolts on. I'd locked him out in so many ways.

And by doing that, I was the one letting Jeffrey Harris win.

I padded to the door and peered out. Rocco was sitting on a chair diagonally from the door, reading a magazine. I unlocked and opened the door and glanced at him, but he was looking down at my feet instead.

"Careful," he mouthed, and I looked down to see Cage.

Cage, at my feet. He'd slept in the doorway. He'd slept in the hall, on the floor, against the door of his own apartment, because I'd asked him to leave. And then I'd felt betrayed that he hadn't come back.

But he'd never left. I stared down at him. He was asleep, but the man across the hall put a finger against his lips, whispered, "He's been up all night."

"Me too." I knelt down and curled around him in that small space. He woke with a start, then held me against him. When I nuzzled his neck and said, "Take me to bed," we were up and I was in his arms, reveling in his strength.

He kicked the door closed behind us, hit the alarm, cradling me all the while.

I was only wearing one of his old T-shirts, which landed on the floor when we hit the bedroom. But he didn't try anything—he just held me. His skin was warm against mine. I just kept picturing how he'd guarded me all night.

"I hate seeing you suffer, Calla. I hate it. That's why you need to let me fix it," he murmured fiercely.

"I'm sorry I freaked out on you. It's just . . . I've never told anyone this."

He brushed my cheek with a knuckle. "I knew there was shit there after our first phone call, babe."

"I was the golden child. I was going to make something of myself. Raise myself out of the working class. Why? So I could use money to shove things under the rug with money?"

Cage stroked my back. "I always had plenty of cash. Doesn't do much good if you're not happy."

I never realized how between two worlds I was. The people involved were paid to shut their mouths and transfer to boarding schools out of the country. Of course, rumors lingered, but there was no denying my status, thanks to my father. Even if I refused to recognize it, the others couldn't. Their parents wouldn't let them. Jameson Bradley was too powerful a force in their lives. "I'm an imposter."

Cage cupped my hip with his hand to drag our bodies closer. "Not to me."

"I didn't want a better life. I wanted my life,

whatever that entailed." I shrugged. "I spent a lot of time pretending and not a lot of time living."

"How long were you working for Bernie?"

"A little over a year. I came home after Grams died and found out I had nothing left. Only the bit in my checking account. I was so angry. I'd been groomed to be this other persona and now I was left with that sham. Because even though my father's name got me into those schools, and even though he insisted on paying the tuition, that's all my mother accepted from him. She'd given me everything else, thanks to the bar, to what she and Grams had worked for. But hey, it's not the first time a man had taken their life savings."

I heard the anger in my voice. I'd thought I was over it. "I should've gotten to know my father. Not for the money, because that's been there the whole time. But we missed a lot."

"It's not too late, Calla. Last I saw, he was waiting for you. Sounds like he'd do anything for you."

"Just like you," I whispered.

"Believe that."

"Some battles I have to fight on my own."

"Not this one," he told me. "Your walls are back up, but I'm already inside. Don't you get that? You walled us in together."

Chapter 20

The next night, Cage waited until Calla fell asleep and then he grabbed the keys to the door at the end of the far hallway. Behind the door was an entire world he'd tried to ignore, but finally, that night, it became clear to him that in this space he might find the answers he sought.

He hadn't been here in years. The last time was the week before he'd shipped out for the first time, and when the familiar pull tugged at him, he almost didn't recognize it.

He made sure to alarm the door behind him so Calla would remain safe in the apartment alone—and the Vipers guys continued to guard the front door to the apartment. Then he took the freight elevator down to the private space on the basement level, but separate from the garage. He was the only one who had access to this space, from above and below.

His hand shook as he unlocked the door and he cursed a string of familiar favorites as he finally got the damned thing to open. And he stood in the doorway, surveying a place where time really had stood still.

Had he moved on? He'd thought so. Thought he'd lost his passion for this. Frankly, it'd been so long since he'd picked up a brush or a pencil to simply sketch, beyond a map of a potential battlefield or LZ that he'd thought maybe he'd imagined his talent.

Fixing bikes or cars was something he'd done most recently for survival, not for joy.

He closed the door behind him, because the thought of anyone walking in right now was unbearable.

He looked at the sketchbook, sitting exactly where he'd left it. He recalled picking it up several times and almost carrying it out the door with him, but in the end he'd left it behind. He ran a finger through the light dust on the cover. Not enough to have collected over the past years. Which meant Preacher had been having the place cleaned.

Scratch that. It meant that Preacher had been cleaning this place himself, because he knew how Cage guarded his privacy fiercely.

And Preacher still believed he'd come back to this room. That he'd come back here, no matter how he'd tried to stay away for a myriad of reasons. He'd tried to escape his Heathen MC past with the Army and then, postenlistment, when he'd realized how bad things had gotten in Heathen territory.

How Eli was no longer unaffected. How he'd known the boy wouldn't be, because Cage had been ten goddamned years old when he'd left, already irreparably scarred. But Eli's mom lived off-compound and had promised to keep him safe. Cage even gave her money and a phone number to call if things got bad, and she'd taken it, because she'd realized how deep she was in. Up to her goddamned neck.

You left him in hell.

And maybe Cage didn't deserve this kind of beauty in his life, not Calla or the art, didn't deserve the way both made him feel.

Maybe he didn't, but he wasn't stupid enough to throw away gifts, not the one in his bed or the one that had been with him since as long as he could remember.

He opened the sketchbook gingerly, like he was afraid to see the past, that maybe it would remind him of the anger and revenge he'd harbored. But it wouldn't matter, because it certainly wasn't dead or buried.

And neither are you.

He stared at the first sketch for a long moment before leaving it for the actual bike, the one he'd just gotten a start on when he and Tals decided it was time to follow in the Vipers founding fathers' footsteps. Enlist, boot camp and deployment. *Hoorah* Rangers. He had the scars, the ink, the mentality to prove he was enmeshed in two brotherhoods so fully that he'd never fully escape either. And he didn't want to, but the Army was the only bridge back here.

He bent down on one knee as he uncovered the bike, like he was begging forgiveness, proposing to work on it again at the same time.

The bike was built from scratch. He hadn't acquired all he'd needed for it, so he'd have to hunt down the hard-to-find parts. With Tals's help, because Tals could procure just about anything. He was the juvenile delinquent and criminal of the bunch, and based on the company he kept, that was saying a hell of a lot.

He touched the cool metal, ran his fingertips along the pattern he hadn't been able to shove from his mind.

He'd promised Preacher that he could restore this. Preacher had never stopped believing in him.

So when had he stopped believing in himself?

He guessed that it didn't matter, since right now he believed in everything again. He knew he'd have to walk through hell to get there, but he was willing, because he saw his paradise on the other side.

Two hours later, he'd sanded and painted the bumper. At first, he was hesitant, and then the right music, the smell of grease and oil, made his hands take over from his head. He blinked, stepped back as he stared at what he'd accomplished, then stared down at his hands.

"Still here," he murmured. And then he locked up, showered to get the paint and turpentine off him so he could slip back into bed, one step closer to healing himself . . . and hopefully, by extension, healing Calla.

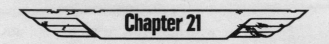

Chapter 21

I'd first called Tenn the night I'd told Cage.

"Do you need me there?" he'd asked, and just hearing him say that was a huge relief. But it was easy with Tenn, because I didn't need him the way I needed Cage.

"I might."

"I'm a phone call away," he'd promised, and when I'd heard Cage leave me after he'd thought I was asleep for a third night in a row, I did call.

Tom was at the door in two hours. Bypassing the alarms. Knocking on the door at the same time he was texting me.

I didn't know what to say, so I just fell into his hug. He carried me over to the bed and curled around me, asking, "When the hell did you sleep last?"

"I feel like that's all I've been doing."

I'd sent him the pictures, because I'd wanted him to see what Cage had. I needed his help and I told him that. "How could he see these and ever think about me the way he did before?"

"He can. He will, hon. You've got to give him credit. He's lived through ugly things. We all have."

"I want to believe you. But I don't know how to bring him back to me."

"You don't need my help, Calla. You know what to do." He paused. "He wants to make sure you're okay. That's what's holding him back. He doesn't think of you any differently. You do."

"Stop being so smart," I told him. And then I changed the subject slightly, to the other worry weighing on me. "The promise he made to me . . . Now that he knows, what's he going to do?"

"You know the answer to that, baby girl."

"Stop him."

He gave a short laugh with absolutely zero humor behind it. "Yeah, that'd work."

"You could try, for me."

"If I thought I could, I'd already have stopped the man from doing other dangerous things, Calla. But the truth is, if he can't do this for you, he'll never be able to live with himself."

"After what he's found out, he'll never be able to live with me either. Never be able to look at me again."

"That's bullshit."

"He hasn't tried to sleep with me, or really touched me since I told him—and that's a new record for us. I'm not an idiot." God, I sounded like a miserable fool. "I'm sorry. I shouldn't have bothered you."

"Do I look bothered?"

"He left me tonight. Snuck out while he thought I was sleeping. That's three nights in a row."

"Could be club business," Tenn offered. "He's not going to go far."

"It doesn't matter—he might as well be a million miles away."

"When you first met him, he promised he was going to make whoever hurt you pay."

"He did."

"And you believed that."

I had.

"Let him."

"Would you?"

"I took care of my own shit, Calla, because I could. If I couldn't have, damned straight I would've let Cage do it."

Tenn was so calm most of the time—so seemingly easygoing that I knew how deeply his pain had to run. It was always the easygoing ones who held the most pain. "I'm sorry, Tenn."

"You did nothing wrong." He paused. "You can rewrite your script, you know. Take control of it. Nothing's bad if it makes you feel good."

I stared at Tenn. "How are you so wise?"

His eyes crinkled at the corners as he laughed. "Christ, woman, you're making me feel old. I'm not wise. Just crammed a lot of life into a small time frame."

"I think you're a miracle worker." I only wished Cage was there to take me the rest of the way.

I must've fallen asleep, because the next thing I knew, I heard semiangry men's voices. I blinked to see Cage standing over me and Tenn practically underneath me. Tenn was lying there, and I was half on his chest. He'd been watching a movie.

Well, porn. A porn movie.

"You're lucky I know which way you swing," Cage muttered to him.

"Maybe I'm bi and never told you," Tenn shot back as he remained curled around me.

"I will fucking kill you."

"Try it, old man," Tenn said, and instead of upsetting me, their interaction made me laugh. Tenn turned to me. "Are you laughing at us?"

"Completely."

"Huh. See if I ever defend your honor," Tenn said with fake insult.

"It's the first time you've laughed in days," Cage said quietly. I held out a hand to him, to pull him down. Once he was settled next to me, Rocco called through the door and walked in.

"Bedroom," Tenn called and Rocco found us. And the porn. And grinned.

"What's up, Roc?" Tenn asked, like he owned the place. I didn't care, because Cage was holding me. I ran a hand along his arm, because I saw something red.

"Paint," he told me.

But before I could question him more, Rocco said, "There's trouble down at the clubhouse. Flores wants to talk to Calla. I figured you'd rather meet her there than here."

"She can come here," Cage said.

"I can go to the clubhouse," I told him.

"Forget it."

"I can't avoid it forever."

"Good thing it hasn't been forever, then," he told me.

Rocco left and returned in a few minutes to let us know that everyone was on their way.

"Everyone?" I asked.

"Flores, that partner of hers—Dom something . . ."

"Her partner's a Dom?" Tenn asked.

"Not a Dom—his name's Dom," Cage told him, and I snorted. Rocco perched on the edge of the bed, then lay down across the width at our feet, and that's how Preacher found us. Watching porn.

"Why are you watching gay porn?" he asked.

"It's a threesome," Rocco pointed out.

Preacher muttered something like "Jesus fucking Christ" and then there was an official-sounding rap on the door. "She wouldn't tell me what it was about. Insisted on seeing you, Calla."

I got up with the rest of them, reluctantly. Tenn turned off the TV and walked with me toward the couch as Cage let the detectives in.

I noted that Rocco walked out then, probably to guard the door. Which I appreciated. I'd had enough surprises.

At least I thought I had.

Detective Flores and, yes, Detective Dom came forward with serious faces. "Calla, I'd like to speak with you alone, please."

"No," Cage and Tenn said in unison. And Preacher too.

"It's all right," I told them. "It's not like you'll be far, right?"

"It's either here or the station," Flores said.

"Do I need a lawyer?" I asked.

"Do you feel like you need one?" she shot back.

"Yes."

"Rocco!" Preacher shouted. He peeked in and Preacher pointed at me. "She's lawyered up."

Rocco came in and sat down next to me.

"You're a lawyer?" Flores asked him, before I could.

"Yes, ma'am. Member of the South Carolina bar." He reached into his pocket and pulled out a business card to hand to her. "Calla, I'll tell you what not to answer, all right?"

I nodded. Cage and Tenn and Preacher moved off toward the kitchen. Flores took a seat across from me, while her partner stood.

"Where was Cage Owens last night?" she asked me pointedly when I was looking at her dead-on.

My gaze didn't waver as I lied. "He was with me."

"All night?"

I smiled. "Yes, all night."

"I suppose that's what you'll tell me about every night this week," Flores said.

"What's this all about, Detective?" Rocco asked. "If you want to question Cage, please do so, but my client's answered your question. Did you come all this way to ask that?" Rocco, who'd just been watching a threesome, was as professional as I'd ever heard anyone, especially if I didn't look at the skull and crossbones T-shirt he was wearing.

Flores didn't pull any further punches, telling me, "Ned Benson's been murdered."

My mouth opened. Closed. I put my fingers over my eyes for a long moment. While there was no love lost between my brother and me, he was still my brother. My head spun and Rocco put a hand on my shoulder. When I looked back up, Dom was handing me water. I took a small sip and then asked, "How? Why?"

"When was the last time you'd seen or heard from your brother, Calla?"

"Don't answer that. Is she a suspect, Detective?" Rocco asked.

"It's a simple question."

It was. "I haven't seen or heard from him in years."

"Years?"

"At least three."

"Satisfied?" Rocco asked.

"Where was he when you found him?"

"He was staying in a motel close to the Georgia border," Flores said.

He'd been that close to here? Was that a coincidence?

"So you and your brother weren't close, then?"

"Not particularly," I told her.

"Any reason?"

I knew better than to answer, because even in my slight state of shock I knew that I had a solid reason to want to hurt Ned. People had killed for a lot less than money.

But she was flipping through that damned pad of hers. "Ned Benson stole money that was earmarked for you after your grandmother died. He also forged your signature on the bar's deed, sold it and pocketed the money."

I didn't say a word.

"All of that on its own would be enough to make me suspect you," she continued. "But there's another piece of evidence that makes it slightly more damning. Because we found some pictures on his computer—of you, Calla."

I glared at her. Blurted out, "Those are private. You're not allowed to see those," even as Rocco put a hand on my arm.

"They're evidence now. Motive."

I looked up. "Motive?"

"He was extorting money from your father. Threatening to go to the papers and put these all over YouTube if Mr. Bradley didn't pay up."

But he did, I wanted to tell her. I kept my mouth shut instead.

"Did you check Ned's bank account?"

"Yes, we did."

"And?" Rocco asked.

"A large transfer of funds was made a month ago."

"I'm not seeing the issue here, Detective."

"The issue is that Cage Owens killed Ned Benson for Calla. I'd accuse Jameson Bradley, but he's got an airtight alibi."

"He could've hired someone," Rocco pointed out, throwing my father under the bus.

"I considered that. But Cage Owens was seen at the motel this week, by an FBI agent who's been part of an undercover sting. I think he makes a very credible witness."

"He's wrong," I said, my voice hollow and raw. "Please go."

"I have more questions."

"They'll have to wait," Rocco told her, then called for Cage, who was next to me in seconds, even as Flores was telling me, "We can do this down at the station."

"Is Calla being charged with something?" Cage asked.

"Not yet." *Not yet.* Oh my God. "You'll most likely be charged together."

"Get the hell out of my house, Detective." Cage's voice was a growl, enough to make Flores start a little. And I figured it took a hell of a lot for that to happen.

When she'd gone, Cage came over to me. Rocco had disappeared into the kitchen with Tenn and Preacher to tell them what happened, I figured.

"You heard everything, I'm guessing."

"Helps that the place is wired," Cage said. "I knew you'd be fine with Rocco, but figured we needed a heads-up. And, babe, I didn't ask you to be my alibi."

"That's right—you're not asking or telling me anything."

"There's nothing to tell."

My mouth opened to ask him if he'd killed Ned. He'd been angry enough to want to. So had I. But instead, I asked, "Do you think it's been Ned all these years and not Harris?"

Ned had been the same age as Harris, but Ned hadn't gone to the same boarding school as I had. My father paid for it and his wouldn't. "I don't know."

"If it was . . . I don't know which would be worse."

"You're trying to push me away, like you think I'm going to do to you."

I blinked and didn't answer. *Damn him.*

"It's not going to work."

"You say that, Cage, but I know better."

"Yeah? You've had a lot of men defending you

against that prick? Because from where I stand, I'm the only one who's kept a promise . . . and I intend on keeping it the whole way."

I swallowed, hard. "Did you kill Ned?"

"No. But I would've if he'd been there."

No hesitation or guilt. Just simple, hard truth. And my simple, hard truth was that it would've been all right with me if Cage had killed Ned for his part in everything.

Chapter 22

After Rocco and Preacher left, I said good-bye to Tenn.

"I'll come back anytime you need me to," he said.

"Are you going back home tonight?"

"Nah. Gonna get in trouble with Tals and head back in the morning. Cage said he'd post my bail if I have a problem."

"I never said that," Cage called. Tenn gave me a hug and then left, and I closed the door and set the alarm. The night stretched out before me. I didn't know what to do. I'd wanted to call my father to tell him, but I wanted to connect with Cage more.

"Hey."

When I turned, he was standing by the locked door. "Hey." I felt shy all of a sudden.

"I've got to show you something. Will you come with me?"

"Of course." I followed him through the door, down the elevator and into the big garagelike space in what looked to the basement.

"I hadn't been working in here," he admitted. "Not until a few nights ago."

This was his alibi.

Cage was an artist. Which explained the moody, brooding parts of him.

"Wait. All this . . . is yours?" I put my hand to my throat. Even though I wasn't a motorcycle enthusiast, that didn't mean I couldn't appreciate what I saw laid out in front of me any less. Custom bikes finished to varying degrees, each piece painstakingly put together to create one-of-a-kind bikes.

My eyes were drawn to one old bike. It looked prewar and it appeared that the refurbishing process was just beginning. "This is your thing."

Everything had been covered in blankets, which now lay scattered on the floor. I saw rows of paints, a half-assembled bike and a sketchbook. I put my hand on it, but didn't open it. My gaze caught on a photograph on the wall, a beautiful, custom bike.

"You made this?"

"Yeah." His eyes looked far away. "That was before."

"Before what?"

"Before I enlisted. Before I decided to become a one-man show, taking down the Heathens single-handedly." His gaze flickered up to the photograph and back down, as if it was too painful for him to look at.

My chest tightened watching him. "And now?"

"I want to. I just don't know if I can, Calla. I know too much. I've seen too much. I'm not the same person anymore."

He had to be lying—whether to me or to himself, it didn't matter. "Are you worried?"

"When you do shit like this, you have to feel. And I don't want to feel anymore because then—"

"Too late," I told him. "If you already feel, this should be a breeze. Looks like it is too."

The depth and breadth of his talent was apparent the more I investigated the shop. Since no one else was here, I assumed this was his baby and his alone.

"Does anyone help you?"

"Sometimes Tals will, for the complicated stuff I can't fix alone."

"Do just MC members buy these?"

"No. Before I went into the Army, rock stars

and celebrities bought them. Figured it was time to pick it up again."

I pulled myself up to sit on one of the tables so I could survey the place. He climbed up next to me.

"I told you that the Heathens surrounded me in that parking garage. I knew those men, Calla. I grew up with them."

"I don't understand."

"My brother, Troy . . . He was the one who gave the orders to kill me."

I opened my mouth, then closed it. Because, based on my family experiences, it wasn't all that unbelievable. "So your brother joined the Heathens?"

"He was born into the Heathens MC. Just like I was."

Calla's mouth dropped open. He put a finger under her chin and gently pushed up.

"Sorry," she said. "It's just . . ."

"Fucked up?"

"That sums it up pretty well," she agreed. "Is it bad there?"

"You have no idea, Calla."

"So tell me."

"You're already too involved.

"In for a penny."

"Why? Why would you want that?"

"You took on my burden."

"Willingly. No strings."

"Why?"

"Because." He skimmed her cheek with his knuckles.

"Exactly." She mirrored his actions. "I'm here, Cage. Not because I have to be. Stop trying to lock me out. As a wise man once told me, your walls went back up, but I'm already inside."

It was only fair that she learned what she was getting into. He'd given her zero choice, and staying here wasn't an option forever. Nothing lasted forever, but goddamn, he was going to try with the woman sitting across from him. "I couldn't tell you before. For a lot of reasons."

"I understand secrets, Cage."

He ran a hand through his hair. It had started to grow out a little, not enough to make him feel completely like him yet, though. "My father's the president of the Heathens. Troy's my half brother. So is Eli, but he's only fifteen."

"Where's your mom?"

"She died when I was twelve. So did one of my sisters." He paused. "Heathens have been dealing in drugs for a long time. Meth especially. It's cheap and easy to make and sell, addictive as anything. Heathens run it down the coast. They started when I was about seven or eight. It had never been par-

adise, because it was a violent MC, but once the
meth came into play, it was never the same."

"What happened to your mom?"

"What happened to a lot of other Heathen old
ladies. She got addicted to the drugs." He paused.
"I left, Calla. Left at ten and met Preacher. And
he'd told me I could stay with him, that I didn't
have to go back."

"But you were ten."

"It didn't matter. I knew my responsibilities."
And still, a big part of him wished he'd never
gone back to his house that night.

If he'd just stayed at Vipers . . .

But he was worried about his sister. He was
worried about his mom too, but he was also mad
at her, because she wasn't doing anything lately,
for herself or for her kids for two years. Cage had
stepped in to help as much as he could, but he
was twelve fucking years old, and he wasn't supposed to be mom and dad to his ten-year-old
twin sisters.

Didn't mean he didn't try. "I'm the ultimate trai-
tor in their eyes," he told her. "If I'd been patched
in already, it would've been really ugly when I left.
Although it was pretty damned ugly anyway."

"What happened?"

He took a breath and he told her his secrets.

The fire choked him. He wasn't sure what was

happening, but even though he was still in that partial dream state, he was still born and bred to an MC. He'd always been able to function easily postslumber, out of necessity. From the time he could remember, it was always, "You take care of your mother and your sisters, you hear, boy?"

And Cage had, loud and clear. Learned to shoot at six, was carrying a piece pretty much everywhere except school by eight and, now, the weapon was in his hand even as he covered his nose and mouth with a towel he grabbed from the chair as he fought his way out through the smoke.

He'd woken when the living room was already filled with smoke. When he'd fallen asleep, his mother had been asleep in the chair next to the couch. As he reached out, he realized that the chair was empty.

Had she stumbled to her room? Lit a cigarette and fallen asleep in bed? He'd caught her doing that before during the day, but that night, he'd slept deeply, and he'd woken and cursed as he yelled for his mother, his sisters . . .

Their room was next to his parents'. He could barely make it past the hallway bathroom before he started choking. The ceiling had begun to fall in and he got out of the house in time, before the entire thing burst into flames.

As he stood, feeling the heat from the fire

scalding him, he remembered the tree house. He ran there.

Marielle was in the tree house. Sometimes, at night, she snuck out there to read.

"I smelled Mom's stuff," she said, referring to the meth, "so I climbed out. Couldn't sleep with the smoke."

He put an arm around her, kept her close, because it was crazy all around the house with fire and police and the Heathens, who didn't trust the firefighters or the police, revving their bikes and trying to cover up the fact that Cage's mom was responsible.

"You keep your mouth shut," his father growled when he saw him.

Somehow, it was all blamed on him. An angry kid . . . playing with matches, doing drugs . . . His school record showed a history of fighting. His record was sealed, because it was from when he was a juvenile. He'd done the time because he'd been too numb to give a shit about anything else. It was easier to take the blame than to fight it. His sister could stay with his father—the one thing he could say was that he'd never hurt Marielle. Unlike their mom, his father treated his girls like gold. After Sally's death, he kept a very close watch on her.

Even so, as soon as she turned fifteen, Cage got her out, thanks to a boarding school in Florida where Preacher pulled some strings. Marielle had gone willingly and she'd been in Florida ever since.

But lately, she'd been worried about him, had been threatening to come back. Especially when she heard about his near-death experience.

He blinked and he wasn't smelling the smoke anymore, wasn't in that front yard or the juvenile detention center. He was with Calla and she was hugging him.

When she pulled back, she asked, "Was any part of it good? Because why go to another MC?"

"Where else was I going to go, Calla? Foster care?" He paused. "This is a violent, addictive lifestyle. I was born into it, yes, but it's also in my blood. In here."

He hated telling her this shit. The look of horror in her eyes was something he wanted to wipe away, not watch grow stronger.

But he pressed on. Because if there was one important thing he learned in the Army, it was that letting someone know who they were up against and why made for a more effective soldier—and ultimately, a more effective mission.

"The Heathens are in fucking ruins. Just like my family," he started. "The money they're bringing in should be enough to make everything good. But it's brought in nothing but ruin."

"The drugs."

"You think he'd know—no, you'd think he'd care."

"So your father and your brother, they don't do the drugs."

"No, they're smart in that regard. Most of the brotherhood doesn't. In fact, if you're caught doing drugs as a Heathen member, you're out. But they don't give a shit about their women. They keep them clean while they're breeding, but that's about it."

"Breeding?"

He shrugged. "S'what they call it, babe. Not saying it's pretty, or that I agree. If I agreed, I'd still be a Heathen. And what I went through to get out and get in Vipers? That wasn't pretty either."

"And no one stops them?"

"They don't sell the meth in their own town, so everyone thinks they're wonderful. Took that trick from Preach. Difference is, we don't sell drugs at all."

"Guns?"

"We ship them out of the country," he said.

"So they're trying to push meth into Skulls?"

"Among other things. They've got a prostitution ring."

"So they drug the women, then pimp them out. I hate them."

"Emotions will get you every time."

"In this case, I consider them a bonus."

He tapped on his heart. "Preacher gave me a second lease on life."

From childhood, his few good memories centered on the bikes and the open road, anything and everything that happened away from the clubhouse.

MCs fucked you up good. But they were what he knew, and he was damned well and determined to believe in Preacher's Vipers. Because Preacher had saved the Vipers from a fate similar to the Heathens, had shoved the Vipers out from under the weight of drugs and shifted them toward the equally dangerous gunrunning.

But gunrunning wasn't destroying families from the ground up, not in the all-pervasive way drugs were. A mother with a gun could protect her baby; a mother on meth could not.

"Where's your sister now?" Calla asked.

"She's still in Florida. But she wants to come back."

"And?"

"And I won't let her. No one knows where she

is except me, Preach and Tals. And Tenn, of course. I need it to stay that way."

"She's mad at you for that."

"I think she's beginning to hate me," he admitted, careful not to let Calla see how much that shit broke his heart. "My family—what's left of them—would destroy her. My mom . . . by the end, she was all fucking strung out. She wasn't herself anymore. And my sisters were scared of her, but they needed her so much. I tried, but it wasn't the same."

He stopped before his voice broke. Calla was staring at him, her hand on his arm, rubbing the ink there, tracing the symbols there. And when he was able to talk again, he told her, "We might be above the law here at times . . . but we don't pull that drug shit. I will never let that into my town."

He paused, then told her part of the answer she'd been looking for. "I got out of the Army. Took the trip back here. That same night I came back to Vipers, they had a big welcome-home party for me." He didn't want to go there, but he did. "Heathens crashed it. They heard I was home and they wanted to fuck things up. Two of our guys died. Because of me. And the next day, two high school kids OD'd on meth, sold to them by the same Heathens who crashed the party."

The Heathens were taunting him, basically telling him, *You love your town so much, we'll destroy it.*

She looked so sad as she said, "So after all that . . ."

"I left. Didn't say anything. Packed up some shit and took off. Let it be known I was going rogue. Heathens could hunt me down."

"You were hoping they'd follow you and leave Vipers alone."

"Yeah."

"But why is Preacher so mad?"

"You've got to get permission to go rogue. If he'd known what I was planning, I wouldn't have gotten it." He took a deep breath and continued. "The number I gave you . . . it's to a locked safety-deposit box. There are recordings in there that could take down my father and Troy. I was going to turn them over to the DA for their RICO case. If I could take it back, I would."

"I know. I can't unmemorize it any more than I could erase you from my mind. And I don't want that."

The Heathens left him hollowed out inside, and both Vipers and the Army had slowly filled the void, but they'd also made him a more efficient street criminal.

They'd also given him Calla. Calla, who touched the scars on his neck. She'd been there with him when he'd come back from the dead. Now it was up to him to help her bury her ghosts, no matter what it took.

Chapter 23

After Cage and I went back up to the apartment, the now too familiar separation between us began. The closeness we'd regained with the reveal of his bike art—and the way we'd communicated—was still there when we got into bed. But I'd remained fully dressed in sweats and didn't push anything, although he wrapped himself around me while we slept.

I'd say the lack of sexual willingness was my fault, that he was simply giving me space, but of course I assumed he didn't want to touch me because of the pictures.

The next day we both hung around the apartment, under the weight of Ned's death. We didn't hear anything from Officer Flores, although I swore my heart skipped a beat every time the phone rang or someone knocked on the door. But it was just the guys checking on us, bringing us food.

By nightfall, I'd snuggled into the couch to watch a movie, not wanting to go back into the bedroom. Cage was downstairs for a while and I heard him moving back and forth, but I didn't think anything of it.

Finally, he sat down next to me and put my feet in his lap. He rubbed them a little, the massage making me groan a little.

"That's nice," I told him.

"I'd do anything to make you feel good, babe. Anything for you—you know that."

We weren't talking about massages any longer. "I know, Cage. You keep your promises. But I don't want you to do anything that will stay on your conscience."

"Trust me, nothing I've got planned will make me lose a second of sleep."

It wouldn't for me either, and maybe I wasn't supposed to think like that, but I did. Because lately, especially after staying at Tenn's, I couldn't help but think how many other girls Jeffrey had done this to, because I couldn't have been the only special one he'd "chosen." Anyone that sick didn't simply stop after one.

But I didn't want to think about Jeffrey now. He'd taken up too much of my life at this point.

"We're going to figure it all out, Calla. But I care more about driving him from your mind, your heart, than I do about wiping him out right now. You're more important."

"You've gone a long way toward doing that already."

"Yeah, but I haven't gone far enough."

My belly fluttered a little with nerves, but I didn't say anything, waiting on him to elaborate, but all he asked was, "Do you trust me?"

"Yes."

"Good. Wait here, then." He went into the bedroom and called me in about ten minutes later. He'd obviously put some thought and planning into it. There was a clean drop cloth draped over the bed. A camera. A video camera. Paints and brushes.

I looked between him and the setup.

"I've thought a lot about this. I've always known that art of any kind can heal."

"Tenn thinks so too." I hadn't been surprised by the porn he'd been watching.

"Yeah, Tenn got me thinking," he admitted. "You ready to help me create something new?"

"More than."

"Good. All you need to do is get out of your clothes and lay down on your right side. I'll do everything else." As he spoke, he was opening the paints. I slid down the sweats and my under-wear, and then my sweatshirt. My T-shirt was thin, and I wasn't wearing a bra.

He turned to look at me, then moved closer, skimmed his hands along my bare hips and then up my sides, taking the fabric with it. When he pulled it over my head, he looked down at my naked body, murmured, "Beautiful," and kissed my shoulder.

Then he picked me up and placed me on the bed. "Curl up."

Curl up, like I'd been in those pictures. In that moment, I understood exactly what he was go-ing to do, and warmth filled me to the point I was sure I'd cry and ruin everything.

But I wouldn't, because doing this would heal me. It would heal us. So I laid down with my head on my arm, my legs pulled up a little. He arranged me a little and after he put the video camera on the tripod, I understood why. The an-gle wouldn't let the camera see anything more than simple bare skin, but it would capture the entire transformation. I would be covered by my pose, by his body and, finally, by the paints.

"Just relax," he told me, then grabbed a brush and began to mix the paints while I watched his back. When he turned to me, he was intent on his mission. I kept my eyes focused on Cage's face.

This was different, like being reborn, and I didn't want to go back to that dark place in my memory.

The tickle of the brush on my hip bone put my nerve endings into overdrive, but I kept still. I bit my bottom lip to stifle the giggle, then realized I didn't have to. This was about regaining my happiness, owning my memories and making new ones.

He grinned, his eyes flickering up to meet mine for half a second before concentrating on me, in much the same way I'd seen him focusing on his bike. To be put in that same all-important category was important, on so many levels.

While he worked the brush on my hip, his hand drifted to my sex. I gasped softly as his fingers slid between my folds, the sensation of his rough hands and the tickle of the brush leaving me wanting to beg. But I didn't have to, because he fingered me to an orgasm quickly—it wrenched out of me as if to say, *Finally*. Reminding me that I was still okay, that Cage wasn't defining me by what Jeffrey Harris did to me. Reminding me that, really, I was the only one who could hold myself in that cage.

He bent his head between my legs and he licked me to another quick orgasm. He kissed his way along the back of my thighs, and then he fully concentrated on the painting.

I was fully relaxed, sleepy from the orgasms. As Cage's vision began to grow in scope along my side and thigh, I was amazed. He was decorating me like a sleek, strong, roaring bike, built to slice through the bullshit and handle whatever the world gave me. I was steel wrapped in all the pretty, and no one could mess with me. I'd always felt like that around Cage, but more so now.

My body was streaked with a mixture of blue and silver paints, gradations of gorgeous, purposeful streaks that snaked up my side and grazed the underside of my breast. The brush hit every place I'd been drawn on, erasing those scars that no one but I could see and putting something entirely more beautiful in their place. He'd drawn something on me that I wanted to remember forever. He took pictures then—Polaroids—and showed me. The pose was the same but the look on my face was different. And I wasn't alone, because Cage's work was there, protecting me.

"I want this to be permanent."

He smiled. "It might be more fun if I can paint you anyway I want. Anytime I want." And then he turned the camera off and he took his clothes off. He didn't ask, and I was glad—I didn't want to be treated like some gentle thing anymore. I wanted him to take what he wanted, the way he'd done since we'd met. I planned on doing the same.

He came up behind me—I was still on my side and he entered me, holding up my thigh so he could fill me completely. "Mine," he said. "You've been mine since I called you, and nothing's going to change that."

I shuddered through another orgasm at his words, contracting around his cock and making his groan join mine in stereo. I was vaguely aware that I shivered, that he was taking me into the bathroom.

Boneless in the tub, leaning back against him, his erection throbbing as it rubbed between my ass cheeks as he patiently washed whatever paint hadn't come off on its own. He'd let the water out a few times, running the handheld over me so I wouldn't get cold as he replaced the old water with new, clean water. And still, the blue and silver swirled in the water around me, as lazy as his motions.

"Thank you," I murmured.

"Your trusting me means everything, Calla. You have to know that."

I did. Because he'd made me a part of his art, part of him, and he'd transformed the most painful memory of my life into something amazing.

*　　*　　*

He helped Calla out of the tub, dried her off, got her into the bed after moving the paint-splattered drop cloth.

His hand had trembled a little when he'd first dipped the thin brush into the paint. He'd composed himself, had to because he'd known how important this was. He'd known it needed to be so fucking perfect.

He'd erased the past and covered it with the promise of the future.

There was so much he'd bottled up, never really letting it out, because there was something inside he always wanted to keep hidden. With Calla, there was a great deal already exposed.

Calla moved then, began to kiss her way down his neck, then his shoulders, giving special attention to the scarred one, her breath catching when she saw his back.

"Survivor," she murmured as she ran her fingertips over the areas that still ached at odd times. The doc had told him that skin pulled as it healed, knitting up to become stronger.

He didn't think he was any stronger than he'd been, because how strong could one person get? He didn't want to become a machine.

He shuddered under her touch. When she put her mouth to the ragged scars and kissed them, he barely held it together. And then she went back up and did the same thing to the unscarred side.

"You're not going to have this freedom for too much longer, baby, so enjoy it while you can."

"You were more compliant in front of the camera."

"I'm never compliant."

"I said more, not completely." She traced his nipple with her tongue. "Besides, I like you this way."

While she writhed lazily against him, his hands dragged over her body, rough to her smooth. She moaned as the pad of his thumb found her clit. As she anchored him against the mattress, he watched her face contort with pleasure. He wanted to consume her, loved watching her breath hitch, loved being wrecked by her.

Afterward, they lay tangled in the dark, her hair splayed over his scars, and he knew he loved her. As if she'd read his mind, she hugged him a little harder.

Chapter 24

Cage had cocooned me away for days while we waited for more news about Ned. As his next of kin, I was responsible for his body, but the coroner wasn't releasing it yet.

I still hadn't called my father to tell him. I was pretty sure he'd heard the news by now, but since we'd had a father-daughter relationship that centered on not talking, I was thinking that getting in touch with him might look suspicious.

Even though I wasn't guilty.

Tonight, Cage was going someplace with Preacher. And I agreed to stay put, with Rocco watching out for me, just in case Flores decided to pull something. But while Cage was getting ready, his phone rang, and he came out of the bathroom, half dressed, saying, "No, I don't think so."

He glanced at me and I frowned. "Hang on." He

put his hand over the phone. "The tattoo shop needs a hand tonight. But if you're not up for it . . ."

"I'd even tattoo if that would help you."

"You just want out."

"If you were here, no."

He smiled. "I know you're going stir-crazy." He spoke into the phone. "Rocco will bring her in. Give her half an hour."

He hung up. Pulled his shirt on and grabbed for his cut while pocketing his phone. "Gotta run, babe. I can pick you up from the shop or Rocco can bring you back here. Up to you."

"Okay." Being with Rocco was easiest, I guessed, because Flores would hesitate to pull anything when I was with my lawyer. All in all, things were quieting down and I was hoping—praying—that this would all go away.

Cage had been checking my e-mails too, and he'd said there had been nothing new coming through. I hadn't been able to look at the old account, so I'd given him all the info and opened a brand-new one.

I was getting a lot of fresh starts these days. "Will you be late?"

"Not sure."

I would not act needy. "Okay."

His voice dropped an octave. "I'll be sleeping next to you tonight, babe."

"You'd better be."

He kissed me, a definite promise to that effect, and then called over his shoulder, "Don't you dare get tattooed without me there."

"I'll try not to."

I didn't know what to wear to a tattoo shop, but I didn't have many options. I put on the jeans and tank top I'd washed, but then discarded it for a black wifebeater I found in Tals's closet. I wore my bra underneath, so I showed a lot of skin, and I pulled my hair back and put on makeup for the first time since the night of the bar.

I smelled Cage on the shirt—on me—and I looked damned good. I needed that.

Rocco looked like he approved, if his rumbly hello and gaze up and down my body was any indication—and since he obviously knew the deal between me and Cage, I was safe with that gaze. Having the Vipers' approval was a good thing.

Rocco drove me in his truck, big and black, with a slight tint to the windows. He kept checking the rearview, but turned to me and said, "We're clear."

He parked behind the clubhouse and we cut through the alleyway to the shop.

"Holly'll show you the ropes," Rocco told me. "You'll stay till closing and then she'll bring you to the clubhouse next door."

I froze then. Cage hadn't mentioned that part.

I didn't want to make a big deal of it—I was only going to the clubhouse to meet Rocco, not to hang out. Obviously, Cage had kept my meltdown a secret, which I was grateful for. "Sure, that'll work."

Rocco nodded. "You just text or call if you need me. I'd hang here, but I'd rather check things out from next door."

"Because of Flores."

"Yeah." He glanced at the blond woman who walked up to us, and she nodded to him. "Calla, this is Holly."

I hadn't seen Holly around before, because I would've definitely remembered her. She looked like a model. She was at least six feet, and somehow still managed to look completely feminine and graceful. She wore old jeans that looked painted on and a tank top that showed off a delicate sleeve of tattoos, and her long blond hair hung in a sheet halfway down her back. "You must be Calla."

And to top it off, a crisp, brilliant British accent.

She gave me a head-to-toe once-over. "You'll do, but maybe you can dress a little sexier?"

"I thought I was just taking appointments."

"Nothing around here is 'just' anything."

Rocco put a hand on my shoulder and he'd

disappeared before I could turn around. When I faced Holly again, she said, "I didn't really want you working my shop tonight, but I owe Preacher. So let's try to not make this a miserable experience."

"Wait—Vipers doesn't own this?"

"They own the building, but this business is mine," she said, her eyes cutting me like daggers.

"Okay, wow. That's cool."

She pursed her lips together, like she'd heard it a thousand times, and pointed to the phones. "Just answer and check the book."

I stared at her, then walked behind the counter. The book didn't look particularly full and I made the mistake of saying so.

"Lots of walk-ins," Holly told me, sounding bored at having to deal with me. "And a lot of them just want to get close to the club, so they come to hang out. Makes the place look busier, which attracts more business."

She shrugged and pointed at the appointment book. "Before you schedule, you've got to find out what exactly they want. And if they don't know, they need a fifteen-minute consultation appointment before they can book the real thing."

"Do a lot of people back out?"

"A lot of women come in for their consultation and end up having sex with the artist in the back," she said with a shrug. "It's a big deal to be marked by a Viper, but a one-night stand doesn't get you in the club as an old lady."

"What does?"

She smirked. "You're really interested, honey?"

"I'm here, aren't I?"

"For now. But we both know that you don't really belong." Holly's tone was clipped and condescending. "You don't know anything about this MC or any MC."

"Cage brought me here."

"Guys do all sorts of dumb things for gash," she conceded.

"I'm working here tonight, so if you're not going to show me how to run this, is there someone else here who can?" I asked sweetly.

"You look like you've never worked a day in your life."

"I've worked every day of my goddamned life, so cut the shit," I hissed under my breath, then smiled as the man in leather approached the counter. "How can I help you?"

Holly snorted and walked away. *Bitch.*

I'd figure it out myself. How hard could it be?

Chapter 25

The ride Cage was supposed to take with Preacher the night after he'd arrived back in Skulls had been pushed off until things were calmer.

Unfortunately, losing the detectives' tail took a bit of work, but they were able to use all of their very distinctive bikes to throw them off track. Rocco and Tals headed in the opposite direction—on Preacher's and Cage's bikes—while Cage rode Tals's bike and followed behind Preacher on Rocco's Harley. It was just like the first time he'd ridden behind the head of Vipers, wondering if Preacher was bringing him into the woods to kill him.

He'd been sixteen. That's how fucked up his life had been. That's how he'd thought, even after so many years of Preacher paying for his school, his clothes, his life.

That night, Preacher had given him a probie cut. "Nothing will change if you don't put it on, Cage. You'll still have my support—financially and otherwise—until you're eighteen. After that, the financial shit stops but nothing else does."

He'd stared at the cut for half a second before nodding and letting Preacher help him shrug it on. Because he believed in Preacher, and the Vipers. And he believed in the MC life, since that was all he'd known.

He'd followed Preacher's example, had gone into the Army and done his time. Between Preacher and the Army, he'd become the man he wanted to be. The man he'd need to be to shoulder the responsibilities of being second in command of Vipers, which was where Preacher told Cage he ultimately wanted him. For now, Tals was filling that role, and Tals himself told Cage he didn't want it. Ultimately, Tals would be a much better enforcer, and he'd enjoy that job far more.

Before he could accept that, though, he had to take down his family. And now, it was finally time. "I should've been honest with you about going rogue. But after that fight . . . when we lost Cal and Marsh I . . ."

Jesus, he didn't want to go back there. A night of celebrating, of being back in his element, the

Vipers all around him, all shot to shit in an instant. A single Molotov cocktail flung through the window of the bar. He remembered the screaming, the choking smoke. He and Tals and Preacher easily made it to the doors, opening them to let people and smoke out . . .

Right into the arms of the waiting Heathens. And Cal and Marsh had taken the brunt of it.

"I know, Cage."

"What do you know, Preach? That if it hadn't been for my return, those guys would be alive? The bar wouldn't have been destroyed? Women wouldn't have been scarred and terrified?"

"Taking the weight of it all on your shoulders isn't smart, Cage. The Heathens want to bring us down—you're a convenient excuse."

"You can't tell me there wasn't a vote called after that," he said.

"Is that why you left?"

"I didn't want to make any of you choose. If I thought I could let go of the cut, I would've. But that's something I'd never do."

The men stared at each other as Cage bared his goddamned soul to Preacher.

"Fine. I can understand that. But you still could've asked for our help in this, even though you were rogue." Preacher crossed his arms and stared him down, and goddamn, the man still had the power to make him feel ten again. "Why didn't you?"

"It's not your fucking responsibility."

Preacher nodded. "Never said it was, but maybe I'd want to help."

"Not your battle. You've done enough for me. More than enough. I couldn't ask—"

"You could've. You should've. But since you didn't, I've gone ahead and started working toward it. Guessing you'd like to help."

Cage's head shot up. "Don't get involved, Preach. If something happened to you or the club again—"

"Something will happen. Something is happening, Cage. Can't keep the meth out of Skulls on a wing and a prayer. You saw those men the other night—they might've followed you and Tals into Skulls, but Tals isn't stupid. He recognized them. They're the ones working with the Heathens to push the meth in here, to scare the shit out of the residents and the cops, so no one says a word. We've got to do some major damage control. Now."

"What do you have in mind?"

"Follow me." Preacher walked a few feet, then moved behind some trees and pointed. "Go lift the trap door. Disarm it first."

"Are there cameras?"

"Waiting for you to tell me, Army guy."

"Fuck off," he muttered, since Preacher was one himself. "What the fuck is this?"

"Drug tunnel," Preacher said. "Now you know why I needed the C-4."

"I know they dig this shit in California, but here?"

"They're getting smarter."

"If they're so smart, how'd you find out about these?"

Preacher smiled. "You know what they say about a woman scorned."

"One of the Heathens women told you this?"

"Troy's old lady."

"You slept with my brother's wife?"

Preacher shrugged. "Whatever it takes. She needed a shoulder. And revenge. And I got her the hell out of Dodge. She's safe, hidden, and she'll get clean."

Goddammit, Preacher always knew how to pull it out of the fire for me. "When?"

"When I left you in the hospital."

"I thought you were just pissed."

"I was. If you hadn't been in such bad shape, I'd have beaten the shit out of you myself." Preacher pointed at him. "I waited for you—I could've done this months ago, but I fucking waited for you, kid."

Kid. Shit. Cage forced himself not to smile.

Taking out the tunnel was step one in dismantling the Heathens' power. Cage's father and his brother were too well protected for him to take out. He'd seen that himself and wore the scars to prove it.

Because he'd gone it alone. And even the baddest of assassins had some kind of backup.

When he was in basic, he'd learned that no man is an island. And he'd known that in his brotherhood, but he'd forgotten it along the way.

But he'd gotten one hell of a reminder.

Now he set the C-4 with the igniters and waited. Because he and Preacher didn't want to take out the Heathens who'd come to patrol the drug tunnel. No, he was planning on framing them.

There were neighbors close enough to hear the explosion but not be hurt by it. No innocents would be harmed by this—it wouldn't make up for all the people the Heathens had already hurt, but it was a start.

Hitting the Heathens where it would hurt them most would anger the MC and put their relationships with the connections they sold the drugs through in disrepair.

It looked like they'd gone from just making it themselves to buying it in larger quantities. Or maybe they were doing both, but either way the fact that they'd needed a tunnel made Cage think that more than just meth would be coming in.

"Think Havoc knows about this?" he asked Preach. Because even though their compound was hours away, they owned this stretch of land, although why was anyone's guess.

"Back end of their land, so I'm guessing no, or they would've taken care of it a long time ago." Preacher ran a hand over his shaved scalp. "Then again, who the fuck knows if they're in on this? I'm thinking that not giving them a heads-up is the best idea."

"Agreed." It was time to start dismantling the Heathens from the head down, and a war with Havoc wasn't something any of them wanted. "Ready when you are, Preach."

"I've been ready for this since you were ten, Cage."

Cage ignored the tightness in his throat as he pressed the button and watched the tunnel blow sky high.

Chapter 26

The night passed quickly, thanks to a constant stream of men and women, all hoping to get a glimpse of one of the Vipers. But tonight, no one with the familiar patch on their cut came in. I got looks from men, sneers from some of the women, but it was fine, especially because Holly wasn't there the whole night.

She'd gotten quiet at some point after being the life of the shop for a couple of hours, calling out to people as she tattooed a man's shoulder. And then the wisecracks were gone and then she was gone. She'd left me with a woman named Gigi, who was in the back now, counting up one of the registers while I finished taking the last of the money from the young girl who'd come in and given a deposit.

I scheduled the appointment, but I could tell she would back out.

"I'm almost done, Calla. Then we'll go to the clubhouse," Gigi called. My heart sank, because I'd managed to forget about that for a while.

I was just about to go lock the door when the bells on the door jingled and I looked up to see a teenage boy wearing a leather cut with a probie patch.

"Where's Cage?" he asked. I stared at the patch and then at him as alarm bells went off in my head. He was young, sure, maybe sixteen at most, but he was also a Heathen.

"He's not here. You can check next door." I tried to sound casual.

"Not going into a Vipers clubhouse." He pointed to the Heathen patch. "Can you call over for me?"

I glanced down at the phone and back up at him, the confusion no doubt obvious in my eyes.

"You're new," he said.

"Very."

I held my breath until he said, "I'm Eli. Cage's brother."

Eli, not Troy. "Oh. Oh, okay. Is he expecting you?"

"Definitely not." He paused and looked at me, but I didn't see any kind of connection there, and maybe he didn't know that the Heathens had me on some kind of hit list. "You Cage's old lady?"

"We're friends."

He put his tongue in his cheek and pushed it out. "Cage doesn't have women friends."

"Maybe you don't know him all that well."

He smiled, the way only a teenage boy could when the devil was at his door. And then he said, "I'm in some trouble. He said I could come to him, but I lost his phone number."

"He'll be back soon." In truth, I'd debated pulling out the cell phone to call him, but I decided that I liked Eli's vibe and didn't have anything to worry about. Although I really didn't understand the Heathen thing. Unless . . .

I pointed to his jacket. He looked at the patch and back at me.

"I'm not going to hurt you. I really just want to talk to Cage." He glanced behind him. "You want me to lock this up?"

Gigi called, "A few more minutes, Calla, and then Rocco's coming to grab us!"

Okay, that was good. Although it made Eli tense up. "Yeah, just hit the lock, okay? I'll talk to Gigi about letting you hang out here until Cage comes back."

I should've been bone tired, but I was buzzing. Maybe I'd crash soon, but for the moment I was just fine.

And really, I should never say or think anything like that and tempt the universe, because shit went to hell in the next few moments.

"Yeah, that'll work. Gonna hit the head." Eli went to use the bathroom and I was about to go talk to Gigi when the glass door shattered inward. I ducked behind the counter to avoid the flying glass.

There was a bat. I held it in my palms, wondering if I should get up or not.

In the end, that choice wasn't mine. Someone grabbed the back of my shirt and dragged me up, but since the counter was between us, the hold was awkward. I managed to pull away, my shirt nearly ripped off in the process. I held one hand to my chest, the other firmly curled around the bat as I focused on the leather-wearing Heathens in front of me.

My first thought was that Eli had somehow played me, but I dismissed that quickly. My instincts had been sharpened since I'd let Jeffrey Harris take advantage of me.

"Where's Cage?" one of them demanded.

I found my voice. "You could've just knocked."

The biker grinned, but it wasn't friendly. It was predatory, and I chilled. "Come here, sweetheart."

I held up the bat. He held up a gun, and I froze. And that's when gorgeous Holly came in, swinging a shotgun wildly. She was distracting enough

in just a T-shirt and striped barely there underwear, her hair as wild as the look in her eyes.

"Get the fuck out of here," she said in her clipped
British tones. She sounded so proper even when
she was cursing, and for a moment it almost
worked. The Heathens blinked at her; then the biggest one smiled and stepped forward, still holding
his gun as he went to grab Holly.

Holly walked toward him and fired. It hit the
big Heathen in the thigh and he howled in pain.
She shot again, toward the other men, who cursed,
grabbed their friend and dragged him backward
through the shattered glass of the door.

Everything after that happened so fast. I un-
froze, because Holly buckled to the ground, holding the shotgun and rocking a little. Eli came out
and cursed and told me, "Gotta get out of here
before the cops come."

I thought he was talking about himself, but he
pointed to Holly and me. "I'll take care of some
of this—get her to the back."

While he killed the lights, I bent down as sirens rang in the distance and focused on Holly.
"Holly, listen to me." Holly's eyes were vacant as
she looked at me. "Holly, we've got to get out of
here. Just give me the gun."

But Eli was pulling it from her hands instead.
"I'll get rid of it and the carpet. Get out of here."

The idea of handing a scene-of-the-crime shot-gun to a teenager went against everything I'd ever known, but I did it anyway. "Holly, come on."

I pulled her up and the three of us went out the back, grabbing Gigi, who seemed to be in shock as well, and locking the door as we did. Eli disappeared into the woods and Holly and I went through the alley silently and into the club-house. Once inside, I looked her over. She had blood splattered on her shirt. I ripped it off her as Bear came out and said, "All right. A show."

"Police are after her," I snapped. "She shot a Heathen. Alarms are going off next door."

Rocco was next to me, demanding, "Why didn't you press the alarm?"

"I didn't know there was one," I told him. Holly mumbled something. "And Cage's broth-er's getting rid of the gun."

"Cage's brother?" Rocco repeated as he grabbed the T-shirt and lit it on fire.

There was a knock on the back door. "That's him."

"He can't come in here," Bear protested, but I was beyond listening. I let him in and Bear went from angry to relaxed in seconds. "Hey, Eli."

Eli stood in the doorway. "I got rid of it."

"Good job, kid," Rocco told him.

"Not a fucking kid."

"Right. No. Come on—I've got an idea." Rocco motioned for him to come inside, and after a long moment's hesitation, Eli did. "Go wait in Cage's space, all right? Take Holly."

Eli led the tall woman by the elbow. She turned around toward me before she allowed that, though, and she squeezed my hand.

Halfway through the demo of the tunnel, several Heathens came charging up the hill.

"Better than Havoc," Preacher muttered to himself as he drew his knife with the pearl handle, the one rumored to have come from the founder of the club. The knife he'd taken by force from the last president of Vipers nearly twenty years earlier, when he'd had enough of the man's shit.

The knife he'd killed the man with, in the middle of the clubhouse, and left him lying in the middle of the floor, daring any of the others to step forward and fuck with him.

A balls-to-the-wall move—one he'd been too young and stupid to even consider not trying. Impetuousness had served him well back then. These days, he believed thinking things through was a man's best friend.

Back then, a few of the guys had come forward to challenge him. They were no longer in the club, but he'd left them among the living. But the former president . . . after what he'd done to a woman, the daughter of a member, there was no way Preacher could look in his face daily or pretend to take orders from him.

You didn't fuck with women or children. That was a rule he drilled into his MC members' heads. The Heathens didn't live by those rules, and because of that, he had no problem at all taking their lives.

Cage came over to him and looked at the dead bodies at Preacher's feet. Three bodies in all, but one of them was moving.

"I'd have called if I couldn't handle it. Go back to your explosions," Preacher told him.

Cage just shook his head and left, muttering something about crazy motherfuckers.

An hour later, they'd buried the two Heathens and blown the drug tunnel to the sky. Cage and Preacher left the other Heathen handcuffed to his own bike, C-4 in his pockets and the remains of the tunnel next to them.

It wouldn't take care of his father and Troy—not immediately. But the fallout would throw enough suspicion on the Heathens to keep them busy for a while. It would also deplete their drug supply, and their cash flow. And hopefully, make them several more enemies.

All in all, a good night. Until he saw the flashing lights two blocks before he and Preach got to the clubhouse and pulled over. They checked their phones and saw the alarms—Cage realized they'd been out of range.

Preacher dialed, a hand on his shoulder to keep him from bolting, because Calla was the first thought in his mind.

"Started in the tattoo shop? What the fuck?" Preacher growled, then hung up and made a few more calls, cementing their alibi for the night before they drove past the shop and into the clubhouse.

Of course, the goddamned police chief was only too happy to see them.

"Looks like a brick was thrown in the window. Seems like the shop was closed at the time. We're just being extra cautious."

"And I certainly appreciate that, Officer." Preacher told him as Cage slid into the clubhouse, his heart pounding out of his chest. Bear pointed and he took the stairs two at a time, slammed the bedroom door open and found Calla, pale but unharmed, sitting on the bed. She'd been curled up and started when he'd burst in, but she met him halfway. He scooped her up in his arms and just held her close. She was trembling but holding him tightly.

"Babe, what the hell . . . ?"

"I didn't want to worry you. I know you said emergency, but by the time it became one . . ." She trailed off, shook her head.

The creak of the floor behind him made him turn, ready to strangle the next person who came near him. He hadn't been prepared to see his stepbrother.

"Hey, Cage."

"Eli, what's going on?" The fact that he was even in the clubhouse meant something was completely fucked.

"He saved me and Holly. Well, Holly saved us and then Eli protected us from the police," Calla explained, her voice strong enough to make him believe she was okay. He looked between them and saw an understanding had blossomed between his woman and his brother, and that a bond had already begun to form. Life and death would do that to you.

"Is that true, Eli?"

Eli nodded, but he looked troubled. "She wouldn't have needed saving if I hadn't fucked up in the first place."

"Eli, no," Calla started, but Cage put a hand on her shoulder and motioned for Eli to continue.

"They followed me here. They had to. I thought I was being slick but . . ."

He looked miserable.

"Why'd you come here in the first place?" Cage asked.

Eli shrugged.

"I think you two need some time alone. I'll go check on Holly." Calla touched his back and then Eli's arm on the way out. Her look implored Cage to go easy on him, and Cage would. He just wouldn't let Eli know that.

Cage watched Calla move from the main section of the clubhouse before he said to Eli, "You know how many times I've reached out to you?"

Eli shrugged. Now the kid was going to pull the cool act.

"Does your mom know you're here?"

"Doubt it." He paused. "I spent the past week at clubhouse."

Cage almost growled out loud. Eli's mother had promised that Eli would spend minimal time at the clubhouse. Eli had seen Cage as the enemy before this. Cage saw a scared kid behind the teenager in the probie cut, forced to be a man too soon.

"Why?" he demanded harshly. More so than he'd intended.

Eli's jaw tightened. "I was moving there permanently, at Dad's request."

"Dammit, you were supposed to stay . . ."

"Like you did? You left."

"Eli—"

"Heard it before."

"You'll hear it again."

Eli turned away from him and Tals stuck his head in. "Cage—a moment?"

Cage said to Eli's back, "We're not done," and the boy just grunted.

"Way to parent," Tals told him.

"Like you could do better?"

"Mommy Dearest could've," Tals informed him seriously. "Take a step back. He finally did what you wanted—he came here. Don't push him back out the door."

Holly was already asleep, helped along by whatever meds Rocco had given her before he and Bear took the bullet out of her thigh. I'd heard her moaning, and it had been a struggle to stay out of the room myself. Once Preacher arrived, he seemed to have that same struggle.

Rocco said he'd stay with her overnight at the clubhouse, but then Preacher said Rocco should drive us home and that he'd stay. That got a raised eyebrow from both Tals and Rocco, but I didn't question them. Tals quickly decided he would stay to stand guard, in case the Heathens tried to come back. Rocco drove me and Cage and Eli back to the apartment. Once Cage got Eli settled in, he came back to where I waited, by the windows.

"Babe." He circled his strong arms around me. I tried not to tremble and failed miserably. He pushed me against the wall, his body holding me down and protecting me all at once, like a human shield. "Please tell me that blood on you isn't—"

"It's all Holly's," I said quickly. "Rocco helped. He took the bullet out of her thigh. Said there's going to be a scar. I wanted to take her to the ER but—"

"Babe, stop. You don't have to relive it."

But I was—worse than when we'd been at the clubhouse. I'd been calm there, out of necessity, but here I was losing it. I was babbling. Spinning. And then I realized that he must've faced demons of his own tonight, because the look on his face was so tortured. "Just hold me."

He did, and for a long while it was just us, standing on top of the world. "Calla, I had no idea Eli would come by."

"I know." For Eli, I had to hold it together. I wouldn't let him feel guilty for any of this. "Holly . . . if she hadn't been there . . ."

He grimaced. "I'm thankful she was. Otherwise, Eli would've taken action."

"Holly was like a wild woman. She was possessed. What's her deal?"

Cage ran a hand through his hair. "She was hurt a while back. Her old man was killed pretty brutally in front of her. He wasn't one of ours, but his MC didn't stand by her."

"I thought that's what you guys did."

"They claimed he'd sold out his club. That he was trying to get out. If someone hadn't killed him, his own MC would've. If you want out, you've got very few options."

"And Holly?"

"They hurt her. The MC kicked her out, took over her business and left her with nothing. She came here to start over."

There had to be a reason, but it didn't seem to matter. No wonder she'd freaked out so badly. "But if the violence scares her, why come back to an MC?"

"It's all she knows. MCs are where she's comfortable. What she likes."

I tried to wrap my mind around that and only semifailed. "How's Eli?"

"Not admitting much. Trying to pretend he's fine. Furthest thing from." He sighed. "My father's going to be calling me soon."

My heart broke for him. "So now that Eli is here, they'll try to hurt you again?"

"Better me than him. But at some point he's got to decide to tell them he's staying here. I'm just giving him a little breathing room to do so."

"He's a baby."

"No, he's not. Not in this world."

"What about getting a court order?"

"We don't need that. The Heathens—my father won't go to the courts for help, and even if we did, it's not a code of justice he'd bother to follow." He hung his head. "I never should've let him stay there that long."

"The last few years . . ."

"I spent trying to kill his father," he finished.

"Well, when you put it like that . . ." I murmured, then continued. "The thing is, there are always going to be Heathens. If you stay in this world, it's always going to be a fight. Is it worth it?"

"Always has been. Always will be."

"Then I'm in."

"The Heathens can stay. It's my family I want out of there. That's who I'm exorcising. The rest of those motherfuckers . . . they can stay and try to fuck with the Vipers. But my family? That's personal, and I'm handling it." He buried his face against my neck. "I promised to keep you safe, dammit."

"You can't be with me twenty-four/seven."

"I should've been here."

"It's my fault." Eli stepped out from the shadows and Cage's face turned pale.

"No, nothing is your fault," Cage said quietly, and I nodded in agreement.

"I put your woman in danger. I'll go back."

"You're not going back," Cage told him.

I watched the scene, imagining a young Cage being as stalwart as Eli was at the moment. I pulled away from Cage and went to stand with Eli. "Eli took care of things."

"Yeah?" Cage moved closer to both of us and put a hand on the back of Eli's neck, and the teen couldn't stop a grin from escaping. "Good job."

"I was trying to make up for everything," Eli confessed, like he couldn't hold it in any longer, the look on his face breaking my heart.

"There's nothing you need to make up for," Cage told him.

"They found you that night because of me," Eli confessed.

I tensed, but needn't have worried.

"And your calling the cops saved me. You risked everything by doing that, Eli," Cage told his younger brother firmly, before getting up and dragging the boy into a hug.

"I can't go back there, Cage. I feel like I'll fucking die if I do," Eli admitted quietly.

I wanted to hug both of them.

"You're not going back. Ever. You belong here. You saved me and then you saved Calla. You've more than proven yourself to Preach."

"Suppose I don't want the life?" The question burst out of him like a surge of gunfire, but the only damage in this case was the fear I saw etched in his face.

"Is that what you're worried about? That the only reason I'd let you stay is if you join Vipers?"

"You had to."

"Fuck no, I didn't have to. I wanted to. I didn't want it any other way, but Preacher wouldn't let me join until I was sixteen. Until I saw what Vipers was about, and if I hadn't wanted to? He would've paid for college."

As Cage spoke, Eli's eyes lit up. "Really?"

"Yes, really. You stay with me. If you want out of the life, you're out. Simple as that. I want you to have all your choices open to you."

"It really doesn't matter to you?"

"The only thing that matters is that you're happy. And that you're a good man. From what I've seen, you've already gone a long way toward that second part."

Eli's shoulders slumped with relief. "I didn't know if there was room for me."

Cage put a hand out to me while looking at

him and said, "There's room, Eli," as he gave my hand a squeeze.

There was room for all of us, Cage was telling me.

"You don't have to hover over me like I'm a child."

Holly's clipped, cold tones never sent him away, although that's exactly what she was looking to do.

Preacher ignored her and pulled a chair right up to the bed. "And if I wanted to, I'd lay the fuck down next to you," he told her.

She stared at him. Blinked. Because she knew it was a promise, not a threat. "What the fuck's happening, Preacher?"

"There's going to be hell to pay."

Her eyes were glassy, from the pain and the meds to combat the pain. She'd refused her anxiety meds, and Preacher didn't push them on her. But Christ, there was no way she was getting through tonight without a nightmare.

"It's not Cage's fault," she told him. "Which means it's not yours."

"What makes you think I'd take the blame in the first place, woman?" he demanded. She snorted softly and didn't answer. And she was probably the only woman—the only one—he'd let get away with telling him his business. Like he didn't know it.

Still, the reassurance was good to hear. Even if he'd never admit it.

She was watching him, a small smirk on her face, because she knew.

Taking Cage back into the MC—bringing him into it in the first place—wasn't ever something Preacher thought about twice. He'd taken over the MC when it had been in the worst possible shape and he'd dragged it back to where it was today. He didn't want a piece of shit he couldn't be proud of representing him. He liked action. Danger. He didn't mind stealing a car or two either. But the drug shit? No way.

When he'd taken Troy's wife to bed—and he'd done it several times, because he could—he'd made her a lot of promises he knew he'd never keep.

There'd been a lot of women in and out of his life. But none like Holly. And even though he would end up sleeping next to her tonight, that would be all they did. She wasn't ready. Probably never would be. And he'd ruined enough women.

"You've got blood on your jeans," she pointed out, her words slightly slurred.

"Didn't have time to change."

"Vigilante justice?"

"Best kind."

"Am I in the wrong place, Preacher?" she asked softly. "Maybe I should go retire somewhere warm and safe . . ."

"Maybe you should," he told her, his voice just as quiet. But she was already asleep, or pretending to be so she wouldn't hear his rejection. Again.

And he wondered why doing something for someone else's own good was always easier than doing it for himself.

"Preach?"

He turned toward Talon's voice, then got up, covered Holly and followed the man into the hallway.

"Sorry to bother you, man. But some of these guys are freaked about Eli being here."

"You one of them?"

"No," Tals said without hesitation.

Chapter 27

The next day, Rocco stayed with Calla while Cage and Eli went to the clubhouse in the early-morning hours. Tals said he'd stayed up all night listening to the police radios and other MC chatter and he hadn't heard anything about the Heathens missing one of their own. And this was big goddamned news. MC wars had been fought over much less.

"This shit's going to start a war, Cage," Tals said.

"Maybe you could announce the obvious," Cage shot back.

"Goddammit, Cage. I was there, okay? I fucking sat by your bed, thinking you were going to die," Tals told him. "Don't pull this shit on me."

Cage swallowed hard. Wanted to say that it would've been better if he'd been DOA, but that wasn't true. It wouldn't have solved anything. "Eli called he cops. If he hadn't . . ."

He trailed off and watched Preach and Tals turn to Eli for confirmation. Eli nodded and Cage said, "If our father finds out . . ."

"Fuck that. I'd be more worried about Troy," Tals spat. "Not that you have anything to worry about. He's never getting close to you again."

Preacher turned his attention to Eli, asking, "Do you want to stay here, with Vipers protection?"

"I want to stay here with Cage," Eli said, choosing his words carefully. Cage wasn't the only one who noticed that.

"How do you know he's not a spy?" Crook asked. He was a year older than Preacher, another lifer in the MC, and when Cage shot him a look, he shrugged. "Come on, Cage. You're as suspicious as we are. Just because he doesn't sit at the table doesn't mean he won't learn a lot of shit."

"I'll leave and take him with me," Cage told him.

"Ah, Cage—come on, man," Crook muttered.

"For the good of everyone. If that's what it takes." Cage stuck his hands in his pockets.

"We don't let our own just walk away when there's trouble. And you are our own, Cage. Have been for a long time now," Preacher said.

"You wanted me to stay away."

"As much as I wanted you to come back," Preacher agreed. "Either way, I would've been okay, as long as you were happy."

"What makes you happy, Preach?"

Preacher smiled like he had the greatest secret in the world. "You've got to figure it out for yourself. Never made this easy for you. Not starting now."

Eli's phone began to ring. He stared down at it for a second, then looked up at Cage. "It's Dad."

"Give it to me," Cage told him.

"I can do this."

"Put it on speaker when you answer," Cage told him.

With the men around him, Eli did as Cage had asked and their father's harsh voice demanded, "Where the fuck are you, boy?"

Eli winced and seemed to lose his resolve.

It was all right, because Cage had enough for both of them. "He's with me."

"Cage? You send that boy back to me right now."

"No. Never."

"You want more of a war? Almost dying the first time wasn't enough of a rush for you?" his father demanded. "I'll make sure the job's done right—because I'm doing it this time."

"I want to stay with Cage," Eli said. "It's not

his fault. He didn't ask me to. I came to him. It's my choice."

"You don't have a choice, boy. You're mine. You're a Heathen. Patched in. Did you tell Cage that?"

Eli swallowed hard and Cage cursed mentally. Being patched in was a whole other problem, one they both knew well. Eli had worn his probie patch into Vipers, no doubt because he'd known it would gain easier entrance.

"We'll deal with it," Cage replied.

"You want to be the one to cut the tattoo off your brother's back? Because you know that's the only way he's out."

Eli paled and Cage put a strong hand on his shoulder. "You're a fucking bastard. But you're not laying a hand on him."

Cage hung up on his father, then asked Eli, "Did they force you to patch in?"

Eli's expression said it all. And really, when they'd offered it to him, how could the kid say no?

"How big's the tattoo?" Tals asked quietly.

"Between my shoulder blades," Eli said.

Cage's heart sank. That was really fucking big, the span of the skull and crossbones taking up the majority of space. Black ink.

The doorbell rang.

"Liquor shipment," Rocco said.

"Eli, go with Rocco," Preacher ordered. Eli hesitated until Preacher said, "Trust us, Eli."

Eli turned to face Cage. "I do."

When he was gone, Cage blew out a frustrated breath. "Not a lot of options."

"So fucking antiquated."

"They're trying for one-percenter status," Tals said quietly. "I heard it from Tenn, who's been in touch with Havoc."

"Like they haven't murdered enough innocent people—now they'll be forced to so they can keep their rep," Cage muttered.

Preacher was nodding in disgust, because he'd obviously heard the rumors. "So what about sending Eli to Havoc?"

"Protection in return for what?"

"Sometimes Havoc doesn't want anything in return for protection."

"It'd be the last place my father would think to look for him. But what kind of life's that? He'll be surrounded by an MC. And he says he wants out. If that's what he wants, I'm behind him," Cage said.

Preacher looked pained. "He could go to your sister, but it's risky."

"We cover up the tattoo."

"Anyone who looks at his back will know what it's covering. Especially in a kid so young," Preacher said.

"So we dismantle Heathens completely. I don't see any other option," Cage said fiercely.

Preacher laughed, but there was no humor behind it. "Sure, let's take the easy way out." He ran his hand over his shaved scalp. "Christ, Cage . . ."

Rocco and Eli came back then. "Eli's got some information for us."

Everyone turned to Eli, who said, "Dad's got help now. This guy just came in a couple of days ago and offered to smooth the way into a new territory."

"Great, so they've got a guardian angel," Preacher muttered.

"More like twenty-five percent of their new-territory profits in return for a smooth run."

"Only person who can promise shit like that is the law."

"He's not a cop," Eli said with certainty. "But he's not a civilian."

"Fed," Tals muttered.

"Which means he could be investigating or on the take," Rocco pointed out. Either one wasn't good.

"You didn't get a license plate, did you?" Because Cage was certain the guy gave a fake name.

Eli smiled and the resemblance between them hit Cage right in the solar plexus. "I memorized it."

He wrote it down and Tals went to run it.

Cage steered Eli to a private corner, sat him down. "I don't care if you don't have information—you know that, right? Even if you came here with nothing but yourself, it would've been fine."

"Sorry about the patch."

"I was going to come get you," Cage told Eli. "Preacher and I were going to bring you back here, with me. For good. Whether you wanted that or not. I shouldn't have left you there alone."

"I'm not your responsibility," Eli said, as if he was repeating a line someone told him over and over.

"Damn straight, you are. You're also still just a kid. You want out, you're out. But you're also dealing with my rules, and I don't think you've had that before, so you'd better get used to it."

Did those words seriously just come out of his mouth? Even Eli looked surprised, but not unhappy. He grumbled, "Great, so I'm here and I'll still have no decision-making power," but there was no hiding the expression of relief he wore.

"You're fifteen. Keep doing what you're doing—

keep making good decisions and you'll be fine." He squeezed Eli's shoulder. "You're here. You're only as safe as the decisions you make."

"Yeah, I hear you." He stared at Cage. "Are you going to be able to do this? Go to war again against Dad and Troy?"

"Are you?"

"Hell, yes," he whispered.

"Then so am I."

Chapter 28

There were several Vipers guarding the apartment while Cage was at the clubhouse with Preacher. After the previous night, going back there was less of an option, but I was restless.

I heard another Harley approach and I glanced down to see Bear, who was carrying bags of food for the guys.

In a very short period of time, I'd come to anticipate—enjoy—relish—the loud distinctive roar of a Harley and I could differentiate between a single bike and two or even three at this point.

I knew Cage's bike too. I could pick out its sound above the others. I didn't tell him that, but it was something I loved knowing.

Was I fooling myself, thinking that Cage and Eli and I could be a family, within the MC's family?

I took the key to Cage's private space—he'd

shown me where I could find it—and I let myself down the private elevator into his world. Except it felt like our world, our place of secrets. There were times I'd just sit here, watching him for hours, neither of us talking.

I stood inside the garage work space so I could feel close to him. It was locked down, but I should've told someone where I was headed. But I couldn't stay in the bedroom, not when I was on the verge of another panic attack. I needed space, and lots of it. In the middle of Cage's workshop, I found it.

I ran my hands over an unfinished metal bumper, the coolness of it under my palms enough to soothe me. Ground me, until I swore I could feel Cage's energy flow from the bike to me.

I'd made it through the hard part tonight. And while that was the truth, how many harder parts did I have to endure?

Was it worth it?

"Cage is," I whispered, wanting to fold up on the table with his custom parts and sleep. But I was too cold, too wired, too scared to death of my dreams.

Finally, I did drag a blanket around me and curled up on the old couch. I must've fallen asleep, despite my reservations, but when I woke, Cage was in the room with me.

Blinking sleepily, I watched him. Bent over the bumper, he was painting the details with a small brush, concentrating so hard he'd sucked his bottom lip between his teeth. He'd tied his hair back with a bandanna and the hard rock music blared into his headphones, so loud the sound escaped. I'd been in here before when he played it out loud, when the music made the whole place seem to shake.

The motorcycle's base was a deep blue. The streaks of silver and black were scattered and I could only imagine how they'd look as the bike zoomed by.

He looked over at me. Smiled. Took the headphones off, lowered the volume and unplugged them so music filtered through the entire space.

"What was it like, before this war?" I asked.

He didn't seem surprised by my question, but he put the brush down and came to sit next to me. I shifted to make room, sat up and folded into his arms as he told me, "It's always been dangerous. That's the draw. But the Heathens aren't patrolling Skulls twenty-four/seven."

"But now that you're back . . ."

"It's going to get worse before it gets better." He sighed. "We could leave, you know? Me, you, Eli. Go live by Tenn. Go anyplace."

"What would happen to the town without Vipers?"

"Beyond going to hell with the drugs? Shit, I don't think many people realize how much real estate we bought when times were bad here. The mayor does. The police do too, which is probably why we don't get harassed more. But we don't put people out of business or party in their neighborhoods. And I'd hate to relocate and give up my home. But I would." He looked at me. "Do you think he's going to be okay?"

"With you in his corner? Yes." That made Cage smile, and I liked making him smile. "I wouldn't mind being fifteen again and having a do-over."

"It's the first time you've talked about that without fear in your eyes."

"Maybe because I just realized I'm getting my do-over right here, right now. You took what was all fucked up and you turned it around so I could heal." All those years, trying to fuck away the memory. It had never worked, because it hadn't been with the right person.

Cage made me feel powerful.

Correction: Cage just made me feel.

I stood, walked over to him and wrapped my arms around him. He buried his face in my neck for a moment, murmured, "So fucking soft, Calla." He licked along my collarbone. Sucked, hard enough to leave a mark. I shuddered, on the brink of orgasm. It would take a single touch from him—the tweak of a nipple, a finger rubbed on my clit, even another hard suck, would slam me over that edge.

As if he knew, he did little more than pull down my sweats and underwear. And then he slid down my body, inserted himself between my thighs and had me put one leg over his shoulder. I was upright only through the combination of sheer will and his strength. And I was under no illusion that it was mainly the latter.

I was half naked. He was dressed, his face buried between my legs as electric currents shot through me, the quickness of the climax unsurprising.

I trembled but his arms were strong around me as he rose and wrapped me around him. I buried my face in his shoulder. "You made me come alive, Cage. You made me really live. And I don't ever want it to end."

He tightened his grip. "Good. 'Cause I'm not planning on going anywhere, babe."

When he'd first come back to the empty apartment, Cage had known exactly where Calla had gone. He'd found her resting so comfortably in the space, and had been ready to pick her up and bring her to bed when he'd seen the sketchbook on the chair, not the table where he'd left it.

It was a new one he'd just bought the day before to start framing out new jobs, since he'd put out the word that he'd be taking orders again. He flipped through to find the first twenty or so pages taken up with sketches and a signature with a jagged *E*.

At least the old man gave us this. Because their grandfather had been the artist in the family. His father was a good mechanic, but he'd never had the patience for putting together a bike from scratch.

But Eli did, at least from what these drawings indicated. And he had the potential for a talent well beyond Cage's . . . if he kept practicing.

Cage would gladly make room for another artist in his garage, but what Eli needed wasn't in this space.

He needs you, Tenn had told him that morning. But Cage had learned that sometimes giving people their freedom to grow was the best gift you could give them.

Chapter 29

Cage was dealing with finding Eli a tutor for his GED. He couldn't enroll him in school without bringing child protective services down on him in some fashion. For the moment, there was a fragile peace and getting the law involved would make it much worse. I understood that, because in this situation Eli would be placed back with the Heathens, or in foster care. I wasn't sure exactly which would be worse, but Eli threatened to run if CPS got involved.

I was going to hang around the apartment, but Preacher came to pick me up. I was surprised to see him, but when I went to let him in, he shook his head and said, "Let's take a ride and get something to eat."

He had his truck, a dark gray Suburban that rumbled as he drove it. We parked in town and walked through to the small restaurant. It was a warm day, so we sat outside. It was the first time I really got to people-watch and I enjoyed it. A couple of other Vipers members came to join us, and there were others going about their business in town.

As the afternoon wore on, I watched the men and women, cognizant of what Cage had told me, that most of the general population didn't know the contributions Vipers made. But maybe it took an outsider to notice, because I could see easily how the town treated these men, and me by extension, with a mixture of fear and gratitude. I saw it in their eyes—the little boys who watched the leather and Harleys with a gleam of awe as mothers and fathers hurried them by. Fathers, maybe a little more slowly, and I definitely saw some mothers looking over their shoulders.

Everyone has a wild side.

I also saw it in the giggle of older teenage girls as they gazed on the bikers for just a little too long.

The dichotomy was fascinating.

The town definitely knew that Vipers was a big part of their infrastructure.

"Does it bother you?" I asked Preacher after two teenage girls focused on him, giggling and reddening like he was a celebrity, until an older woman sternly shooed them away and glared at Preacher as though he'd encouraged it.

Which, for the record, he hadn't.

"What? That I'll never be invited to Sunday dinner?" Preacher asked now. "Fuck 'em. They should be grateful."

He couldn't hide the hurt and it actually made me want to shake these people a little. Although, in theory, a little bit of fear put the best kind of separation between the town and the Vipers. Best for both, because enemies could easily use that relationship against Vipers. Anything that left the MC vulnerable wasn't good, and so pretending to only give a shit about their interests protected the town from all the things that went roar in the night.

I dropped the subject and we ate. Talked about Eli and school, and his art.

"Cage showed me some of his stuff. The boy's good," Preacher said.

"He should go to art school."

"We don't have that around here."

They did in New York. That made me think about my father, and the fact that I hadn't been in touch with him. I felt guilty about it, but the investigation surrounding Ned's murder was ongoing. At least it was the last time I'd called to check, because no matter how much I couldn't stand him, I couldn't let him be buried in a pauper's grave. "Do you think Officer Flores contacted my father?"

Preacher nodded. "And I'm sure he knows exactly where you are."

"You think so?"

"If you were my daughter and I heard you were hanging around an MC, I'd know."

The thought of Preacher with a daughter made me smile—I couldn't help it. Because the idea of a wild guy saddled with a daughter to worry about was some kind of sweet revenge.

"I know what you're thinking, Calla," he chided. We finished lunch uneventfully and then we got back into his truck.

When I saw we were heading toward the clubhouse, I must've tensed.

"Cage told me you have a rough time coming here," he said. "It's quiet now. I need your help."

I didn't ask why, just nodded, because certainly they'd helped me. Granted, they'd almost gotten me killed too. But once we were inside the clubhouse and I saw it was quiet, I relaxed slightly, until Preacher pointed down the hall and said, "I can't get through to Holly."

"You think I can?"

"I think she won't be able to resist being a bitch to you, no."

"And that's a good thing?"

"Better than zoning out and crying, yes," he said firmly, pointing. I walked down the hall with only slightly less enthusiasm than if I'd been going to the electric chair.

I knocked on the half-open door and saw Holly lying on her side. As soon as she glanced up and saw it was me, she straightened, propped herself on the pillow.

Even with no makeup and with messy hair, she managed to look haughty. And I didn't even have to say anything before she started in.

"What, none of them could get through to me, so they figured, send in the rich girl?" Holly asked. She was wearing a T-shirt and shorts, her leg still bandaged, and her gaze flickered over me for a brief second before turning back to the TV. She was changing channels incessantly.

Finally I said, "I'm not a rich girl."

She turned the TV off and stared at me. "I'm sure Cage told you how I came here."

"A little."

"Well, let me explain it, Calla, so you can understand the difference between you and me. Because I don't want you to become deluded into thinking we could be friends."

I crossed my arms, leaned against the wall without saying a word.

She continued. "I fell in love with an American when I came here on vacation with some friends."

I wanted to say, "You had friends?" but I didn't. She smirked, like she knew what I was thinking, then went on. "I was eighteen and Mickey was thirty-five. He said he'd take care of me, and he did. I never went back, told my family good-bye and moved in with him. He was part of the No'Ones. They're based out of Tallahassee. And we were together for ten years. One day, the MC members came in and cornered me in our shop, the one Mickey and I bought together. I didn't know it was mortgaged under the club's name, so really neither Mickey nor I had any rights to it. And the president of the club demanded to know where Mickey was. I'd thought he'd gone to the gym, but I knew something was very wrong. I tried to get in touch with him, to warn him, but no luck. They tied me up, waited for him to show, and then they bashed his head in with a baseball bat while I watched. They untied me, told me to get out, and here I am."

She sucked in a breath and I struggled to do so as well. There had to be more to the story, but I wasn't about to push. She was telling me this for shock value, but to what end? "I'm sorry, Holly. I can't imagine."

"Of course you couldn't."

"You're still going to be a complete bitch to me?"

"You got my shop shut down. I had to come in and save you because you got sentimental and let your lover's brother inside. He's a Heathen, Calla. The same MC trying to kill Cage and you. Fucking daft, you are. Go back and play with your rich friends before you get this MC in big trouble."

"Mickey got killed for something you did," I said now.

She blinked. "What did you say?"

"A guilty conscience always recognizes another." I walked out, although I couldn't be smug about it, because I'd hated the look on her face. I'd been right. And whether or not Holly was someone the MC should trust wasn't entirely up to me.

Preacher had heard the entire thing. I didn't like the look in his eyes, but he didn't say a word when he drove me home and walked me up to the apartment. When Cage opened the door, all Preacher said was, "Thanks for talking to her," and walked away.

"What was that about?" Cage asked.

"I don't think you want to know."

Cage had managed to get Eli a tutor, and he was in Rocco's apartment with her now, so Rocco could supervise. I told Cage about my lunch with Preacher and a little of what happened with Holly.

"Did you ask Preacher to take me to lunch?"

"You couldn't go anywhere on your own."

"Ever?"

"I didn't say that."

"Okay, good."

"But for a long time. And you can only go where you'll be supervised by club guys."

"What?"

"Did you think you could just stroll around and go shopping?"

Honestly, I hadn't given it any thought at all. My future was all a big, yawning abyss and I didn't know what I was supposed to do or feel. "For how long? And don't say, 'For as long as it takes.'"

To his credit, he didn't say it, but just pointed at me when I said it.

I threw my hands in the air and turned my back. I should be grateful, not frustrated to the point of tears, which would spill down my cheeks soon if I didn't pull it together. I bit it back because, with or without Cage, I'd be in a lot of trouble. Without him, I'd have no place to go.

"Calla." His voice rough to my ears, and his hands rough to my skin. I couldn't stay angry at him. And that was the problem.

"I need to know there's an end point."

"I'm trying to get us there."

I knew that Flores was trying to bring trouble down on me and the MC because of Ned. I knew that. I also knew too much about the Heathens. But I couldn't stay caged forever. "You have to let me do something. I don't have any money of my own. I'm a burden to you."

"This is my fault. And you're not a burden."

"Maybe it is your fault, but I'm not used to being taken care of."

"Get used to it," he growled.

"No," I told him. "Don't get all sexy and possessive and ruin what I'm trying to say."

"Sexy and possessive, huh?"

"Don't," I warned.

"I'm listening."

"I have to at least make my own money. That's important to me."

"I'm not keeping you with me out of guilt, Calla. If that was the case, you wouldn't be sharing my bed. But the other stuff, I get that. It won't be forever that you're hiding, but I can get you a temporary ID. Actually, it's good for you to have something."

"No."

"No? Jesus, women are fucking confusing."

That gave me a momentary grin. "I think it's time I just used my own ID. My own money. Because isn't it better that way? The more it's out there—"

"The more questions you'll get. The more the Heathens will know about you."

"Like they don't already."

"Fuck." He ran his hands through his hair as he paced. I thought about how I'd grabbed his hair the night before when he was between my legs. He caught the tail end of my expression, even though I tried to school it and smiled. "I swear, you think about sex as much as I do."

"That's not a bad thing."

"Not at all, babe. What is a bad thing is thinking you can go up against the Heathens and win. They don't value life, especially female life. This isn't like going up against the law. I've got to fight like with like, or this won't work."

I buried my head against his chest. "I don't play the rescued-princess role well. The fact that you tracked my phone—"

"Not changing that," he said stubbornly.

"I'm surprised you haven't found a way to plant a tracking device on me. Wait—" I stared at his smirk.

"Maybe you'll need to strip to find out?"

"Nice try." But he didn't have to try . . .

"How about the bar? Amelia's already said she'd be happy to take you on."

I wore an armful of bracelets from that very first night I'd met her. "Thanks, Cage. I'm just . . . trying to find out who I am."

"Take your time finding that out."

"Are you?"

"Every damned day, baby," he told me. And he was serious. Completely.

And that afternoon, Amelia showed me the ropes in the bar while Cage and Preacher played pool. As evening rolled around, it got more crowded.

I was better here. I wiped down the bar, served drinks, managed the crowds with a little help from the bouncers.

I was back in my element. I'd done this regularly during the summers when I could escape from the boarding schools. I'd grown up watching Mom and Grams do it. I'd spent summers learning to bartend when I was much too little to even think about it.

Last time, I'd been too focused on Cage and fitting in to appreciate being back behind the bar. This time, all the memories flooded back to me. I inhaled the scent of oiled wood and stale beer and good whiskey. Smoke mixed with the leather and I swore I could hear the conversations that had happened here, like ghosts in the wind, whispering in my ear, telling me about the good old days.

Chapter 30

After Amelia closed up, she shooed me away. "I've got guys to help clean up. Your man's waiting for you."

He was, and he'd been very patient all night, especially because I'd been too busy to do much but serve drinks. I walked out with him and he put his arms around me. "Let's take a ride."

"In bed or on your bike?"

He grinned. "Bike first."

He handed me the helmet and I got on behind him, but before we could go, I heard Vipers bikes circling back toward us.

"There's trouble," Preacher called.

I held on and Cage gunned the bike after him. We were headed to the clubhouse two blocks away, where Eli was left with Holly and plenty of other Vipers to guard them both. But as we pulled up, I saw a pile of men. Cage stopped the bike and we both got off quickly. He ran toward the group with Preacher and I saw Eli waiting in the alley.

"What's going on?"

"Heathen Enforcers," he said. "They came for me."

I looked and watched the man whose hands—always so gentle on me—were now beating several Heathens senseless. Tals was pulling Cage away and the men were starting to separate, even as a police siren sounded.

"Shit, they had to be watching," Eli muttered. It was true—the clubhouse was in a quiet area, especially with the tattoo shop being closed, which meant that the Vipers were under surveillance.

The Heathens and Cage and his guys stood across from each other, none of them moving as Detective Flores got out of the car. "What's going on here?"

"Just a friendly discussion, Detective," Preacher said.

None of the other men said a word.

"You look like you've been fighting," she commented.

"No, ma'am," Preacher said, and none of the Heathens argued. "They were just leaving."

As Flores's partner stepped in between the

men to ensure that was happening, I looked down the alley and saw Holly there. Her cheek was bruised, her lip bleeding, and she held a metal pipe down by her side. She put the pipe down and came to join me, just as Detective Flores reached me.

"I'm sure this somehow ties back to you, Calla." I didn't say a word. Her eyes flicked over me, and then Holly. "What happened to you?"

"Nothing," Holly said in that cool tone of hers. She put a hand on my shoulder and stared at Flores while I stared at her, wondering who the hell this pod was and what she'd done with Holly. And then I saw her eyes flicker over Flores's shoulder and I followed her gaze to a man getting out of the back of Flores's car. "Who's that?"

Flores didn't turn around, but gazed at me. "It's the witness who saw Cage at Ned's motel room door the night before he was murdered."

"But not the night of, right?" I asked, and then I went mute, because he was here. Standing next to Detective Flores, taller and broader than he'd been back then.

But his eyes were still as dead as a shark's. My hand was at my side and I reached for Holly's wrist and squeezed, hoping that would some-how clue her in that I needed help. I glanced at her too for a second, and she looked back at me with fierceness in her gaze. She squeezed my shoulder and didn't take her hand away.

"Calla, this is Agent Jeffrey Harris, with the FBI."

"I don't understand why he's here," I said to Flores, refusing to look at him.

"He was part of an undercover sting," Flores told me.

Suddenly the pieces of the puzzle fell into place with a sickening clarity, made worse by the fact that I couldn't tell her about any of it.

"Calla Benson?" he asked me, like he didn't know. Because neither of us was supposed to admit to anything—that would break the rules of the confidentiality agreement.

I stared at him, unwavering and unashamed. He wouldn't break me again. Let him sweat.

"Calla? We need to talk," Flores told me.

"So talk."

She grimaced a little and motioned to Jeffrey. "The FBI is involved, Calla. You need to tell us what you know, starting with what happened the other night at the tattoo shop."

I shrugged. "It was pretty boring. And Holly's a class-A bitch."

Beside me, Holly snorted. "She's not the greatest employee."

"You're playing a very dangerous game, Miss

Benson. I'd rethink your position, if I were you," Jeffrey told me.

Before he could say anything else, I saw movement out of the corner of my eye, and Cage and Preacher and Rocco were heading our way. Jeffrey slid back toward the car and Detective Flores handed me her card.

"You need to get in touch, Calla, and soon."

She walked away just as Cage got to me. Only then did Holly let go of my shoulder.

Chapter 31

We didn't stay outside. Instead, we went back into the clubhouse to regroup and then decided that we were safer going back to Cage's building. We drove in different cars and bikes, took different routes and made sure there was no one tailing us.

I refused to go into a panic attack—it was only by sheer will that I didn't. And when Cage tried to get me to take one of my pills, I said to him, "The FBI agent, Jeffrey . . ."

His eyes widened, jaw clenched with anger. There was no last name on the e-mails, but there was a first.

We didn't talk about it any further on the ride back to the apartment. He held me tight as he brought me upstairs and just murmured for me to breathe, which was a surprisingly effective reminder.

In an hour, we'd regrouped in Cage's apartment. Holly was there, with Preacher, Rocco, Tals and Eli. We had the usual guys guarding downstairs and several more at the clubhouse and the bar.

The bar. That part of the night seemed like it had happened years ago. I had held myself tight up until this point, but now, facing the reality that Jeffrey was somehow involved with the Heathens was too much for me.

Cage sat next to me, practically vibrating with anger. But when he put his hand on my shoulders, his touch was completely gentle.

I didn't say anything, gnawed my bottom lip and nodded.

"What's Jeffrey's game?" he asked finally.

"He said he saw you at Ned's motel the night before he was murdered. He's working on some kind of undercover sting," I said.

"He's Flores's witness?" Cage asked.

"He must've followed me here," I said. He wouldn't have to keep track of me to send me e-mails . . . and I never changed my e-mail address, because I didn't want to encourage him to search me out. And it's not like I've been hard to find. Until now.

"He's the guy who met with the Heathens," Eli said quietly.

"Someone want to fill me in?" Preacher asked.

"That man hurt Calla," Holly said.

All I could do was nod.

"Is there a restraining order?" she continued.

"Yes, but it's not . . . official. There was a binding agreement," I said. "It's all confidential."

"You're going to have to call your father, Calla," Cage said.

I nodded. "Not right now, though. Please."

"Why don't we leave them alone," Holly said. Holly had saved me tonight, more than she could've known. Or maybe she did. She and Preacher and Rocco left, taking Eli with them to Rocco's apartment for the night.

Once they'd left and Cage locked up and came back into the kitchen, I told him, "You're going through enough. You've gone through enough— I don't need you fighting my battles."

"It's part of my battle now too." His face darkened with anger, none of it directed at me, but I still hated seeing it there.

He strode over to me. Picked me up, put me on the counter and moved between my legs so we were nearly eye-to-eye. "I'm protecting you, Calla. I don't give a shit if you don't want it or not—you don't have a choice in that. You're mine. I'm going to make sure nothing ever happens to you."

"He'll stop at nothing. He'll take away anyone I care about—and now that I was getting closer to my father, I had someone else to worry about. And Jeffrey Harris knows exactly how to find my father. Everyone does."

"Your father has enough money to hire body-guards. Yours are built in."

"He'll go after you."

"He already has," Cage pointed out.

"No one can stop him."

"No one's ever tried, babe," was all he said. I shivered.

"You're calling your father tomorrow. I'm sure he's worried sick."

"I know. But as good as he's been the last two times I talked to him . . . there's so much history there. Most of it is my mom's fault. I'm seeing that now. But suppose I'm wrong?"

"Suppose you're not?" he said. "Bernie wasn't the type to do favors for assholes. If he thought your dad was trying to hurt you . . ."

"I hate it when you're logical," I told him, and he just got that look—I knew he wanted to laugh but he held back.

"Maybe you should hear him out."

"Maybe you should stay out of it."

"I can't, Calla. You invited me into your life—"

"Because you dragged me into yours—"

"And I'm here. I'm not leaving. And that means I have to help you stop fucking hurting yourself over something that was never your fault or Jameson Bradley's."

"And I'm here." I blinked at him.

"And I love you, Calla."

"Damn you, Cage. Just damn you. Because you know I love you too."

The next morning, while Calla slept, Preacher came over. He was tense as hell and Cage let him pace for a few minutes before saying, "What's going on?"

"I've got some information. It's not good."

"Tell me."

"The Heathens are planning on taking Eli back with Harris's support. He's got a file on us that supposedly has us running meth. And shows you and Tals at the scene of Ned's murder."

"All bullshit."

"Of course. But the Heathens have his full support. We get taken down, they push their meth into Skulls and it's all over."

"I've got the intel for the RICO case, Preacher. That'll cause a lot of reasonable doubt."

"Right. They know that. And they haven't found the safety-deposit box."

"And they don't know for sure if Calla knows about it."

"I don't think that matters."

Preacher was right. All they had to do was

take her and they knew Cage would give it up. Or they thought he would. Cage would hunt them down and kill them for touching her—he'd find a way to not let that happen.

By keeping her on lockdown forever?

"Shit," Cage muttered.

"After I talked to the Heathens, I spoke to Harris."

"What the fuck?"

"He contacted me. Said he'll walk away from the Heathens, leave them hanging—and leave Flores hanging—if you let Calla go."

"What the fuck? Let her go where?"

"Anywhere away from you."

"Please tell me you got this on tape?"

"You think he'd let that happen? Besides, he didn't come straight out and say this. It was implied enough that I got it. Guy's obsessed with her."

That made sense. Sending her those pictures a couple of times a year ensured she was locked in his prison, unable to even think about trusting another man, thanks to Jeffrey's reminders. But she had finally broken through and trusted Cage, and Cage wouldn't let her go. "I hope you're not asking me to turn her away."

"Did I fucking say that?" Preacher yelled.

The rage inside of him boiled over quickly, but he forced himself calm so he could plan. "I'll fix this."

"I know. But first you have to tell her."

"Why? So she can feel guilty?"

"Because if she finds out, which she will, she'll be angry you didn't trust her enough to make the right choice."

"What is the right choice, Preach? Because I know what the goddamned right choice is for me."

"What's going on?" Calla was standing in the doorway, her eyes still full of sleep.

Preacher looked at Cage and said, "I'll do this if you want."

"Do what?" I was instantly on alert. I could feel the tension bleeding off both men. "Did something else happen?"

With a glance at Preacher, Cage told me about Jeffrey's deal with the Heathens. About what he wanted Cage and Vipers to do with me.

"You're not going anywhere," Cage growled.

I tugged my arms around myself and nodded. "It'll be everywhere soon. Why would he want that?" I asked. "It will expose him. That's the deal he made with my father—if we didn't say anything, he wouldn't. The second one of us fucks up that game of chicken, all bets are off."

"He's planning on saying that you loved it," Preacher said flatly.

"What?" Cage asked. Apparently this was the first time he was hearing this too.

Preacher shifted. "He's got a group of guys who said you begged them to do it. That it was part of a hazing for a secret sorority at the school you went to."

I ground out, "But I didn't."

"I know, Calla."

It was never going to end. As Cage came to me, I heard Preacher leaving. When the door shut, I said, "He'll use me against you, so you lost your leverage."

"I'll find it again. Don't you worry about that."

I wasn't. What did worry me were Jeffrey Harris's last words to me, all those years ago in my father's lawyer's office. I hadn't known that Jeffrey would be there, as well as the boys who'd been involved—maybe no one had. And when I froze, he looked at me and mouthed, "We're not through."

I knew what that meant. "Take the Heathens down."

Cage shook his head, ground out, "At your expense? Never."

"You have to, Cage. There's nothing more Jeffrey can do to hurt me. It's done, it's over."

"It's not done until I say so," Cage said, and I knew better than to contradict him. "He's not going to keep his word, Calla. Don't you get that?

He's going to find a way to arrest us, and then he's going to keep coming after you. And Vipers. It will never end if we give in."

Cage's phone rang then, and he looked at the number, frowned and passed me the phone. I saw *Bradley Industries* and I picked up. "Dad? How did you—?"

My father breathed out a sigh, a surprised one. "Yes, Calla—I called the Vipers clubhouse. After I called a man named Tenn—I traced back the number you called me from. Are you okay?"

"Yes. No. I don't know." I took a deep breath and opened my eyes to see Cage watching me. "He's sending me pictures."

"Who?"

"Jeffrey."

"Since when?"

"Since a few months after you paid him," I said quietly. "It never stopped. He's been doing it since then. And he's threatening me again. Me and the man who saved me."

"I'm coming to you."

"You don't know—"

"I know exactly where you are now, thanks to Tenn. You're lucky I haven't landed a helicopter on the roof of the Vipers clubhouse or Cage's building," he said.

Chapter 32

I told my father to come to Cage's apartment instead. Without the helicopter.

He came alone, driving a nondescript rental car, according to Rocco, who met him in the underground garage. The last thing we wanted was for Jeffrey to know Jameson Bradley was in town.

My father stepped into the apartment. I'd only seen him in person once—and that had been a haze. The experience was surreal.

He was my family. Down to the color of our hair. My breath caught, and even though this reunion was happening under the worst of circumstances, I ran to him.

He caught me in his arms with the grace of someone half his age. I'd expected him to be cold and aloof; instead, he was strong and comforting. And when we pulled back, he looked over my shoulder to where Cage was standing.

It was only then that I remembered my anger. "Why didn't you try harder to see me before this?"

"Calla, I did try—"

"Right. Really hard, I'm sure. Like your helicopter couldn't have just landed in the bar's parking lot if you were that desperate to see me."

"There was a restraining order against me," he said quietly, and before I could say I didn't believe him, he took two pieces of paper from his pocket and handed them to me. I grabbed them and read them as best I could, through tears and the shaking of the paper in my trembling fingers.

"I don't understand—it's saying that you can't come near her or me. Because . . ."

"Because she lied," he said flatly and handed me an envelope. I recognized my mother's handwriting immediately. "I didn't know about you until you were fifteen. Inside, is her apology. I never wanted to show you any of this, Calla. I really didn't. If it wasn't for the fact that you're in immediate danger and I need you to believe me . . ."

I did.

"We can talk more about this, but there are pressing matters, Calla. I'd like to get you out of here and get you someplace safe."

"I don't think so."

Cage's voice. As I watched, they stared each other down and I swore I heard music from the O.K. Corral, expected one or both of them to draw at any moment.

Finally Cage said, "You served."

"Eighty-second Battalion."

Army. These men were both Army. How did I know so little about my own father? How could Cage know that just from looking at him?

I studied them for a second, noticed they did have the same bearing. Maybe there was some kind of secret way of knowing.

And suddenly, the two men I figured would be enemies had their heads together, talking about making plans. For me.

"First I'd like to talk to Calla a bit, though," my father said.

"I'll go grab us some dinner," Cage agreed. He gave me a kiss before he left, and my father and I sat down and dealt with the topic at hand.

"I wanted to prosecute. Your mother was worried about what it would do to your social status. She wanted that for you, Calla, for right or wrong. I should've fought her harder, but she convinced me that a lengthy trial would be too much for you."

"Wait—you wanted to bring the police in on this?"

"Of course." He ran his hands through his hair, his eyes sad. "I don't want to do this, play the 'Disparage Your Mother' game. She did what she thought was best."

"She knew I didn't want any of those trappings."

"She thought you deserved them."

"And what did you think?"

"I think that rich, poor and everything in between comes with its own set of problems. But I wanted to strangle that boy with my bare hands," my father said fiercely. "It was only through the intervention of my friends that I'm not in jail today and I'm still pissed at myself for listening to them. Because sitting in jail, knowing that fucker was dead, would've been worth it. But they convinced me that keeping it quiet was the best for you. That something like that could ruin a fifteen-year-old."

"It did ruin me," I said quietly. "But if it had gotten out, it would've been worse. You buried it, and I'm grateful. But I shouldn't have tried to bury it for myself."

"I'm so sorry, Calla. I just wish you'd told me earlier, because he broke an order not to contact you."

"I couldn't prove it was him," I said. "I don't know how he involved Ned. But I'm guessing he used Ned for a while, and then killed him. Although I can't prove that either. Jeffrey's trying to frame Cage for that, and based on what the detectives saw in those pictures . . ."

My father's face hardened and I said, "I told Cage to just let it go public. He refused and—"

"Of course he refused. That's not going to happen. Over my dead body."

"That's what I'm afraid of," I whispered. "I just found you and Cage. I don't want to lose either of you."

"I'm not going anywhere." He studied me. "Cage is good to you."

It wasn't a question, but I nodded anyway and said, "Very. And I'm good for him."

"It's not where I'd like to see you, but I'll be damned if I stand in the way of someone's love."

If I'd been allowed to know what I knew now . . . I could've had a different relationship with him. And then, I might never have met Cage.

I hugged him, like any daughter would hug any dad. "It's not too late for this, is it?"

"Never, Calla. Never," he said fiercely. "Are you safe here?"

"No. They never would hurt me, especially not Cage. But I'm hurting them."

My father paused. "I'm sure they can handle

it, Calla. But you want out—I'm coming to get you."

Before I could tell him I had no place to go, he'd added, "And you'd come home with me.

"This isn't the life I'd have chosen for you," he continued. "What father would?"

"One who grew up in an MC?"

"Wiseass."

How had I not known my father had a sense of humor? A stab of pain at all the wasted time tore through me, and tears ran down my cheeks.

"Calla, honey . . ."

"It's okay. I'm just . . . I'm sorry."

"For what?"

"That I spent so much time hating you. Thinking you hated me too."

He didn't say anything, just grabbed my hand and squeezed. "That's behind us. We can talk about it—we will talk about it—but for now let's concentrate on fixing this business that's been haunting you once and for all."

"Cage fixed it. He fixed me," I explained. I wouldn't go into detail, but my father seemed to understand.

"And you think you can live the rest of your life attached to an MC?"

"I don't know. But I know I can live with Cage for the rest of my life, if he'll have me."

Chapter 33

I dragged Holly with me to the gym. She'd finally come out of her room, and although the tattoo shop was open and running, she'd refused to step foot inside. There'd been no signs of the police finding anything else but a rock through the window and so it had been filed as a nuisance report.

So far, so good. Rally dropped us off at the gym and we went right inside. I felt a little silly being bodyguarded most of the time, but I think Holly definitely appreciated the extra presence.

Once inside, she jumped right on a treadmill and began to run. I did the same, and for half an hour there was just the music from my iPod and the pounding of my pulse and my feet in a steady rhythm. The stress of everything fell away easily, and I made a mental note to get here more often.

I much preferred running outside, but I'd take what I could get.

Holly stopped a few minutes before me, and she was still stretching when I finished. I wiped my face with a towel and gulped some water down.

"Good run, yes?" she asked. It was good to see her smile. I thought about how I hadn't liked her at first, and how fast things could change.

"We've got to do this more often."

"I'd love to take a swim and then sauna. Are you in a rush to get back?"

"Nope. Go for it. I'm going to do some free weights and then I'll meet you in the steam."

She patted my shoulder as she passed and I headed for the weights.

If I'd seen Detective Flores ahead of time, I'd have turned my ass right around. But I didn't notice her until I was practically on top of her, since she was lying down doing some bench presses.

"Hello Calla."

I nodded in her direction and went to grab some weights of my own, feeling distinctly uncomfortable. All the good high from my run went flying out the window. I barely got the five-pound weights settled in my palms when she was next to me. I looked at her in the mirror, not turning when she said, "I think we should talk."

"On or off the record, Detective?"

"I'll be doing the talking, Calla, so you can file it whichever way you'd like."

I wished I could tell her that I wasn't in the mood for listening to lectures, but for the good of the MC—for my own good—I put the weights down and followed her out the back door. There was a small patio area with a couple of benches and she motioned for me to sit next to her. I did, turning to sling an arm over the back.

She took a long, unhurried drink from her water bottle, took her time capping it. She looked around and motioned. "This is a beautiful town."

I nodded, taking the "I didn't have to talk" thing to heart. She smiled for a brief moment. "I grew up here. Went to school with some of the younger members of the Vipers. They've been here longer than I have. One might begin to think they're something of an institution, as if they have the right to do whatever they want because they're a part of the town's history."

I knew all about the history of the Vipers, how the MC had started with a friend of Preacher's father, and how Preacher finally took it over and got rid of all the bad shit. His words, not mine. Bad shit to Vipers equaled drugs.

"I remember when Preacher came and cleaned house. We all thought that the MC would actually go legit. But that didn't happen. Sure, they got rid of the drugs, but not the guns or the violence. And they bring other violence into Skulls Creek, whether it's their fault or not. Calla, I've seen girls like you chewed on and spit out by these guys, time and time again. When a Viper gets through with you, there's nothing left. Doesn't matter if you're a mama or an old lady—the same thing will happen."

"Sounds like you have personal experience?" I asked, unable to stop the wiseass comment.

Her expression shuttered, but she nodded briefly. "My sister."

"Your sister dated one of the Vipers?"

"No, one of the Heathens."

I lifted my chin. "That's not the same thing at all, Detective."

"Bullshit. Cage is a crossover from the Heathens. That just proves to me that these guys are interchangeable."

"They're not angels, but they don't pretend to be. They do a lot of legitimate business in this city, don't they? Look at the buildings they own. The stores too. They don't bring their problems within the city limits."

"Drugs are being pushed in here because of them."

"Drugs are being pushed everywhere," I pointed out. "Without Vipers, I'd hate to see how easily it would happen. There's always going to be an underworld of criminals. Sometimes it takes bad guys to fight bad guys. And sometimes it's hard to tell the difference between the good guys and the bad guys."

"You're really naive to believe that."

"You don't know my background at all."

"I can tell just by looking at you. Rich bitch looking for a bad boy to make her feel good. You'll slum for a little bit, but, honey, get out while you can." She got up then, effectively ending the discussion. And then she turned. "I'll find a way to take them down if it's the last thing I do. Consider that a warning. And I won't go easy on you or any of the women there. You're as complicit as the men you hang out with. Try that on for size."

I didn't want to. I didn't break her gaze, forcing her to when she finally walked away, shutting the heavy steel door behind her. I didn't want to go in and let Holly see me upset, but Detective Flores's words definitely had an effect. If I didn't know better, I'd think that Cage asked her to talk some sense into me.

He didn't want to let me go, he said, but he

also hated the idea of me staying. I'd never been more confused in my life.

I put the towel over my face, let it stay there for a second and then pulled it down slowly. When it got past my lips, I opened my eyes. And I tried to scream.

Chapter 34

I blinked and coughed. I tried to remember where I was, what had happened. My mouth tasted awful, like some kind of medicine.

He'd stuffed a rag into my mouth when I'd started to scream. And now Agent Jeffrey Harris stood over me as I lay on the ground, immobilized. My hands were tied above my head, and when I tugged them I felt that they were tied to something in the ground. I wouldn't take my eyes off Harris, though. My legs were similarly tied, but I was thankfully dressed.

Maybe he was just going to kill me.

That was my thought—and honestly, if that happened, I'd be lucky. I couldn't take another violation. I'd barely survived the last one.

That's when he put the knife against the center of my chest, right between my breasts, and dragged it down, slicing my shirt, bra and shorts right down the middle. Cutting my skin, and I watched in horror as my body was exposed and blood welled along my breasts and belly. He stopped at my crotch, put the knife down and ripped the shorts and my underwear in two, leaving them in tatters.

I shivered, from fear, the cold, the cuts . . . and he laughed. Took out the gag and I spat, "You . . . fucker."

"You crossed my path again, Calla. That's a sign we weren't done yet."

"I won't stay quiet this time."

"I know. But you're not going to have a choice." He shrugged as he ran a finger over my nipple. "It wasn't as much fun for me when you weren't awake. I bet you're even more of a fire-cracker in bed these days. Have to be, to catch the eye of one of the Vipers guys."

He rubbed a hand on his chin as he stared down at his ringing phone. He pressed the screen and I heard, "You got the bitch?"

"She's ready and willing," he said.

God no . . . no . . .

I hadn't realized I'd started screaming until he grabbed the gag and began to stuff it inside my mouth again so I couldn't say anything, let alone breathe. Because I'd started to panic, hyperventilate . . . and I did the only thing I could think of. I head-butted him, hard. He looked stunned the first time, and I did it twice more before I passed out.

When I woke again, we weren't in the woods. I was lying on a table in a place that looked a little bit like the Vipers clubhouse, but the wood paneling was darker. I was on a hard, raised surface—it took me a second to realize it was a pool table. And it was far too quiet.

"Place is soundproofed," Jeffrey told me. My head jerked toward the dark corner and the sound of his voice. Had he just been sitting there watching me? "You'll make a great present for the Heathens. Especially Troy."

No. Not Cage's brother. "You're a sadistic bastard."

"You make it sound like that's a bad thing."

I swallowed hard. Stared at the ceiling instead of him. "Why?"

"Really? That's what you want to know?"

"Yes. I get why now, why here. Your symbolism's not exactly original, but I'd expect that from someone whose family had to buy him into private school." I heard a snarl, knew I was pushing my luck, but didn't care. "How many other girls have you done this to? How many women?"

"More than I can count, but none of them were

like you. You were really special, Calla. My first. They say you never forget your first."

"You fucking bastard."

"It'll be nice to have you awake for the whole thing. I'll film it this time, and once the Heathens have their way with you . . ."

God, he'd let them kill me. Or was I supposed to beg for my life?

I wouldn't give him the satisfaction. "Cage will find you, Jeffrey. I can't feel sorry for myself knowing what he'll do to you when he finds you."

I thought I saw him pale slightly, but maybe it was just wishful thinking on my part. I heard the bikes pull up—Heathen bikes—and when I looked back up at Jeffrey, he was smiling.

I closed my eyes when I heard the doors slam open and the rough voices began to yell. God, this couldn't be happening. I kept my eyes closed even after I heard fighting, because if I didn't look, none of this would be real.

It was only when I felt a familiar, rough touch on my cheek and heard his voice murmur, "Calla, baby, I'm here," that I opened my eyes to see him.

"I don't want you to see me like this," I told him.

But Cage shook his head, even as he shrugged his jacket off to cover me.

"I'm just happy to see you." His eyes were wet, his voice hoarse, and I felt someone working the ropes on both my arms and legs. He touched my face again.

"You . . . the Heathens . . ."

"We stopped them at the bottom of the hill. Rode their bikes up to surprise Harris. Thank God we found you in time."

"Thank you."

"Jesus." He touched my bruised forehead and then my lips and my neck and I realized he was making the sign of the cross over me, blessing me.

"I want to walk out of here," I told him when I was untied. He gave me his T-shirt to put on, wrapped blankets around me, slid his jacket on over everything.

Rocco was by the door and Preacher was there, watching us without watching.

"Where's Jeffrey?" I asked.

"He's here," Cage told me. "Eli, can you take Calla to the truck? Connor's there waiting."

Cage kissed me; then Eli came to my side. I didn't understand why until Cage moved away and I heard Jeffrey Harris's scream, almost a howl. I met Eli's eyes and he nodded. As he led me away I looked over my shoulder. Rally and

Preacher were holding Jeffrey for Cage, and although I didn't see everything, I knew what the blood between Harris's legs meant.

He'd never do this to another woman. He'd never haunt me again. This was justice. And the police were nowhere to be found.

I thought about all of that as I let a boy who was more of a man than Harris would ever be lead me to the safety of a waiting truck. Connor, from the backseat, said, "Preacher said to go to the clubhouse. They'll meet us there. Cops are on their way."

Eli pulled away and I said, "Wait—you're not—"

"Not old enough to drive? I've got a license," he said, like that was all that mattered.

I was so grateful to be safe, I didn't care. He'd turned up the heat because I was shivering, then said, "Cage is right behind us, okay? He'll come to you as soon as he can."

"He saved me," I whispered.

"Yeah, he did."

"Again."

"He's good at that." He grabbed another blanket from Connor and handed it to me. As I spread it over my legs, he said, "You're going to be okay, Calla."

"So are you," I told him, and his expression tightened. "He won't let you go back."

"Cage might not have a choice."

"Cage always has a choice."

Sometimes, knives were far more effective than money or power. Cage stood over Harris's crumpled body as the man sobbed.

Harris would die here. Calla's file would be anonymously sent to the FBI with her name redacted. They would also get pictures of what he'd done to her—two of them, because that's all he could stand to let Preacher snap before he ran in to rescue her.

Thank God for Holly . . . and for Detective Flores. When he'd figured out where Calla was, Cage had sent Flores on a wild-goose chase, because she'd have simply taken Harris into custody. And that wasn't nearly good enough for him.

"That one's for Calla. The next one, that's for Eli. And the last one will be for me," Cage growled, his hand curled around the knife. He wiped it on the grass next to Harris's face and he forced the man to look at him. "Rot in hell, motherfucker."

And then he walked out of the Heathens clubhouse and away from any guilt, because for this, he had none.

"Now what?" Preacher asked.

"I'm resisting the urge to find the other two who hurt her," Cage said, with a barely suppressed fury. He never liked being this angry when he had a job to do, but this was far too personal not to be. "But first, let's finish what we started with the others."

"Let me, Cage."

"They're my problem, Preach."

"I know. But let me." With a hand on Cage's shoulder, Preacher said, "Go to your woman. Tell her she's free. Tell Eli he's free. Tell him that with a clear conscience."

Rocco watched the exchange. "I'll drive you, Cage. Rally and Tals will help Preacher."

The Heathens, including Cage's father and Troy and the others who were going to hurt Calla, were tied up at the bottom of the hill. Five men who wouldn't be alive come morning.

He grabbed Preacher in a one-armed hug and let Rocco bring him to the rest of his family.

Chapter 35

There would be too many questions at the ER, and although I didn't want to be at the club-house, I knew it was the best place to be. Because the police would come here soon, and they'd see what happened to me. They'd put two and two together, but I wouldn't admit to anything, because no matter what I said, it would indict the man I loved.

Holly helped me shower, got me dressed and settled me onto the couch. She gave me something to calm my nerves and wrapped me in blankets. I couldn't stop shaking, and I knew I was in a little bit of shock, but that would wear off when I saw Cage come in, safe and sound.

After an hour, Cage came in. He kissed me, then went to shower, as did Rocco. When he came back to me, he was dressed in clean clothes. We were all sitting there watching a movie when the police cars came to the clubhouse, with Officer Flores coming to check on me.

I was bruised, but calm. I told her that someone dragged me into the woods and tried to assault me, but Holly scared them off. And no, neither of us knew who it was.

Preacher and Rally and Tals came in then, all of them looking clean and fresh . . . and reeking of booze. Flores eyed them suspiciously.

"Detective Flores," Preacher boomed. "Nice of you to join us."

"I was just leaving. I suppose you have alibis."

"About six of them," Preacher agreed.

Flores rolled her eyes.

When she left, I fell asleep in Cage's arms. When I awoke, we were all there, in the same spot—Tals and Preacher and Rocco and Eli and Holly— collapsed on the couches, with other members of the MC watching over us from various corners of the clubhouse.

Yes, this place could end up feeling like home after all.

Detective Flores came back to the clubhouse in the morning. I was sitting outside drinking coffee when she sat down next to me. I tensed, because she had to know what had happened by now.

"Agent Jeffrey Harris is missing."

"Really?" I sipped my coffee. "That's a shame."

"It seems like he went crazy, murdered about six men from the Heathens MC in cold blood. Word on the street was that he'd agreed to help them move their drugs, but then he'd turned on them."

"Sounds like there's no harm, no foul, then."

"By all accounts, Jeffrey Harris was a decorated agent," Officer Flores told me. "I haven't been able to find evidence to the contrary."

I wanted to scream to tell her exactly what he'd done to me. "I'm sure he's got friends who vouch for that."

"Many of them," she agreed. "Several of whom tell a very interesting story about a time at a party when a young girl tried to get him in trouble."

"Really?" I shifted.

"They wouldn't give a name," she continued. "But there was talk of some pictures. Like the pictures I found in your brother's possession the night he died."

I stared straight ahead. "I don't know what you want me to say."

"Are you all right, Calla?"

I turned to her. "I am now. So you'll excuse me, Detective Flores, if the line between the good guys and the bad guys is pretty much god-damned blurred for me."

She nodded. "You know where to find me if you need anything."

"No offense, but I hope I never will."

She gave me a small smile before disappearing around the corner.

Chapter 36

I rested for a week before I went stir-crazy. Cage was with me the majority of the time, but today he had things to do. He didn't specify what things, but I assumed it had to do with cementing Eli's place with him.

Eli's mom was scared of retaliation. Cage made sure she was hidden until he could figure out the next steps. I knew Cage's sister also wanted to come back to Skulls too.

Eli and I went down to the shop next door to grab a quick soup and sandwich. Rocco was waiting outside. Eli had been drawing and I'd been lounging on the couch watching a movie, so I was dressed in sweats and a T-shirt. Eli wore jeans and a T-shirt, and without the leather vest, he looked younger.

He went to grab sodas and I prepared to order.

The woman behind the counter eyeballed me, saying, "You're a new one."

I raised a brow but didn't say anything beyond, "I'll have a number two on white bread and a number four on a roll, please. And two tomato soups."

She rolled her eyes and put the soup into takeout containers, made the sandwiches in front of me, muttering all the while.

"Is there a problem?" I asked.

She shoved the wrapped sandwiches at me, then put the containers up behind it. "You're one of theirs."

I didn't say anything. Eli came up next to me and I swore I heard a mini Cage-like growl. The woman froze, stared at him.

"Can I just pay?" I asked.

"Fine," she said. When I handed her a twenty, she said, "I've gotta grab change in the back."

"Are you okay?" Eli asked.

"Fine." And I was. I was also tired and stressed and still very worried about him and Cage and waiting for the other shoe to drop but . . .

She stormed out of the back and punched the register keys. She handed me change and shoved the food into a bag and Eli took it for me.

I didn't know what she was so angry about. I was the one who should be angry, since she was talking about a revolving door with the Vipers and their women. But that was in the past . . .

"She didn't come back with change."

"What?" Eli asked.

"She said she had to go to the back to get change. But she came back and used the register." My last words were drowned out by the roar of motorcycles. Eli pushed me behind him and Rocco was coming toward us as a big guy got out of a van.

He had a Heathen patch—and a gun trained on me—and with his free hand, he pointed between Eli and the van, saying, "Come with us and no one gets hurt, Eli."

"Eli, don't you dare go with him!" I called, but it was too late. Eli was at the door of the van and the gun was no longer pointed in my direction.

"He's the president of the founding Heathen chapter," Rocco told me, holding my shoulder like he was worried I'd try to run and grab Eli.

The president looked at Eli, then at Rocco. "Tell Cage to call me. The kid'll be fine until then."

Of course, it couldn't be over as easily as cutting his father and oldest brother out of his life forever. Eli was still at risk, because even though the feds and ATF were all over that particular Heathens chapter, there were still others to answer to, including the main chapter. The original.

Cage took Tals with him to the bank where the box was being kept. They took it to a different bank, used a different code to lock it up tight.

"That takes care of Calla's involvement at least," Cage said.

"You're not that naive," Tals told him. And no, Cage wasn't. But they all knew that having anyone they loved in their lives made them vulnerable.

He was willing to take that chance, if she was.

"What? Rocco, slow the fuck down," Tals was saying into his phone. Then he paled. "Okay. Got it."

He hung up and said, "Cory's got Eli. Took him and said you need to call him."

Two hours later, we sat in front of Cory, the president of the original Heathens chapter, who told Cage, "You sold out your family. And Eli's still a probie, which means he's still Heathen property and you're no longer a Heathen."

"My family patched Eli in. He's fifteen. They tattooed him. He's not just a goddamned probie," Cage growled. "You think that shit's cool, maybe you deserve to be taken down too."

"Way to stay cool, Cage," Tals said through

clenched teeth. "We're going to die if you're not careful."

"Your friend's the smart one," Cory said.

"First time anyone's ever accused him of brains," Cage said. "And I wouldn't count on us being the ones to die."

Tals put his head in his hands and groaned. "We have RICO evidence against all of you. We'll leave it alone if you give us Eli and leave Vipers the fuck alone."

"I never agreed to that," Cage said.

"But you're agreeing to get us dead," Tals shot back.

Cory studied us carefully. Tals slid the key to the safety-deposit box across the table. "Only copy of the key and the tapes."

"You could've used these against all of us— been rid of us once and for all."

"I'd like to believe one bad bunch didn't spoil all of you."

"Been watching this war for years, son." Cory was pushing sixty. "Tough choice."

"No, it wasn't," Cage told him.

"Get Eli's tattoo covered." Cory took the key and stood, knocked on the door. Eli came in, looking nervous but none the worse for wear.

Cage and Tals guided Eli out of the building

where Cory held the meeting—a neutral place, except it included a ring of Heathens. But none of them were familiar faces, which made Cage breathe a sigh of relief.

Once they'd driven far enough away to consider themselves safe, Cage growled to Tals, "I can't believe you did that—just handed over the tapes."

"You wanted to."

"I was about to, but you wouldn't shut up."

"Can't believe I made a copy of the tapes either," Tals told him.

"When?" Cage demanded, and when Tals shrugged, Cage sighed. "You got the numbers from Calla."

"She didn't think you should ever give up all your evidence. But the fact that you were willing to, for family? That says it all."

Chapter 37

"We can remove it, but it'll hurt. It'll never be completely gone," Cage told Eli honestly. "Or you can cover it with another tattoo."

"Either way, there's always going to be a reminder," Eli said. "But maybe some things you shouldn't forget, if they bring you to better things."

"So fucking smart for fifteen. So much smarter than me."

"I . . . ah, speaking of smart," Calla started. "My dad and I might've done something. See, there's this school for artists in Manhattan . . ."

Eli's eyes lit up.

"And we showed them your drawings," she continued. "It's midsemester, but they'll make an exception."

"Wait a minute—is the only reason I got in because of your dad?"

"It didn't hurt, but, Eli, they wouldn't take you if you didn't have the talent." She turned to Cage. "I don't want him to leave here—but he doesn't want this life."

Cage stared between Eli and Calla. "Calla, your dad can keep an eye on him?"

"He's already got his guest suite set up. For you and your mom," she said to Eli.

"I see no reason the kid shouldn't get a shot," Cage said, putting his arm around Calla.

"Wait till I tell Mom!" Eli said. He gave Calla a hug, then Cage, then went to make the call.

"I can't believe you did that."

"Are you mad?"

"No. Not at all. Jesus, Calla . . ."

Cage was staring at me, his eyes dark with lust when he said my name.

"I'm here, Cage. You're not getting rid of me."

"And here I thought you were getting ready to run," he admitted. "And I couldn't blame you. You've gone through hell. And while this part's over . . . there's still a dangerous world out there for us. You could go to your dad's. Start over."

"I did start over. Especially once I realized that you really wanted me here. That we belonged together."

"I sense a 'but.' "

And there was. I didn't want to sound un-grateful but . . . "You have your thing, Cage. I don't have mine."

"I'm your thing."

"You know what I mean. I can't sit around all day waiting for you. Helping out at the tattoo shop and the bar here and there is fine and all, but . . ."

"Why rush it?"

I waved my arms. "You were born with this."

"Sometimes you're born with it. Sometimes you stumble into it."

"Supposed I never find it?"

"Suppose you do?" he countered. "Being with me won't stop that, will it?"

"No, it won't. But I have a plan."

He smiled. "Bet you do."

"Amelia said Preacher promised to find her someone to manage the bar, that her role was just temporary."

"Here we go," he muttered.

"So I was thinking, with the experience I have, maybe Preacher would hire me."

"That's really what you want to do?"

"For right now, yes. From there, I'll figure it out."

He sighed. Stared up at the ceiling. "Okay, fine. And Preacher said yes when I asked him."

"What? Cage, there you go, doing that protection thing again!"

"Damned straight. Learn to love it."

"I do. I love it. And you."

Cage's expression softened. "I've loved you from that phone call, babe."

I stood and moved to sit in Cage's lap, asking, "Who are you, Christian Cage Owens?"

"Just a broken guy, Calla. One you shouldn't be forced to stay with."

"No one's been forcing me for a while," I told him.

"I worry, Calla. I really fucking worry that this life is too violent for you."

"Soft with steel underneath, remember?" I wasn't teasing with those words.

"You'll never get used to it."

"So you're not?"

"No," he said firmly.

"Then how do you do it?"

"I got better at dealing with it."

"Then so will I."

Cage fisted a hand on the table. "You shouldn't have to, dammit. You should be—"

"I want to stay here with you. *Want*—not have to. Because someone needs to protect you." I ran my open hand over his fist and he laughed then, a look of disbelief, but ultimately he looked pleased. His hand unfisted and he slid his palm against mine.

He stopped laughing when he saw I wasn't. Then he said, "Okay, yeah, Calla. You're right. You have to stay and protect me."

It was my turn to laugh, which he quickly muffled with a kiss, a kiss that did that *Bang— you're naked* thing that seemed to happen around him. Because I belonged in this world—and I belonged with Cage. I also belonged to him, but the best part was that Cage also belonged to me.

Acknowledgments

Writing a book is never a solitary endeavor, and I'm so grateful to the following people for their help and support.

For the awesome Danielle Perez, whose insights and patience are always invaluable and appreciated. For Kara Welsh and Claire Zion for all their unwavering support, and for everyone at New American Library who helps make my books a success. And I have to give a special shout-out to the art department for their most awesome covers!

For my friends, writing and otherwise, and my readers—the support, encouragement and laughter you supply is more important than you'll ever know.

For my family, who understand why I spend so long in the writing cave, and who are always waiting for me—usually with dinner—when I crawl out.

Don't miss the first novel
in the Section 8 series by Stephanie Tyler,

SURRENDER

Now available from Signet Eclipse.

Prologue

Zaire, twenty years earlier

The explosion threw him forward hard, the heat searing his body, debris cutting into his back as he covered his face and stayed down. Darius didn't need to look back to know what had happened— the bridge had exploded. Simon had purposely cut off their last means of escape. It would force their hands, Darius's especially.

"Darius, you all right?" Simon shook him, yanked him to his feet and held him upright. His ears would continue to ring for months.

"How much ammo do you have?" he called over the din. Couldn't see the rebels yet, but he knew they were coming toward them through the jungle.

"Stop wasting time. You go." Simon jerked his head toward the LZ and the waiting chopper about thirty feet away, crammed full of important rescued American officials and the like.

Already precariously over capacity. "Go now and I'll hold them off."

Simon had always had a sense of bravado and a temper no one wanted to deal with, but one against twenty-plus? Those odds were not in the man's favor. Darius shook his head hard, and it was already spinning from the explosion.

"You are no fucking help to me," Simon told him. "I can't watch your back this time, Darius."

"Fuck you."

"Leave. Me. Here."

"If I do that, I'll come back to just a body."

"You're never coming back here." Simon's teeth were bared, ready for battle—with the rebels, with Darius, if necessary.

"If we both fight, we've got a better shot," Darius told him.

"You would tell me to leave if things were reversed, Master Chief, sir."

Simon stood straight and tall, hand to his forehead, and Darius growled, "Don't you dare salute me, son." Their old routine. Simon managed a small smile, one that was as rare as peace in this part of the world.

"Don't take this from me, Darius. Let me save your goddamned life. You have your son to think about—I won't take you away from Dare."

Dare was in middle school—his mother had already left them both, and pain shot through Darius at the thought of leaving his son without a parent.

Simon knew he had him, pressed on. "The team will always need you, and me—well, you can always find someone who can fight."

"Not like you."

"No, not like me," he echoed. "You go and you don't ever return."

Darius didn't say anything, and for a long moment they were silent, listening to the rustling that was still a couple of miles away. The blood was running down his side, and if he stayed in this wet jungle much longer with a wound like that . . .

"There's one spot left for a ride home." Simon told him what he already knew. "That seat is yours."

"I'm half-dead already."

"You think I'm not?" Simon asked, and Darius flashed back to a younger version of the operative in front of him, walking along a dusty road two miles from Leavenworth.

Darius had gone from being a Navy SEAL, fresh from capture in an underground cell where he'd been held for twenty-two days, to a medical discharge, to a phone call inviting him to join a very different kind of team. The CIA was creating a group—Section 8. For operatives like him. They'd have a handler and all the resources they'd need. Their only rule: Complete the mission. The how, when and where were up to them.

He was maybe the sanest of the group, and that was saying something. Simon always had the look of a predator, occasionally replaced by a childlike wonder, usually when Adele was around. If you looked at the team members' old files, you'd see everything from disobeying orders to failing psych exams to setting fires.

But if you knew S8, you'd see the mastermind.

The wetwork expert. The demolitions expert, the one who could handle escape and extractions with ease. They could lie and steal and hack. They could find any kind of transport, anytime, anywhere, anyhow, that could get them the hell out of Dodge.

In the beginning, they'd been nothing more than angry wild animals, circling, furious with one another and their circumstances. But once the trust grew, it was never broken.

Separately, they were good. Together, they were great.

And now, three years later, two S8 operatives stood near the wreckage of a bridge in Zaire and they were both about to die.

"If you could save fifteen people . . . or just one . . . ," Simon prodded.

"Don't you pull that trolley-problem shit on me—I've been to more shrinks than you and I'm not leaving you behind like this," Darius said, his voice slightly vicious. But they both knew he'd relent. He'd done everything Simon had asked of him, and this was for the good of the rest of the team.

"They'll never recover without you," Simon told him. "You're the goddamned heart of the team."

"And you're my best goddamned friend," Darius growled. Simon's expression softened, just for a second.

"Just remember the promise," Simon warned.

We don't try to find out who's behind S8. No matter what.

Neither Darius nor Simon believed what had happened today was a screwup their handler could've known about. But their promise referenced him specifically. They knew they'd been brought together by the CIA, but their handler picked the jobs, gave them orders and anything else they needed. Once they started distrusting him, it was all over.

"I'll remember," Darius told him now.

"Good. Go." This time, Simon's words were punctuated with a push. Darius barely caught himself, and when he turned, Simon was already running in the direction of the rebels, the crazy fucker confusing them with his contrary tactics. Because who the hell ran toward the bad guys?

Darius made his choice—he was a liability, so he made his way to the helo, pulled himself on board and shoved himself into the pilot's seat. Within minutes, the steel bird was grinding gears, rising above the heavy cover of jungle. As the chopper blades cut the air smoothly with their *whoompa-whoompa-tink*, Darius turned the helo and stared down at the man who'd left himself behind as Darius took the rescued civilians—aid workers, a diplomatic attaché and other Americans who'd been working in the area—away. He'd never take credit for the glory on this one, though. Simon could've sat in this pilot seat as easily as Darius did.

There was a chance Simon could fight them off. There was always a chance. And as he watched for that brief moment, he hoped beyond hope that Simon could win, fight his way out of the mass of humanity that was trying to kill him simply because he was American.

One last glance afforded Darius the view he didn't want—the mob surrounding Simon. It was like watching his friend—his teammate— sink into a manhole as they swarmed over him.

Section 8 had ended at that moment, at least for him. He'd later learn that their handler had agreed, and the group of seven men and one woman who'd been thrown together to work black ops missions around the globe with no supervision and very few, if any, rules, had been officially disbanded, the surviving members given large sums of money to buy their silence and thank them for their service.

He would have to explain to the team why he'd left Simon behind, although they'd know. They'd get it. They all prepared for that eventuality every single time they went out. It was part of the thrill.

There was no thrill now as he watched his best friend die. And he didn't turn away, stared at the spot until he couldn't see anything anymore, and knew he'd never get that image out of his mind.

Chapter One

Twenty years later

Dare O'Rourke believed in ghosts because they visited him regularly.

He woke, covered in sweat, shaking, and immediately glanced at the clock. He'd slept for fifteen minutes straight before the nightmare. A record.

The screams—both those in the dream and those that tore from his own throat whenever he allowed himself the luxury of sleep—would stay with him as long as he lived, wrapping around his soul and squeezing until he wished he'd died that terrible night.

A part of him had, but what was left wasn't a phoenix rising from the ashes. No, Dare was broken bones and not of sound mind. Might never be again, according to the Navy docs, who said the trauma Dare had faced was too severe, that he wasn't fit for duty. He had no doubt those doctors were right, wasn't sure what kind of man he'd be if he *had* been able to go the business-as-usual route.

He'd never be the same.

The CIA felt differently. *You'll survive. You'll recover. You're needed.*

And even though he knew the world needed rough men like him, no matter how fiercely the government would deny his existence if it came down to brass tacks, he told them all to fuck off and went to live in the woods. He was no longer a SEAL, the thing that had defined him, the job he'd loved for ten years.

Dare had prayed for many things that night in the jungle, including death, but none had been answered. And so he'd stopped praying and holed up alone and just tried to sleep through the night.

Three hundred sixty-three days and counting and not an unbroken sleep among them.

Three hundred sixty-four was a couple of hours away, the day giving way to the dusk, and the car coming up the private road couldn't mean anything but trouble.

Three hundred sixty-three days and no visitors. He saw people only when he went into the small town monthly for supplies. Beyond that, he remained on his property. It was quiet. He could think, whether he wanted to or not.

As for healing . . . that would all be in the eye of the beholder.

He rolled out of bed, flexed the ache from his hands before pulling on jeans and a flannel shirt he left unbuttoned. Barefoot, he went out to greet his guest.

He met the car with his weapon drawn, put it away when the car got close enough for him to see the driver.

Adele. A member of the original Section 8—a black ops group of seven men and one woman recruited from various military branches and the CIA. All loose cannons, none of them taking command well. All of them the best at what they did. A real-life A-Team, except the reality wasn't anything like it was portrayed on television.

Dare's father—Darius—had been a member, was MIA and presumed KIA on a mission last year. At least that's what Adele had told Dare.

All Dare knew was that S8 had officially disbanded when he was thirteen, and for years, its members worked black ops missions on their own steam. Until they'd gotten a call—that call—the remaining six members and one last job. Back into the jungle they'd sworn not to go back into. *A mistake to go*, Darius told him. *We're too old.* But they were still strong, with plenty of experience. And they went anyway.

Four men never returned. Adele and Darius did, but they were never the same. Refused to talk about it and went off on more unreachable missions until they'd both disappeared more than a year ago.

Dare had wanted to assume that the secrets of the group were all dead and buried with them.

Fucking assumptions would get him every time. He knew better. His father and Adele had come back from the dead more than once.

Adele took her time getting out of the car. She

was stately looking, at one time considered more handsome than pretty, with short hair and kind blue eyes, a thin frame that belied her strength. It was hard to believe she was as deadly as the men she'd worked with.

"I have a job for you," she said when she reached the porch he refused to leave. No preamble, all business. The only thing contradicting her deadliness was the frail frame she now carried.

She was sick—he could see it in her pale coloring, the darkness shading the skin under her eyes. His heart went out to her; she'd been the closest thing to a mother he'd ever had, even though she'd been far more like a mother wolf than a nurturer.

But it had been enough. "I can't."

"You're not broken, Dare." Adele sounded so damned sure, but why he wanted her reassurance, he had no idea.

He jerked his gaze to her and saw her own quiet pain, which she'd carried, kept so close to the vest all these years. "It was all a setup."

Adele neither confirmed nor denied, but the truth of his own words haunted him.

It was a setup . . . and you were supposed to die.

A Ranger had received a dishonorable discharge for rescuing him against a direct order. Dare would never forget the soldier's face, and he doubted the soldier would ever stop seeing his.

Two men, bound by pain.

He closed his eyes briefly, thought about the way he'd been found, nearly hanging from his arms, up on a platform so he could watch the entire scene being played out in front of him.

The villagers. His guides. American peacekeepers. His team. All slaughtered in front of him.

The fire came closer now . . . and he welcomed it. Had prayed for it, even as his captors laughed at his predicament, spat in his face. Cut him with knives and ripped his nails off one by one. There was nothing he could offer them, nothing they would take from him.

He'd offered himself multiple times. They refused. He must've passed out—from pain, hunger, it didn't matter. He clawed at the wood, his wrists, forearms, fingers, all broken from trying so hard to escape chains not meant for humans to fight against. It hadn't stopped him—he'd been nearly off the platform, ripping the wood out piece by piece, when the worst of the rape happened in front of him.

It would've been too late.

Could've closed your eyes. Blocked it out. Let yourself pass out.

But if they were going to be tortured, the least he could do was not look away. And he hadn't, not even when they'd nailed his hands to the boards, not for twenty-four hours, until everyone was dead, the village was razed, the acrid smell of smoke burning his nose, his lungs. The sounds of the chopper brought him no relief, because he knew they'd save him before the fire reached him.

The group of Army Rangers had been going to another mission, stumbled on the destruction by way of the fire. They'd come in without permission, the Ranger who'd saved him taking the brunt of the blame, or so Dare had heard later.

Dare hadn't gone to the hearing for that soldier who'd saved him. It wouldn't have helped either of them. In the next months, Dare was sure the soldier would be found dead under mysterious circumstances, another in a long line of men who'd interfered in something S8 related.

He turned his attention back to Adele, who waited with a carefully cultivated pretense of patience. "Why come now?"

She hadn't seen him since right before that last mission. Hadn't come to the hospital. Hadn't called or written. And while he'd told himself it didn't bother him, it had.

"Your sister's in trouble."

Half sister. One he'd never met before out of both necessity and her mother's insistence. He didn't even know if Avery Welsh knew he existed. "I thought she was well hidden."

"We did too."

"Where is she?"

"On her way to the federal penitentiary in New York—or a cemetery—if you don't hurry."

"Are you fucking shitting me?"

She twisted her mouth wryly. "I assure you, I'm not."

"What did she do?"

"She killed two men," Adele said calmly. "The police are coming for her—she's about forty-eight hours away from being sent to jail for life. Of course, there are other men after her too, and they make the police look like the better option."

So the men who were after her had tipped off the police. "She's what—twenty-two?" A goddamned baby.

Adele nodded. "You'll have a small window

of opportunity to grab her in the morning at the apartment where she's been hiding."

"You want me to . . ." He stopped, turned, ran his hands through his hair and laughed in disbelief. Spoke to the sky. "She wants me to help a killer."

"Your sister," she corrected. "Is that a problem?"

He laughed again, a sound that was rusty from severe underuse.

Avery had been secreted away with her mother before she'd been born, the relationship between her mother and Darius brief once she found out what Darius's livelihood was. But after that last mission, everything S8 related seemed to die down. Until Darius went missing. Until Dare was almost killed.

Until Adele showed up on his doorstep, dragging the past with her like an anchor.

"She's a known fugitive and I'm supposed to hide her?" he asked now.

"She's family—and she needs your protection."

He turned swiftly, fighting the urge to pin her against a column of the porch with an arm across her neck. The animal inside him was always there, lurking barely below the surface, the wildness never easily contained. "What the hell is that supposed to mean?"

Adele hadn't moved. "Don't make me spell everything out for you, Dare. You know you're still wanted. Why wouldn't she be?"

"I can't do this. Find—"

"Someone else?" she finished, smiled wanly. "There's no one but me and you, and I'm about to buy the farm, as they say. Cancer. The doctors give me a month at best."

"I'm sorry, Adele, but—"

"I know what happened to you. But we protect our own."

"I didn't choose to be a part of your group."

"No, you were lucky enough to be born into it," she said calmly.

"Yeah, that's me. Lucky."

"You're alive, aren't you?"

He wanted to mutter, *Barely*, but didn't. "Where's my father, Adele?"

She simply shrugged. "He's gone."

"Yeah, gone." Darius had been doing that since Dare was six years old.

"They're all gone—the men, *their families*. All *gone* over the course of the last six years. Do you understand?"

He had known. Dare had kept an eye on the families left behind by S8 operatives. Even though Darius had growled at him to stay the hell out of it, he'd found a line of accidents and unexplained deaths. They were all spaced widely enough apart and made enough sense not to look suspicious to the average eye.

But he wasn't the average eye. This was an S8 clean-house order, an expunging, and Dare knew he was still on that list and there was no escaping it.

For Avery, he would have to come out of hiding.

"Hiding won't stop your connection with Section 8," Adele said, as if reading his mind.

"I'm not hiding," he ground out.

"Then go to Avery—show her this from Darius."

She handed him a CD—the cover was a photograph of Avery. He glanced at the picture of the woman, and, yeah, she resembled her father—the same arctic frost blue eyes—but her hair was light, not dark. She was really pretty. Too innocent looking to have committed murder, but he'd learned over the years that looks could never be trusted. "And then what? I'm no good for this."

"You're better than you think."

"Bullshit—I'm just the only one you've got."

She smiled, but it didn't reach her eyes.

He looked at the picture stuck into the clear CD case again, and something deep inside him ached for his lost childhood. He hoped Avery had had one. "I'll think about it."

With that, she walked away, turned to him when she was halfway to her car and stood stock-still in the driveway. The back of his neck prickled. "Best think fast, Dare."

It was part instinct, part the way Adele paused as if posing. She gave a small smile, a nod, her shoulders squared.

He sprang into action, yelled, "No!" as he leaped toward her, SIG drawn, but it was too late.

The gunshot rang out and he jumped back to the safety of the house, cutting his losses. Adele collapsed to the ground, motionless. A clean kill. Sniper.

She'd made the ultimate sacrifice—going out like a warrior to force him to get off his ass and into action—ending a life that was almost over anyway. His father would've done the same.

Now there was nothing to be done here but get away and live. A hot extract involving just himself.

He shot off several warning rounds of his own to buy himself time. He took a quick picture of Adele with his cell phone camera and then went inside, grabbed his go bag and the guitar, then ignited the explosives he'd set up for a just-in-case scenario because, as a kid of a Section 8er, he was always a target.

That entire process took less than a minute, and then he took off in the old truck down the back road, the CD still in his hand.

Adele was too good not to know she'd been followed. She'd trapped him by bringing the trouble literally to his front door.

He cursed her, his father and everyone in that damned group as he motored down the highway, even as another part of his brain, hardwired for danger, made lists of what he'd need.

New wheels.

Guns.

New safe house with a wanted woman.

He threw the CD on the seat next to him and fingered the silver guitar pick he wore on a chain around his neck.

Goddammit, there was no escaping the past.